Praise for

A TOUGH NUT TO KILL

"Warm, witty, and full of Texas charm and feisty characters. Clear a space on your keeper shelf for the Nut House series."
—Duffy Brown, national bestselling author of the Consignment Shop Mysteries

"A family nut tree with some branches missing, sly old ladies, and a tall, dark stranger come to town. Or is he? Chomp into this engaging new mystery series, and it just might Bite-U-Back!" —Mardi Link, author of *Isadore's Secret*

"Elizabeth Lee delivers a delectable mystery that's pure Southern comfort. Readers will go nuts over *A Tough Nut to Kill*." —Riley Adams, author of the Memphis BBQ Mysteries

A Tough Nut
to Kill

ELIZABETH LEE

BERKLEY PRIME CRIME, NEW YORK

THE BERKLEY PUBLISHING GROUP
Published by the Penguin Group
Penguin Group (USA) LLC
375 Hudson Street, New York, New York 10014

USA • Canada • UK • Ireland • Australia • New Zealand • India • South Africa • China

penguin.com

A Penguin Random House Company

A TOUGH NUT TO KILL

A Berkley Prime Crime Book / published by arrangement with the author

Berkley Prime Crime Books are published by The Berkley Publishing Group.
BERKLEY® PRIME CRIME and the PRIME CRIME logo are trademarks of
Penguin Group (USA) LLC.

For information, address: The Berkley Publishing Group,
a division of Penguin Group (USA) LLC,
375 Hudson Street, New York, New York 10014.

ISBN: 978-0-425-26140-8

PUBLISHING HISTORY
Berkley Prime Crime mass-market edition / February 2014

PRINTED IN THE UNITED STATES OF AMERICA

10 9 8 7 6 5 4 3 2 1

Cover illustration by Robert Crawford.
Cover design by Diane Kolsky.
Interior design by Kristin del Rosario.

Acknowledgments

For the wonderful people who get me through long days and longer nights:

Mary Ann Warner, who taught me the kindness of "real" Texas folks.

Patty Sumpter, who coached me until I said "pecan" right. Who brought me biscuits and gravy and is responsible for these extra pounds I'm still dragging around. Who gave me lessons in Southern womanhood.

For people like Mardi Link and Aaron Stander and Doug Stanton, because they keep me going with kindness and belief in their talent, and in mine.

For Carolyn Vosburg Hall, an amazing human being who knows how to get a writer back on track with a simple word here and there; a red pencil mark every so often; and a slightly troubled look that warns a writer to beware of hubris.

For my amazing children and grandchildren and all those children yet to come. Dream big, kids. And turn a deaf ear to the word "no."

And, of course, for Tony.

Chapter One

I was already steeped in the heavenly smell of baking pecan pies and pecan drop cookies when I hurried down, worried, from my apartment over the Nut House, the store our family owned, to find my meemaw, Amelia Hastings, known to everybody in Riverville, Texas, as Miss Amelia, behind the counter, embroiled in her weekly tussle with Ethelred Tomroy.

"I came for one of those 'special' pecan pies of yours, Amelia," Miss Tomroy, a woman of strong opinions and harsher judgments, was saying as she leaned back on her low-heeled oxfords and eyed my grandmother. "From what I hear, you haven't been giving me the right pie. Why, I'm told you make special pies, for special people. If I'm not special—oldest family in Riverville, old as Texas dirt, then who is special, I'd like to know?" She stopped for one of her infrequent breaths. "So I want one of those very 'special' pies of yours, Amelia Hastings. Not one of your regular pies. You know I can make a regular pie as good or better than anybody in this whole town. Don't deny it. Everybody knows my pecan pies are superior to any pie this town can turn out. And don't give me any guff about those judges at the county fair. Biased they are and always have been. It's just that I don't have time on my hands, like you."

Ethelred took a breath and gave me a smug smile, nodding so her steely gray hair snaked out of its rolled bun. "Ya know, Lindy Blanchard, I got better things to do than spend all my days baking like your grandmother here. Rolling out a crust, making up her sauce . . . that's her job, right? Though why you Blanchards let your grandmother keep on working the way she does . . ." She turned back to Miss Amelia and clucked. "You gotta be . . . what is it now, Amelia? You about seventy-five?"

I knew my meemaw wouldn't back down in front of the town harridan. That's not what strong Texas women did, and Miss Amelia had been through enough in her life and seen enough and knew enough about people in general to stand her ground, give back as good as she got, and do it all with that ladylike smile Southern women step out of the womb wearing.

"Why, bless yer heart, Ethelred." Miss Amelia leaned back on the heels of her sneakers and dipped her neatly brushed head of short, no-nonsense gray hair. I watched as she crossed her arms over her apron and hung on tight to her dignity. "Just bless yer heart for all yer concern, but I think I'm still younger than you, unless time stopped and nobody told me 'bout it. You seventy-seven now?"

I had something important to ask her, something bothering me since I'd walked into my apartment a little while before and noticed things on my desk moved and my computer keyboard pulled out, as if somebody had been using it. My swivel chair was turned backward. Maybe I wasn't the neatest dresser in town—jeans and T-shirts being up there at the height of my couture, dirty blond hair caught back in a ponytail held with a red rubber band—but since college, because of my training in biophysics, I kept things around me like an orderly ship captain might: notes and records and grafts and files and pots and numbered plant stakes. I never left my computer at an angle, nor my chair pulled out. And besides that, I felt something different in the air up there. There's a kind of quiet to an empty apartment, like the air goes to sleep while I'm gone and should stay that way until I come back. The air in my apartment wasn't quiet this afternoon. Somebody had been there and I wanted to ask Meemaw if she'd seen anyone near the stairs. With the tour buses stopping and filling the store with people from time to time, it wouldn't be hard for a person to sneak up the enclosed stairway to my apartment. And then the lock—well, that door and lock were about as old as the building—over a hundred years.

I tried to keep a smile on my face while the two women got deeper into their years-old wrangling. I was only back in town from my office at Rancho en el Colorado, the family pecan ranch, to pick up a magazine article I'd forgotten that morning, something about a new kind of nut tree that resisted drought and could be disease-free.

That's my job, my profession. I'm a plant biologist with degrees from Texas A&M. I'd always figured I'd been given so much by the beautiful old pecan trees on the family spread that it was time to give back; maybe help all the ranchers in Riverville, our old friends, since we were in this hard business together. After I got my master's degree, Emma, my mother, built me a gorgeous greenhouse out beyond the barns. With the help of Martin Sanchez, our ranch foreman, I set up a fenced test grove for my saplings. Lots of new plants. New strains. Lots of grafting. I was almost there. A few trees in my test grove could do with very little water, and I had a graft on a GraKing cultivar that was showing great resistance to scab, a kind of fungus that destroys young leaves in spring or can kill a whole crop in wet years. But I couldn't achieve both. Not a disease-free and a drought-tolerant tree all together. Until now. A new group of trees in the test grove. All I had to do was wait out the next year to see if they were as good as I thought, see if I finally had the answer that would solve the ranchers' heartbreaking problems of years with no crops, years when the bank called in notes, years when we said good-bye to decent, hardworking ranchers we knew like family. And especially this year, a drought already hitting the out-budding trees, and at a crucial time for the pecans if they were to be heavy with nuts by late fall.

I was excited about my new cultivars, but I couldn't talk about them to any of the ranchers. No use raising hopes. Still— Meemaw and Mama knew and were both rooting for me.

Standing there, waiting for Ethelred to stop her sputtering about how Miss Amelia knew darned well she was nothing even close to seventy-seven, was trying my patience, but if I got testy with Ethelred I'd hear about it later, in a detailed dressing-down from Miss Amelia, how a Texas woman acts and doesn't act and how we don't want people to think we're rude Northerners—"Do we, Lindy?"

Eventually Ethelred wound down. She heaved a long-suffering sigh and I jumped right in. "Meemaw, could I have a minute . . ."

I motioned back toward the kitchen, where we could talk.

"Not now, Lindy." Ethelred's wind-down had been only a temporary condition. She waved a dismissive hand at me, making my blood pressure shoot up and my tongue swell up with words I'd like to spit at her. "I'm a busy person and I got business here before she goes trotting off."

"Maybe Bethany . . ." I looked around for my younger sister. She was supposed to be helping Meemaw in the store but was probably off on some errand of her own, something to do with her position as head of all the events held at our new pavilion, a beautiful white tentlike structure Emma had erected beneath some of our oldest trees. Bethany's head was so filled with white doves and black ties and pyramids of cupcakes, she could wander off and not remember Miss Amelia was depending on her when the store got busy and people snaked in a line back through the tables of nuts and pecan candies and cookies and gift boxes done up in shiny green paper and tied with green and gold ribbons, all with the family crest—three pecans nested in three green leaves above three wavy lines representing the Colorado River—printed prettily on the labels or tags.

Miss Amelia shook her head. "Sent her home. Nervous as a cat in a room full of rockers, with that big wedding she's got coming up. Had to call about those doves. Somebody in here this morning told her doves make a mess and she started worrying about dove poop on that cake she's got ordered made to look like a big radio studio, 'cause the guy's some newscaster from Dallas, is what she said."

Miss Amelia smiled a sly smile at me. There was something deep down in my grandmother that took great glee in the ridiculous parts of life. Like worrying about dove poop on the overdone cake at an overdone wedding.

She turned to Miss Tomroy, standing with her arms folded and one foot tapping. "So now what'll it be, Ethelred?"

"I'll just take one of those 'special' pies of yours, and be on my way."

"No such thing, Ethelred." Miss Amelia bit at her lower lip and bent to fuss with a row of crooked pecan bars on the crowded counter.

"Meemaw," I interrupted, keeping my face straight. I knew she was lying about having no "special" pies and feeling uncomfortable with the lie, especially in front of me. Still, I couldn't help teasing my upright, straitlaced, sin-fearing grandmother, who'd helped raise me and Bethany and my older brother, Justin. And stood by us in our darkest hour, when my daddy, Jake, was killed out in the groves, pinned under the tractor that'd turned over on him.

"You must have an apple pie hidden back in that kitchen. How about a couple of banana creams? Those must be 'special,' " I said.

"Don't you have work to do out there in that greenhouse of yours, Lindy?" She frowned heavily at me.

"If you're not going to tell the truth," Miss Tomroy sniffed, "then just give me one of them regular pies. But I'm not forgetting."

Miss Amelia went back into the kitchen for the pie while I bagged up a box of Pecan Smackers and a package of Miss Amelia's BITE-U-BACK hot and spicy pecan snack mix, which Miss Tomroy plunked down on the counter as she leaned in close, put a finger to her lips, and whispered, "Heard your uncle Amos was back in town . . ."

The words froze me where I stood. Not long enough, I hoped, for Miss Tomroy to notice and gloat.

"Working out at the Conways' ranch, is what I hear. Guess he knew none of you folks would take him in. All that trouble after your father's funeral. Poor Amos." She shook her head sadly. "Always one thing or the other with that boy. Long as he's been on this earth. Trouble, trouble, trouble."

I kept my head carefully bent toward the cash register, ringing up her purchases. Getting no response out of me, Miss Tomroy went back to grazing up and down the aisles. At a counter filled with tote bags, I watched her hesitate above a plate of samples: chocolate-covered pecans. Her crooked fingers delicately probed the candies, pushing one, then another, aside until she found the largest.

When she was back, sucking at nut pieces caught in her

teeth, she eyed me again. "Heard, too, you're real busy out there at the ranch since you got back from that college. Put that advanced degree of yers to any good use yet? Somebody told me you was foolin' with the old-time nut trees. That true?"

She eyed me with her head kinked to one side. "Trees good enough for my granddaddy."

I stretched my lips into a smile I was far from feeling. "You sure hear a lot, Miss Tomroy."

"Keep my ears open." Ethelred brightened, taking my remark as a compliment. "Heard, too, you got experiments going on out there at the ranch."

"Experiments?"

She shook her head, impatient with me. "Everything such a big secret with you Blanchards. For heaven's sakes, don't you realize Riverville's not Houston? Word gets around. Men who work out there for your brother and your mama talk. Think nobody noticed your new greenhouse? Heard about that secret grove of yours? New species of pecan, is it?"

She narrowed her lips and frowned hard at me. "You doing that cloning out there? Hope you don't go fooling with the taste of our pecans. Riverville's been known for our nuts for over a hundred years, you know."

While I choked on a response, she looked harder at me. "What'd you get those degrees in, you don't mind my asking?"

"Horticulture and bioengineering . . . I'm trying to—"

"Bio . . . engine . . . eering, huh? Well, heaven's sakes, don't go starting some kind of plague—with that bio stuff you're doing. Last thing we need in Riverville. Personally— though I'm never one to bring others up short—I just don't cotton to foolin' with what's been our bread and butter for over a hundred years now."

That one took a lot of tongue biting. I ran a few well-chosen words through my head, but was saved by Miss Amelia coming back through the swinging door with the awaited, ordinary pie.

I turned, intending to make a face at Miss Amelia, showing what I thought of Ethelred Tomroy, but Miss Amelia stood carved in ice with the doors swinging back and forth behind her. She stared off, over my shoulder, toward the front door, where someone had just entered, the bell above the door finishing its slight tinkling.

Miss Amelia's face went dead white. She looked as if she was going to pass out right there in front of me. Her hands shook. I watched, unable to move, as the pie she carried shook right along with her. I watched as the pie tipped forward, hung there at the tips of her fingers, then slid in a graceful arc, falling to the floor with the echoing clank of the pie tin and the splat of nuts and sauce.

The spoiled pecans fanned out over the worn wooden floor as the dark, wonderful sauce spread in a rivulet pooling near Miss Amelia's feet.

Ethelred, along with me, looked up from the mess on the floor. She snapped her lips shut, too shocked, for once, to speak.

Miss Amelia's hands flew to her cheeks. Her eyes stayed fixed on whoever was standing at the back of the store.

"My pie!" Ethelred protested, indignation soaring. "Well, for heaven's sakes, what's got into you, Amelia Hastings? Maybe you are getting too old for this job, like people are saying around town. Family can't expect blood outta a turnip, you now . . ."

Miss Tomroy kept talking while I turned to stare hard at the person who had startled my usually unshakable grandmother.

Outlined by pure Texas heat and sunshine coming through the closing front door, a tall, bulky figure in a black cowboy hat hesitated just inside the room. He stood awkwardly a minute then turned and shut the door behind him with a sudden slam, rattling glass and sending baskets of pecans tumbling from one of the back tables.

I wasn't sure at first . . .

The man's face was in shadow. But—the size of him . . . that signature black hat . . . a man in his fifties . . .

My stomach gave a couple of turns.

Amos Blanchard. My uncle. My dead father's younger brother, back after two years away from Riverville. Two quiet years for the Blanchard family. Not anybody I ever wanted to see again in my whole life. Especially not since the night of my daddy's funeral.

I watched, my head buzzing, as Amos hesitated then strolled slowly up one of the aisles, his old cowboy boots echoing across the uneven floorboards.

He stopped at the counter in front of the three of us—frozen in a kind of stop-motion tableau—and politely touched the crown of his tall hat, dipping his head.

"Lindy," my uncle said, acknowledging me. I nodded curtly, not willing to give him an inch more attention than I had to. He'd hurt my mother that night. He'd hurt our whole family. Drunk. Mean. Calling my mother names. I wasn't willing to give him another chance at us. I'd go for his eyes if he started trouble. Southern lady be damned.

Chapter Two

My uncle's face was more worn than I remembered. His dark hair, sticking out from under the hat he hadn't bothered to take off, as all Texas men should when talking to ladies, was touched with gray. He looked older, as if he'd gone through a lot since leaving Riverville. There wasn't an ounce of sympathy in me. Let him be old, and gray, and miserable.

"Miss Amelia." He bowed his head.

"Amos Blanchard. Well, what do you know? Thought you said all you wanted to say the last time we saw you." Meemaw pretended to think hard. "Yer own brother's funeral, wasn't it? When you attacked my daughter the way you did."

Her voice was low, with a slight shake to it. I recognized her warning voice, with something of the rattlesnake buried down deep inside.

I moved to Miss Amelia's side and took her arm.

Ethelred Tomroy, a wicked smile crossing her old face, stood back and crossed her arms over her chest. I guessed she'd forgotten her fallen pie. She frowned hard at Amos

Blanchard. "Hope you didn't come in for something to drink, Amos. You know Miss Amelia's a teetotaler."

I watched as she settled her wrinkled hands across her stomach, leaned away, and waited to see what new Blanchard story she'd have to share around town. "Me and Miss Amelia believe people don't have to be any happier than the Lord made 'em to begin with."

"I didn't come here for whiskey." Amos Blanchard's words were clipped, a small shiver of disgust moving across his tight lips. He didn't bother to look at the woman. "And I didn't come to make trouble, Miss Amelia. Just need to talk to Emma. She around?"

"You're not getting anywhere near my daughter, Amos. You had your chance. You blew every opportunity to work with us. Why . . ." It hurt to watch tears redden Meemaw's eyes, but she held on tight, giving Amos back hard stare for hard stare.

I figured it was up to me to get my uncle out of there. Justin, my brother, wasn't around to take the man on. My mother wouldn't, and shouldn't, see him again. Everything that could be offered to Amos had been offered the day of the funeral. He'd called all of us thieves—stealing his ranch from him. He called my mother a crook, a woman after the family's money—as if she hadn't been a big part in making Rancho en el Colorado what it was today. The man had cursed and roared drunkenly at everyone until Justin, smaller but feistier and younger than Amos, hit him, knocking him to the floor.

That's when somebody called Hunter Austen, my friend since we were kids. A deputy with the Riverville Police now, Hunter had been in and out of our house since the days when we fished the Colorado together and stole more than a few handfuls of pecans on our way through the groves. I was never happier than when my childhood friend came walking in that night, all neat and official in his blue Riverville Police uniform. He recognized immediately what was going on and got Amos out of our house and off to the city jail on a "drunk and disorderly."

The next thing we all knew, back two years now, Amos was gone from town. I'd never been sure that his removing himself from our lives was his own doing or something Hunter planted in his head, to get him away for good. But gone he was and peace settled over the ranch.

I cleared my throat, ready to take him dead-on. "My mother wants nothing to do with you, Uncle Amos."

"I got something I need to talk to her about. It's important. Want to give her this . . ." He stuck a hand inside the old checked shirt he wore and fumbled around, as if he was searching for something in an inner pocket.

"Oh no. Not again," I said and put a hand up to stop whatever he was doing. I stepped out in front of Miss Amelia. "If that's a subpoena, or some other thing you've got planned for us, keep it to yourself. You hurt my daddy bad enough when he was alive. I'm not letting you bother my mama now. Just go away and leave us alone."

"Better listen, Amos," Miss Amelia chimed in behind me. "Me and Lindy will see to it you don't cause us any more trouble. Not one more time . . ."

The doorbell chimed again. Somebody coming in from Carya Street. I choked on things I wanted to say. Bad time for a customer wanting a pie and stepping into this Blanchard drama.

The man who strode in stood at the center of the middle aisle and looked down the row toward where the four of us waited, nobody talking.

I squinted against the bright sun streaming in the front windows. A tall, thin man. Blue uniform. I took a deep breath as he removed a stiff blue hat from his buzz-cut head, adjusted his eyes to the cool dark of the store, and walked toward where we stood. Miss Amelia gave a short surprised "Well, well." Ethelred Tomroy snorted in disappointment. But Uncle Amos said nothing at the sight of my old friend, Deputy Hunter Austen, who seemed to have a habit of riding to the rescue of the Blanchard family.

Chapter Three

There wasn't a noise in the room. Not a creak from the floor; no laughter from Miss Amelia's helpers out in the kitchen. Nobody moved a muscle in the Nut House as Hunter Austen made his way up that aisle of ribbon-wrapped pecan gift boxes toward where we stood at the front counter.

"What do you know," Ethelred said, a satisfied smirk widening her narrow face. "Deputy Austen. Talk about the cavalry . . ."

Hunter Austen dipped his head toward Miss Tomroy. "Ma'am," he said, no real greeting in that voice.

I watched as Amos's body stiffened. He reared back and tightened his eyes half-shut before muttering, "Afternoon, Deputy."

Hunter ignored Amos and greeted Miss Amelia, who looked down at her ruined pie, bit at her lip, then squinted hard at Hunter as if she weren't sure she knew him.

"Lindy." He nodded formally though we'd been friends— and maybe even more than friends—since preschool. Hunter pulled back his broad shoulders, looked from one of us to the other, assessed the situation, and seemed ready for whatever was going on here.

"Saw you walking in, Amos," Hunter turned dead-on to Amos and said in a low, very calm voice. "Thought maybe I'd see what you were up to. We don't want to be bringing this fine family any more trouble now, do we?"

Amos threw his big hands in the air. "No worry on my account." He shook his head hard, making his black hat wobble. "Just here to get a message to my sister-in-law . . ."

"Really?" Hunter's eyebrows soared skyward. "Didn't you get to say everything you wanted to that last time?"

"Nothing like that . . ."

"You got a subpoena or something under there?" He nodded to where Amos pulled his hand from inside his shirt.

"Nothing to do with you, Deputy. At least not yet. Just something—"

"You been drinking, Amos?"

Amos made a face. "Not a drop. Not in almost two years."

Hunter took a step closer to the man and looked him straight in the eye. "Heard you were back in town. Working for Harry Conway, is that right? Conway must be a patient man. Lucky anybody from around here gave you a job at all. Maybe you'd better get back on out there to Rancho Conway and leave these good people alone."

Amos shook his head, thought awhile, then shook it harder. "Can't do that."

"Can't make a man do what he doesn't want to do, Deputy." Miss Tomroy stuck in her two cents.

Hunter did one of his well-known slow turns toward the elderly woman. He fixed those deep blue eyes of his on her and didn't say a word. Miss Tomroy, face reddening, reared back and sniffed once and then twice.

"Could I ask you to do me a big favor, Miss Tomroy?"
Hunter asked politely. "This is official business here, and I
don't want trouble. Be better if you left—if you don't mind."

Ethelred's mouth snapped shut. Every loose gray hair on
her head quivered with indignation. "Why, Hunter Austen.
You're not talking to a stranger here, you know."

"Ethelred, you'd better go," Miss Amelia jumped in.

"But . . . but . . . what about my pie?"

"Come back later. I promise I'll save one for you."

I watched as Ethelred thought a minute. "One of those
special pies?"

"No such thing." Miss Amelia, beside me, drew herself
up to her full five feet nine inches and folded her arms in
front of her.

"I'm asking you to leave, Miss Tomroy," Hunter said again.

With a final "humph," Miss Tomroy stomped to the front
door and was gone, with even the tinkle of the doorbell
sounding aggrieved behind her.

Hunter turned back to Amos. "Now it's your turn, Amos.
I don't mean to be rude, but I'd say you'd better stay at least
a couple hundred yards from every one of the Blanchards
or I'll take it personally that you're trying to bother them
again. You've had plenty of chances here in town. Sheriff
Higsby, like your brother, Jake, and your daddy, too, been
lenient with you, let you get away with too much over the
years. Not going to happen again."

"I got no problem with you," Amos muttered toward his
dusty boot tops as he began to make his way sidewise past
Hunter, moving toward the door.

Walking backward, eyes on the three of us at the counter,
he stopped. "I need to warn Emma about . . . something.
Could be trouble . . ."

"Keep going," Hunter ordered, waving a shooing hand
at him.

Amos stumbled back, off balance, and hit a counter filled with gift baskets holding everything from pecan cookies to pecan bars and pecan turtles. He made a grab for one of the falling baskets, his hand shaking. He took his time fumbling the basket back into place on the counter, straightening the others, then kneeling to retrieve one that fell. Uncle Amos stood slowly, looked up at Miss Amelia and me one last, long time, turned, and was gone.

Once the man was out the door, a final blast of heat striking the three of us at the front counter, there were a few minutes of total silence.

Hunter took a breath, bowed his head, and narrowed his eyes at us. "Hope I wasn't out of line here," he said. "Saw him and thought about last time—at your house—and didn't want him causing you more trouble."

"You kidding?" I demanded. "Anytime you want to play Canadian Mountie and come riding to the rescue, you go right ahead and be my guest, Hunter Austen."

"I didn't even know he was back in town." Miss Amelia leaned forward against the counter, to steady herself. "Oh, what will Justin do when he hears? That boy's got so many hard feelings toward Amos. I'm just worried . . ." She looked out at Hunter. "You know Justin thinks Amos had something to do with Jake's death? Nothing he could prove, mind you. Just . . . a feeling."

"An accident, Miss Amelia." Hunter shook his head. "Happens around here. Mower turned over on him out there in the grove. Nothing suspicious the sheriff could find."

Miss Amelia shook her head impatiently. "You tell that to Justin, Hunter. He won't listen to anybody. With Amos gone, things were calming down. You know, with it being April and the trees out-budding—why, Justin doesn't have time to get his mind filled with all that old misery. There's the spraying, drainage ditches to clear, brush to cut . . . one

of the busiest times of the year for all of us. Now we got this
drought they're predicting. And here comes Amos. I can't
imagine what Justin will say when he hears—"

"He knows, Meemaw," I broke in. "We all knew Amos
was over at Conway's."

"Well, well, and y'all kept me in the dark . . ." Miss Amelia turned her tired, but still pretty, face toward me and I
immediately felt guilty. It wasn't that any of us wanted to
keep her in the dark; it just turned into one of those things
we didn't want to talk about.

Amelia made an unhappy face at me. "So tell me, young
lady, how'd this keeping secrets from me work out for you?"
I knew that stiff voice and figured we'd all be in for a lecture
at some time in the future. "Emma know, too?" she added.

"We had to warn her."

"My poor child. Never a word to me, her own mother.
Carrying this all alone . . ." Grandma's eyes filled with tears.
"And Martin Sanchez. What'll he do? Got our whole place
to run with Justin, and here comes Amos again. You know
how Martin hates the man . . ."

"Why don't I take you home, Meemaw," I offered, to
quiet her. Seeing her this upset broke my heart. "That's
enough for one day. It's almost closing time. I'll get Treenie
out here to take over for the last hour."

"Gotta clean up my mess first." Miss Amelia pointed to
the stiffening pie on the floor.

"Treenie will do it."

"I've got cookie batters all set to go," she argued.

"They'll keep."

"Tomorrow's Saturday. Busiest day in the week."

"Miss Amelia," Hunter interrupted. "Lindy's right.
You've had a shock and you need to get outta here. Go home,
put your feet up. Rest."

"Rest . . . phooey," she mumbled back at Hunter. "Never

had to rest my whole life long. Lost my husband early. Helped raise Emma's kids. Never needed to rest. I just hope people aren't thinking. . . Well, like Ethelred said . . ." She began to fiddle with her apron strings.

Her eyes were shiny with tears when she looked up at us. "You know, what Ethelred said, about me being too old? That's all wrong."

She sniffed hard. "I'll go speak to Treenie. Give me a minute . . ." She stopped when I put up a finger in the air.

"How about a pie for Hunter," I suggested. "He's saved our behinds one more time, you know."

She made a face at the thought of being saved from Amos Blanchard. "Well, certainly, I'll box one up . . ."

"A 'special' pie?"

Meemaw's face turned bright red. "Now, Lindy. I'm not sure the deputy here would appreciate—"

"Oh, he would," I countered. "Believe me, I know Hunter. He'd enjoy the heck out of that pie, and say nothing to anybody else."

"You mean, say nothing to Sheriff Higsby?" Miss Amelia asked, giving me a long look. Deep meaning dripped from her voice. "Or Miss Ethelred Tomroy . . ."

I smiled at her.

"Well, if you're sure . . ." She looked hard at Hunter, who, to his credit, kept his face blank.

"Then . . . Of course, I'll just get one ready and be right back. Gotta tell Treenie I'm leaving. She can handle the store and closing up about as good as I can."

While Miss Amelia was in the kitchen, boxing up the pie for Hunter, I remembered what I'd wanted to talk to her about in the first place. That business up in my apartment. I wasn't sure about it now. It wasn't as if there was a big mess or anything. Just things that weren't right. This wasn't the time to bring it up, I decided. Not in front of Hunter. Not another thing to upset Miss Amelia. I hated dropping any more Blanchard misery on either of them right then.

I reached out to take one of Hunter's wide hands in mine. I shook it a couple of times before letting go, teasing him in a way only old friends can tease. "I don't know what we would do without you, Hunter. I really appreciate you coming in like that."

Hunter couldn't help looking pleased with himself. I liked that about him, that he could color up like a kid. "Anytime he comes back around here, or out to the ranch . . . well . . . you call . . ."

"What do you imagine he wanted to give Mama?" I asked, remembering Amos's gesture toward his shirt pocket.

"Could've been nothing. Or a subpoena, like I said. Wouldn't put it past him. Still trying to get the ranch away from Emma. As if his daddy didn't give him a million chances to prove himself. And your daddy, too. Always good to Amos."

Miss Amelia was back, a white pie box in her hands, green apron gone. Her boxy white purse dangled from her arm.

I smiled at Hunter as he accepted the precious pie. "Call me later," I said. "It's been a while."

Hunter's cheeks reddened up again. "Later," he agreed.

Out on Carya Street, we all said good-bye again, Hunter bending to kiss Miss Amelia's cheek. I watched that strong back in his stiffly pressed uniform shirt as he walked away. I felt my own cheeks heating up. Just a little bit.

He was still only the kid who gave me a bow and arrow for my tenth birthday, when I turned around and shot him in the behind with the arrow, paying him back for the time he threw me in the Colorado with my clothes on.

A good, old friend.

Chapter Four

Driving in under the high wrought-iron gates, with RANCHO EN EL COLORADO—1905 worked into the graceful overhead arch, made me happy. This was the place I loved more than any other on earth. Forty-eight acres of tall, stately pecan trees fronting Highway 71, then stretching along the fertile banks of the Colorado River. Perfect area for pecan trees. Except the Colorado was down in its banks this year, and people were talking about a long, hot summer with little rain. Everybody was worried. Still, we went on, the way we'd always kept on: praying and hoping things would work out. Usually things did work out—except for that one terrible year when the buds withered on the trees in April and the ranchers went deep into debt, everybody suffering together. Which left a deep mark on me. I was only twelve then.

My work on developing a drought-tolerant and disease-free tree began in college. Or maybe back in that terrible April when I stood beside my daddy under our trees and saw the delicate blossoms all shrivel and die.

After grad school, I came back to the ranch to work in a

small corner of one of the barns; not much room for the new seedlings I started. It wasn't long before all my grousing about lack of space led Mama to say my work was as important as any other part of the ranch. She saw to it that I got a brand-new greenhouse—big enough to cover a quarter acre of seedlings, and then I got a small office and next came my fenced-in test area behind all of that.

This was my home: Rancho en el Colorado—a safe place where people like my uncle Amos couldn't get at any of us. This ranch was where people loved me and pushed me to try harder, to excel, to achieve whatever I went after, and I was damned and determined I would pay them back someday.

Miss Amelia, seated in the truck beside me, pulled a neatly folded handkerchief from her purse and wiped hard at her eyes.

The ride home from the Nut House had been a quiet one. I didn't want to set Miss Amelia off again so I left her to her thoughts.

As we curved up the winding drive to the long, low ranch house sitting on a rise among the very oldest of our pecan trees, Miss Amelia reached over and put her blue-veined hand on my arm.

"Ya know, Lindy. What Ethelred was saying back there?" She turned, snapping pale eyes on me. "Treenie came in, mad as a hornet, one day last week. Said people were spreading stories about me. Somebody even asked her if I was going bonkers."

I couldn't help the shocked noise I made. "That's . . . terrible."

"Somebody's telling folks I've been going into Columbus in secret. Seeing a psychiatrist there. That person told Treenie she had it on very good authority I was suffering from 'early onset dementia.'"

"Can't imagine who'd say a thing like that." I pulled to the side of the drive to stop and look her straight in the face. "You're the sharpest woman I know. Always was and always will be."

"Yer darn right. That's what I thought, too. This person told Treenie word is my baked goods aren't what they used to be. That I'm forgetting ingredients." She ran a hand hard across her tight lips. "You know that's not true, Lindy. Truth is, though, an empty bucket makes the most noise. People'll listen. If I get my hands on whoever's spreading this trash about me . . . why . . . I'll . . ."

I grabbed Miss Amelia's shaking hands in both of mine. "You're better than ever. Top of your game. I . . . don't believe people who know you could be so mean." I thought hard awhile. "Who told Treenie all this garbage?"

Miss Amelia shook her head. "Don't know. I was so shocked, asking who said such a thing flew right out of my mind."

She hesitated a few minutes. "Back in Dallas I knew a woman who everybody started saying was too old to go on teaching school. One of the best teachers I ever worked with back there. That was before I married your grandfather and quit my job, you understand. Women didn't go on working back then after they got married, and it was just as well with me. Soon I had your mother and my hands were full. But this woman—her name was Florence Carpenter. She'd been teaching for years even when I got there. All the kids loved her, but one of the new teachers, who came in just before me, started saying how her teaching methods were out of date. Then how the kids were being harmed by someone not up on modern methods. Yeah sure, I'll tell ya—all that rote teaching they got into when colleges started teaching teachers to dumb down our kids. Well, word got back to Florence.

I think she was in her early sixties then. Never had a problem then all of a sudden she was forgetting things. Principal found her in tears one afternoon. She lost her grade book—or someone took it. Not long after that she was gone, retired. Dead in two years because she loved teaching so much and thought maybe she'd been hurting her kids all along. That's what happens when cruel people set out to destroy a person." She nodded along with her own thoughts. "That's what happens."

"Not to you, Meemaw. Never to you. There's nobody in town sharper than you. If anybody is saying anything—look behind what they're saying. Sounds like jealousy to me. And who would be jealous? People like Ethelred, or maybe that gossip, Freda Cromwell. Women who can't hold a candle to you, can't beat your pies at the county fair."

Miss Amelia nodded once and then a second time and then a third time, faster. "You're right, Lindy. Can't let it happen, can I? Not giving in to the mean and small-minded. Guess you always gotta look behind what's happening to you. Who benefits?"

"I think that's a pretty old question, Meemaw. *Cui bono.* Latin. Think about it." I took a deep breath, hurting for this special woman in my life. "And while you're thinking, I'm going to be talking to Treenie. I want to know who she heard it from. I'll take care of them."

"Oh, Lindy." Miss Amelia smiled, but moaned a little, too. "We've got so much going on. Now, with Amos back. Please don't say a single thing to Emma. She'll be hurt for me."

I pulled slowly back on to the gravel drive and drove around to park in front of the house, between rows of stately pecan trees.

I turned to Miss Amelia before she got out of my truck.

"Just like you said before, nothing stays hidden long. Like trying to keep the news about Amos from you. Best we all face whatever's ahead and work through it together."

Miss Amelia "tsked" a couple of times. "We'd better tell Emma that Amos was in. And that he was looking for her. Can't you just imagine Ethelred Tomroy spreading the word already? Telling Freda. Freda passing it on that Amos is causing more trouble." She sighed. "At least it'll give people something to talk about besides me losing my marbles.

"You know, Lindy?" She stopped after opening the door and preparing to slide, stiff and correct, from the seat of my pickup. "I still got this feeling. It's like . . . oh, I don't know. It's like I can't bring myself to believe that Amos is as bad as he seems to be. Troubled, sure. I'll give you that. But I've got this way of knowing people; dealing with them every day, the way I do. Coming into the store, sayin' it's for a pie or candy when I know they come in just to talk, to be a part of something, to hear news and share stories. It gives me kind of, oh, a way of seeing inside people's heads. Sure they got bad stuff going on. We all do. But then there's the rest— the things I sense and give an ear to. That's all they need. Lindy." She nodded hard. "I'm not whistling Dixie. I know folks from the inside out."

I leaned over and kissed her pale cheek. "You are one tough lady, Meemaw. Don't you worry. Like we always do— we'll take it on one day at a time. Together. We'll handle the gossips. Uncle Amos. Whatever's ahead of us. Why, we can handle anything—two fine specimens of Texas womanhood that we are."

Miss Amelia made a face. "I hope you're not pokin' fun the way you do. There's nothing stronger than a Texas lady."

"No such thing," I teased. "But you do know you can't use 'Texas' and 'lady' in the same sentence."

Meemaw couldn't help laughing. "You got a lot of me in you, Lindy. And I'm proud to see it," she said.

Since Mama wasn't in the house to talk to, I got Miss Amelia to lie down in her bedroom, part of the suite Emma had built on specially so Miss Amelia could be a part of the family but still have a little privacy, be where all us kids couldn't get at her and where people coming to the house with disasters at the store had to go through a couple of layers of Blanchards first.

Miss Amelia's room looked just like the woman herself, I'd always thought. Calming blue walls and flowers every-where; good paintings by the best Texas artists: long vistas and iridescent light. These were all the things she'd brought from Dallas after my grandfather died. It was all she had left of a life with a Texas congressman who died much too early.

There was chintz upholstery on the two small sofas in her living room; cornflower blue sheets on her bed; and flowered drapes at her long bedroom windows.

"I think I'm glad you talked me into coming home," she said, heaving a weary sigh. "Seems like right now every time I stand up, my mind wants to sit down on me."

I pulled back the top sheet on the bed, fluffed the pillows, and after Miss Amelia lay down decorously—shoes off, feet neatly aligned on the bed, hands crossed over her stomach—I kissed her forehead and left, closing the door quietly behind me.

Mama was in her office out in the packing barn, where, in November, the pecans got packed and sent off to buy-ers around the world. Packing was a flurry of sudden activity—many workers sorting and filling boxes. No time to stop. We all got involved in packing. Everything had to be done when the nuts were ripe and falling from the trees.

Mama, her streaked blond head bent over a desk covered with papers, blue-framed glasses pushed down to the end of her nose, frowned at first when I walked into her sparely furnished office. When her mind was set on something—like finding an error in the figures or fielding a low-ball bid on her pecans—Miss Emma didn't entertain intrusions lightly. Mama was a pretty woman who was all sweetness and honey one minute and tough as rocks the next. Especially when it came to marketing her pecans for the best price, for finding new markets, and defending her business and her family against all comers.

Miss Emma's middle-aged face—with life and character written in soft lines—went from bothered to happy in a second. "Lindy," she greeted me, "you're a welcome break."

"You busy?" I asked.

She nodded. "But never too busy for you. Just been hunting for your father's Pecan Co-op books all morning. Mike Longway called yesterday. He's the new president and said he wanted to go over the old books, make sure everything was up to date. He said the co-op doesn't have Jake's books from back when he was president and wondered if I'd look for them. Trouble is, I can't find anything. Just his personal check ledgers. Old receipts. Old bills. Nothing directly to do with the co-op. Guess Jake asked Chastity Conway to bring everything up to date when she took over as treasurer, but she says she never got 'em. Next thing Jake was dead and everything was in a mess."

She stretched her neck back and closed her eyes a minute.

"It's just that . . . well . . . I've been all through Jake's files, hunted where he threw stuff in that hall closet, checked out the top of wardrobe." She gave me a knowing look. "You know your daddy wasn't much of a record keeper. Not until I got after him. If I'd left things to Jake, the IRS and every other government agency would've been breathin' down our necks."

She pushed her glasses up on her forehead, and rubbed her eyes with the heels of her hands.

"Can I help with anything?" I offered.

"That would make two of us who don't know what we're doing."

She ruffled through a stack of papers on her desk. "Now I'm hung up on Jake's bills. I thought I'd taken care of everything but I found one . . . Oh well, I'll go through the check ledgers. Can't imagine it wasn't paid. Still . . . odd to find it at all."

"What's got Mike Longway worried?" I asked. "Or just the new president rattling his saber?"

She shrugged. "He's talking about a problem at the bank. I'll do what I can, but how would I know? It's been two years."

I cleared my throat and took a chair opposite Mama, pulling it close to the desk.

Miss Emma leaned back and sighed. "Your daddy never was a man for order—except where the trees were concerned. But you wanted to tell me . . . what?"

I cleared my throat and bit at my bottom lip. I'd much rather go on talking about Daddy, but I had this Uncle Amos story to tell.

"Somebody came in the store while I was there this morning, Mama."

"Let me guess. Your uncle Amos. I've been expecting something ever since I heard he was back in Riverville, but if he bothers Miss Amelia . . . Why, I swear I'm taking a shotgun and going over to Conway's myself. Why'd Harry hire him in the first place? Thought he was a friend of ours.

Now he's given that miserable . . . well, you know what I'd call him if I wasn't a lady . . . giving him a job right next door, like he did . . ."

She blustered on awhile then stopped, smiling a chastened smile. "Guess you better tell me what happened before I explode in a million pieces and mess up my office."

"He asked to see you."

"What for?"

"Didn't say. Just that he's got something for you and wanted to warn you. Don't know what about. Probably some crazy idea he got in his head."

"Maybe he's suing me. That's 'bout what I'd expect from the man. Jake, like his daddy before him, kept hopin' Amos would straighten up, get off the booze, and become a man. Then your daddy was dead and Amos worse than ever. Best thing that ever happened was Amos leavin' town the way he did. Too bad he came back at all. I don't wish harm to nobody on God's green earth, but I'd like Amos to just go away and stay gone for the rest of his life."

"Hunter Austen came on in," I continued. "He saw Uncle Amos and was worried about us. I don't like to bring up bad memories, but you know Hunter was there the night of Daddy's funeral. He saw for himself what Uncle Amos gets like when he's drinking."

"Hunter can't always be around to save us," she sighed. "Good man. Still interested in you, if you ever get around to thinking about settling down someday."

I frowned hard at Mama. Sore subject. Me heading straight for spinsterhood. Been going on since I moved into the Nut House apartment. "I've got my work right now, Mama. Until I'm sure I'm doing the right thing . . . well, Hunter, or any other man, can just stay away. And I wish you'd stop pushing . . ."

Mama threw her hands in the air. "Don't go flying off

like a mad crow. Just saying . . ." She thought awhile. "So what was it he wanted to give me?"

"Don't know. Hunter drove him out before it got settled. I don't think he'd give whatever it was to anybody but you. Hunter thought 'subpoena.' Maybe not. Uncle Amos was kind of quiet this time. Didn't seem mad at us. I don't think he was drinking either. Maybe bein' gone the way he has been, he coulda changed."

"Yeah, Lindy. Like a leopard growing stripes. You don't want to stand around holdin' your breath, waiting for that to happen. Doubt he's changed one whit. He's been stayin' right next door there, with Harry and Chastity, had plenty of time to call me, if that's what he wanted. Didn't say nothing to nobody about wanting to see me and make up for all those bad times. Just nothing—couple weeks now." She shook her head.

"But, Mama, you and Daddy already paid him plenty. He still gets money on our gross profits. Why's he think he deserves more?"

"You tell me. Could be part of this Blanchard thing we all buy into. You know, pride in what Jake's daddy and his daddy's daddy, before him, accomplished here. How much our name means in Riverville. Heck, how much the name means in all of Texas, if it comes to that. Kind of hard to let go of, I suppose. You know, the family pride part."

"You gotta earn that pride. That's what Daddy always told me. You gotta earn it by working the ranch, by standing up for the rest of the family. Uncle Amos never did any of that."

"Woulda just killed Jake, all this wrangling with his brother. Looks like Amos figures on being a problem to us for as long as he lives."

She looked down at her callused hands. "We all work so hard, Lindy. Just a darn shame. Justin heard he was back and went ballistic on me."

No sense going there, I warned myself. "There's something else I gotta talk to you about . . ." I said it tentatively, but it was eating at me.

Miss Emma ran a hand through her thick, short hair. "Okay, let's get this over with."

"Well, Meemaw said not to tell you, but I'm worried. Treenie told Meemaw somebody in town's spreading stories about her. And then Ethelred was there, saying people are talking, saying she's getting too old to run the Nut House."

"Somebody's saying that about Miss Amelia! Nonsense. Not a person in Riverville who doesn't just love Mama."

"Somebody doesn't. Saying she's got Alzheimer's or some such thing. Now there are whispers going around town that her baked goods don't taste right."

"You see anybody not buying her pies? Sales are better than ever. Who'd say such a thing? Can't imagine a soul . . ." She thought a minute. "Well, Miss Ethelred, that woman's jealous as can be of Mama. Thinks she's just as good a baker. Wouldn't put it past her to spread that story around herself."

"I was wondering if Uncle Amos might be doing it. Seems it just got started, maybe since he came back. Like him, to try to hurt all of us."

"Amos can be mean as a rattlesnake, but he's not stupid. We're still his only source of income. Ruin us, he ruins himself."

"Then who?"

"One of those evil gossips we've got here in town. Who knows who'd take pleasure in hurting us? I'll just bet if we ignore the whole thing, it'll go away." Mama yawned. "Don't know why it pours when it rains," she said. "I'm about worn out."

"I hate to do this . . ." I gave her one of my "sorry" looks again.

"Lord love a duck, Lindy. How much do you expect me to take on in one day?"

"Just something . . ."

"Well, go ahead."

"I went back to my apartment this afternoon to get a newspaper article I left there. About a new kind of tree in California. Nuts filled with nutrition. No diseases. I'm thinking of ordering a few, maybe trying a graft on my new cultivars. See what I get."

"Go on," she sat back, sighing.

"Somebody was up there in my living room. Things were moved on my desk."

"You keep yer place locked, don't you?"

I nodded.

"Well, then. Nobody but you was in there. Anyway, I told you, you shoulda stayed right here at the house with everybody else."

"The Nut House is an old building, Mama. Lots of keys around." I swept on past the old complaint and skipped my patter about needing privacy. *A place of my own.*

"Look, Lindy. If I were you, I'd just put it down to leaving too fast this morning and messing things up more than usual. You forgot that article, didn't you? Must've been in a hurry." Miss Emma swiveled her chair around to face her computer screen.

"I don't think so—" I began.

"So how's Miss Amelia now?" she interrupted, tired and at the edge of her ability to listen to any more.

Recognizing a dismissal when I heard one, I got up. "I tucked her into bed for a nap. All of this was hard on her."

"I'll be up to the house soon to see about supper. Just got a little longer here with your father's bills. Then I gotta take a look at something . . . can't put my finger on it but this last bid from the Butcher Brothers seems way too low. Market shouldn't be going down on the pecans. If they're gonna be scarce, market should already be heading up." She frowned and turned back to her computer. "Where you going now?"

"Out to my grove. I'm keeping a close eye on those transplants. I've got five still in their pots, might need to be brought back into the greenhouse tonight. I'm not sure enough to leave them out . . ."

"Maybe it's time you started getting patents on your new stock. I been thinking about it. Some ranchers would look at your work as being worth a lot of money someday. I know . . . I know . . ." She raised her hands to stop my protest. "That's not what you're thinking about. I'm just saying, to be on the safe side."

I wrinkled my nose at her. "I will, Mama. I'll look into it. Just let me get something I'm sure of before we start talking protecting the work, okay?"

"Up to you." She turned her chair away and then back. "Go on now. Better get out there and check those saplings of yours. Kiss every one of 'em, Lindy."

She sighed as she leaned back over Daddy's ledger book. "If I didn't still hope for better, I'd say the only grandchildren I'm ever getting out of you will be a bunch of little nut trees."

I drove under rows of our beautiful trees just coming into bud; across acres that had always been my own magic forest. It was my favorite time of year: spring along the Colorado River. As a child I'd loved skipping under the tall trees, listening as they talked to one another when the wind blew, telling myself I could understand them, that they were happy we took care of them, that they loved all the Blanchards— including me.

My happiest memories were here, when my daddy was alive and running the ranch, when Mama wasn't so harried with work, Miss Amelia not under attack, and when Uncle Amos hadn't been a threat—kept under control by my daddy, who swore he'd always see to his brother, no matter how far he fell into drinking. "And," I muttered to myself, despite Mama's assurances, "when nobody got into my apartment without me knowing it."

I waved to Martin Sanchez, our ranch foreman, as I drove past the barns and through another grove. He was busy mowing the tall grasses. I didn't stop to talk. The sound of the huge mower echoed through the grove. He'd have to shut off the motor to hear me, and Martin didn't like being interrupted while he worked.

I looked around for Justin. Be a good thing to give him a heads-up about Amos coming into the store, but he wasn't with the other men cleaning out the drainage ditches. With so much needing to be done this time of year, I figured he was somewhere fixing another broken-down machine or repairing fences where the wild hogs were coming in, or maybe he'd run into town for more spray. He could even be in Riverville hunting for spare hands, men who waited to be picked up and carted out into the groves to work.

I drove my favorite stretch of two-track alongside the river. I flipped off the air-conditioning and opened my side window, inhaling the thick, river smell of water and vegetation and damp and cool. The river was down when it should have been up, climbing our high banks, but it was still beautiful; running slow; ripples where it crested over old logs; tiny whirlpools where it got ahead of itself.

I passed two old sheds, not used much anymore except for extra shovels and such, and passed places where the bank had been dug out by the hogs. I'd have to tell Justin. He, like everybody else in rural Texas, was always fighting back the hogs that ran wild, mostly coming up into the groves from along the riverbanks, moving along from places where the land was still wild and vegetation grew to the river's edge, giving the hogs cover.

At my greenhouse, I parked around back. I loved the words "my greenhouse," like I was who I had wanted to be since grad school, the person my professors there told me I could be: a helper to all pecan ranchers, to my own family, saving millions that bad years took, and even better, saving the terrible heartache brought to families just like ours.

That was what got me into bioengineering in the first place, that awful year I stood out in the grove beside my daddy, Jake, and watched the blossoms fade. That year the drought during the spring went right on through summer. I told myself back then, when I was still a kid, that I would do something about it. I wasn't going to be like the other ranchers, who bowed their heads and talked about God's will. Things were changing in all sectors of farming now. New kinds of trees and plants. If there was a stronger strain of pecan, I knew I would be the one to find it. Just as David Milarch, the Michigan farmer who cloned ancient trees of the world to save them for the future, did. I hoped to promise a better future, too. A sturdier pecan tree that would save Texas ranches from global warming.

And I was getting close, using clones from our own trees. A process called micropropagation. Branch tips harvested and planted in baby food jars with my own vitamin-enriched gel. New jars, new beginnings. Hundreds in the greenhouse, along with two-year-old saplings, and the four-year-old trees I'd already moved outdoors, into my fenced test grove.

Soon I'd be cutting further back on water, to see how the

trees fared, maybe take the five-gallon buckets away and depend solely on drip irrigation. Then, at the end, if scab didn't attack them and no fungus survived, and the new trees could withstand a drought better than the old trees, and the pecans were as good or better—they would go into the regular groves, replacing dead or fallen trees, some that had been around for as long as 150 years.

The test grove was board-fenced with wire below, driven into the ground to protect the new trees from those feral hogs. I'd put a lock on the gate just so lookie-loos—maybe a workman, or his family—didn't wander in and decide to grab themselves a little pecan tree.

Just getting near my own grove made my heart beat faster. I took a deep breath, taking in the sweetish smell of spring and tree buds and something even sweeter and thicker in the air, then dug down in my shoulder bag for the key.

When I reached out for the lock, it hung sideways, open and dangling from its severed hasp. Somebody had cut the lock, then put it back on as if to fool me.

Nobody should have been in my test grove. There were workers who helped me inside the greenhouse, even planted the trees outside, but at the end of the day, I was always the last to leave. Nobody needed to get inside for any reason.

I reached out and touched the hanging lock, pushing it from where it dangled. I pulled the gate toward me, praying whoever had cut the lock wasn't still in there.

I stepped through the gate and looked around for anyone ready to jump me. It took a long moment before the change in my grove registered. A single long moment before I saw that every one of my trees had been hacked in half, the leafed tops bent to the ground. My precious grove was a ruined forest of dying trees. I couldn't breathe. It couldn't be the way it looked.

I reached out to the first tree in the first row. The strong, young trunk hadn't been cleanly sawed. It was splintered, and jagged, the leafy crown wilting. I walked down each of my precisely laid out, straight-arrow rows. Every tree—destroyed. Nothing left of my years of work.

Chapter Five

I fell to my knees. I couldn't help it. All my perfectly manicured rows—no weeds; every line straight and true. Every five-gallon bucket I filled with water, weighted with stones, holes drilled in the bottom—extra irrigation in this time of drought—all of it destroyed.

I pulled my shoulder bag around my body and dug out my cell phone. There was only one person I could think to call. Everyone would have to know . . . they'd all be sad for me. But Hunter . . . he would help. He would find who did this . . .

"Riverville Police," Sheriff Higsby answered.

I took a deep breath and put a hand on my chest, trying to control the waves of shock running through me.

"Riverville Police," the sheriff said again.

"Sheriff, this is Lindy Blanchard. Is Deputy Austen there?"

"Sure thing, Lindy," the sheriff said. "Just walked in . . ."

It didn't take two minutes to spit out what had happened

there in my test grove. Hunter caught on even as I sputtered the words.

"You stay right where you are, Lindy. Or get the heck out of there—that's even better. Whoever did this could still be around."

I turned to look behind me, at the metal door to my office. The greenhouse was beyond the office. There was only one doorway in. Whoever did this could still be there, doing more damage.

The window to the office was oddly blank—as if someone had covered it. But it wasn't covered. The window swirled with dirty smoke.

"My office!" I screamed at Hunter. "It's on fire . . ."

"I'm on my way," he yelled back at me. "Don't go in there. Lindy. Lindy! You hear me? I want you safe, Lindy . . ."

I dropped the phone, grabbed my purse, and pulled the ring of keys from an outer pocket. I ran up the row of broken trees to the office door, fumbling with the keys, pushing first the wrong key and then the right one into another lock that wasn't locked. I put my hand out to touch the metal door handle—only warm, not blazing hot. I threw the door wide open and stepped inside.

A cone of fire, like a large campfire, burned at the middle of the concrete floor between my long desk and the rows of filing cabinets where I kept my files and plans and daily logs on progress. The open door behind me sucked a whirling plume of smoke toward me. The fire blazed higher.

My fire extinguisher was in a little corner alcove by a microwave oven and small fridge. I grabbed it from the hook next to the sink and ran back to the pile of papers blazing and crackling on the floor—curling separately as they flared and glowed and turned to burning embers spiraling high into the air.

I didn't let myself take in the damage—not yet. I fought the fire, holding hard on to the extinguisher, which bucked back when I pressed the handle, blowing paper everywhere. I chased sparks and flapped my arm at the smoke.

When I looked around at something other than the fire, I saw my file drawers hanging open; a trail of scattered file folders ran from the wall of cabinets to where the fire had been set. Soot covered the walls. It made a greasy, black mess over the floor and kitchen nook and books . . . my exposed desk where my computer should have been . . . but wasn't.

I took a deep breath then coughed hard as I inhaled thick smoke. I wasn't falling down to my knees this time. I was madder than I'd ever been in my life. Whoever had done this would pay . . .

My mind ran to the greenhouse. The door was closed. No window to see if there was more fire, or if anyone was waiting . . .

All my test seedlings in their yellow pods were in there. My two-year saplings. My work. No one had the right to do this.

Maybe I could stand in the doorway and scream and scare them. Maybe I could still save something. My mind clicked fast. Turning and running wasn't in my nature.

But fear was.

Still, if anyone was in the greenhouse . . . every minute I stood there, frightened or intimidated, meant more destruction.

The last thing, right then, I could think about was my safety.

The door was closed but not locked. It didn't lead any-where but to the large, open expanse of greenhouse with its light and heat—for chilly Texas nights—and my young trees and planting tables and bins of soil and tools and hoses and coolers with dormant grafts.

I threw open the door. My body was rigid, expecting an attack. I kept my arms at my sides, fists clenched hard, nails digging into my palms.

Nothing moved. No sound beyond the click and whirr of an overhead blower in the long, echoing building. There were the usual earth and water smells of the sprayers; the cool curls of dampness across the concrete floor—all the familiar markers of who I was and what I loved.

I saw nothing at first, only the gleaming, stainless steel tables that should have held my neat rows of yellow tubes, and black pots with saplings—all divided by genus, and then divided again by test grafts, all neatly held straight by my green metal stakes with a number tag at the top—the numbers recorded in my log books and on my computer.

It was all wrong.

There were no trees on the tables closest to me. Instead, there was chaos. The neatly kept trays of baby food jars were dumped on the floor. Yellow tubes holding my new trees, all the black pots, were upended. Soil—my special mix—covered the tables and the floor like dirty snow. A slight, black haze hung in the air. I stepped into the building. Bright, clean sunlight streamed down from the greenhouse windows, growing hazy as it fell on my emptied plant tables.

I buried my face in my hands for just a minute. That was all the grief I would allow myself. Later—I'd think about what had been done to me, and to my family. Later I'd think about vengeance. Right then prickles of panic scrambled up and down my spine.

That fire hadn't been burning long when I got there. Whoever did this could still be hiding. But the building felt so still and empty.

I looked hard again. Something was wrong at the far tables, nearest the outer wall. Or—something was right. There were yellow tubes there, just as I'd left them.

There was order—row after row. Stock for future years. Tiny, struggling plants. Little soldiers, all in their colorful, plastic tubes.

I stepped forward then stopped to look around, make certain no one was behind me. The destruction, at those far tables, had been stopped somehow. Maybe whoever had done this heard Martin's mower coming closer. They might have heard me pull up beyond the fence.

If I could just touch one tiny tree, I thought. See that they were really okay . . .

I scurried, almost skipping, toward the far tables. My sneakers stuck slightly to the concrete. I slipped once on the dirt covering the floor.

As I turned a corner toward the untouched plant tables, I tripped hard over something and began to fall. All I could do was grab out frantically to stop myself. Unable to grip the closest table, my hands flailed in air. My body seemed launched in space. When I fell, I hit the concrete and scraped my face. The pain was fast and hard. My chest hit the floor. I couldn't breathe; no air left in my lungs. I scrambled back up to my knees and bent forward, gasping as blood ran from my chin.

When I lifted my head and forced my eyes open to see what I'd fallen over, a man lay on the floor beside me, half under one of the stainless steel tables, half out into the aisle.

I pulled away as far as I could get before he reached out and grabbed me.

But the arm didn't move. It lay very still.

The man was face up, his dark head turned away, arms spread wide; feet, in well-used cowboy boots, splayed in opposite directions.

He wore a washed-out plaid shirt and washed-out jeans. Near my right hand, a black cowboy hat trembled on its crown.

Uncle Amos . . .

I crawled toward the body.

Uncle Amos . . . with one of my green metal plant stakes, number tag moving gently, sticking up from the very center of his chest.

Chapter Six

Somewhere in my head I heard a siren, and then the clang of a fire truck, but I couldn't move. Not now. I knelt beside my dead uncle, hands at my mouth, until I heard Hunter's voice, first from the open doorway to the office, then as he pounded across the greenhouse, heading toward me, yelling my name.

When he rounded the end of the row of tables where I knelt, I could only shake my head at him.

"Holy . . ." Hunter stopped dead, then made his way around Amos's body, to take me by the shoulders and lift me up beside him. He pulled a handkerchief from his pocket and pressed the clean white square to my chin, where blood still dripped down to the front of my shirt. "Lord's sakes, Lindy. I guess you had to stop him, but . . ."

Everything after that was a blur: Hunter leading me back outside, taking me to my truck, opening the door, and pushing me up to sit on the front seat, then leaving to hurry to the sheriff's car just pulling in beside mine.

I watched the swirl of firemen running in and then out

of my office. Time passed and the fire trucks pulled away and more police cars and a white van pulled in.

Sheriff Higsby came over to take a look at me, stopping to tip his hat. "Lindy." He frowned as he took in the blood down the front of my blue shirt and my injured face.

"Terrible thing in there." He looked off, squinting up into the late-day sun, over toward the ruined grove. "Suppose that was the only way to stop him."

"No!" I shook my head. "He was like that. I was running to the trees I had left and fell over him."

The sheriff drew in a long, slow breath and let it out as he shook his head. "Doesn't look good. Everybody knows how you Blanchards hated Amos. Not that anybody blamed you. But not this, Lindy. Not even Blanchards can up and kill a man."

"Sheriff, it was like that when I got here. All of it. I saw my trees first, then called Hunter. There was smoke in my office. I ran in and put out the fire. I had to check the greenhouse. It was all I had left . . ."

"So you found him knocking over your trees and . . ."

I shook my head hard enough to start my chin bleeding again. Blood fell on my hand. I pressed Hunter's handkerchief to my face and held it there for comfort. "I told you. He was already dead. Sheriff, somebody destroyed my work. I would have said that it had to be Uncle Amos. Who else hates us this much? But there he is, dead. And it wasn't me who did it."

Sheriff shook his head. He seemed sad. "You gotta look at it from my point of view, Lindy. The mess in there was stopped halfway through. Fire was already set. You come in, catch him, and drop him the only way open to you—a stake through the heart. Come to think of it, seems kind of fitting . . ."

"Sheriff . . ." I moaned. "You've known me since I was born. Do you think I could do that to anybody? Even Uncle Amos?"

He rubbed at his upper lip, sniffed hard, and looked off into the distance, over the truck door. "Anybody can kill, Lindy. Given the right circumstances. Anybody." He hesitated, thought awhile, then said, "Justin wasn't here with you, was he? I know he thought Amos there had a hand in your daddy's accident. If Justin was with you and he came on yer uncle doing what he was doing . . . no question what he would've done. Any man, feeling the way he did about Amos Blanchard and finding him trying to ruin the family— well, wouldn't be called murder, Lindy. We'd call it self- defense. Why, in Texas we'd call that justifiable homicide. I think there are folks here in town that would want to throw your brother a parade. So you see, all I need is the truth and we'll put all this behind us."

I could only stare at Sheriff Higsby.

"Your office's sure a mess," he said after a long pause. "Looks like whoever did this was after your records. Grafting, aren't you? Anything secret about what you're doing in there?"

I shook my head. "I don't have secrets. I don't share my work—not yet, 'cause I don't have anything for sure. But now my records are all gone except—"

"They stole your computer, Hunter says."

I nodded and then remembered what I'd wanted to tell Hunter.

"Sheriff, somebody was in my apartment over the Nut House earlier today. I could see where they were messing with the laptop I keep there. When Hunter came into the store, you know, when Amos was there—I'm sure he told you; I was going to tell him about someone being up there but didn't get a chance."

Sheriff Higsby nodded. "You think it was Amos looking around?"

"Amos would never have gotten by Miss Amelia."

"She's distracted at times, I'll bet. Not young anymore, ya know."

I flinched but didn't have time to think about the implications of what he was saying. "I told my mama and she thought it was nothing . . ."

"Let me get somebody right over there to the Nut House. Seein' as whoever did this was after your work, better secure that place, too. Can my men get in?"

I felt in my pockets for the apartment key then looked around for my purse. "I don't know where my keys are right now, but I think Miss Amelia leaves a key up over the door. Same one probably opens my apartment. Nothing too secure. Never had to be."

I felt a cloud settling heavily in my head. What I had to do was stay quiet until my mother got there. Or even Miss Amelia—Meemaw would stand up to the man, tell him Blanchards didn't kill people and wouldn't want parades thrown because a man was dead.

As if in answer to a prayer, Emma's old black pickup pulled in behind the sheriff's car. Emma and Miss Amelia both got out at a run. Emma pushed the sheriff aside and leaned in to take me into her strong arms. I closed my eyes and rested my head on Mama's shoulder. From behind her came the sheriff's protesting voice, and then Miss Amelia, loud and angry and peremptory, the way she could get when her children were threatened. "What's wrong with you, Willard Higsby? Our girl's had a terrible shock and you badgering her? Why, shame on you. Just shame on you, Willard. Now you get the heck away from our Lindy and go find yourself a killer. Poor Amos . . ."

Her voice trailed off as she followed the quickly retreating Sheriff Higsby back toward the greenhouse building.

Chapter Seven

There was nothing comforting about being back in the ranch house. Nothing reassuring about the dark, exposed beams of the living room, or the low sofas and chairs. It was more a place where the real horror of what I'd just gone through settled in.

Hunter hovered over near the low archway leading into the living room but stayed away from me. He was going in and out as Sheriff Higsby ordered.

I couldn't stand to look at him right then. It was as though my best friend had turned against me, in this, one of the worst times of my life. It was as if he'd joined the other side, unable or unwilling to reach out a hand to help me.

I couldn't process what had happened. Couldn't work through stumbling over Uncle Amos's dead body. Couldn't work out that Hunter had been the first to accuse me of killing him. As if he didn't know me at all.

We were all together now, but sitting apart. Justin, still in work clothes—blue shirt and old jeans—his dark head bowed, sat on a low sofa across from me, hands clenched between his knees. Miss Amelia, her arm around a sobbing Bethany, sat upright and alert on another sofa. She looked over then blinked a few times as if she was surprised to see me there.

Poor Mama. She sat with her worried eyes going back and forth, policeman to policeman, then to me. She smiled and nodded nervously.

From time to time, Justin stood and shot a question at whichever cop was near him. Getting no answer, he'd sit back down and tap his foot angrily, muttering to himself. I could see my brother was bursting to chase these men out of our home but was holding himself in tight.

We had to talk—all of us—when the police were gone.

We knew what Sheriff Higsby was thinking, that he had the killer right there in the room. I'd be thinking the same thing if I were the sheriff, I figured.

First there was Mama, who detested Amos, and here he was back, probably planning to get the ranch away from her.

Then there was Justin, who still thought Amos had something to do with our daddy dying. He never accepted the coroner's verdict of "Accidental Death."

And me. All anybody had to do was look at my work and know I would feel murderous if I caught Uncle Amos in my greenhouse, destroying everything in his path. But I didn't kill him. Mama wouldn't hurt a flea. And Justin—if he was going to kill Uncle Amos, he'd never have done it in my greenhouse. The last thing Justin would do was implicate me in anything this awful. And anyway, my brother might be tough when it came to protecting the groves, firing a guy who needed firing, standing up to anybody trying to hurt the ranch—but despite what the sheriff said, Justin was no killer.

All I could think, sitting there drawn into head-lowered misery, was how I wanted to get back out there and clean up the mess, then begin my program all over again.

Bethany moaned against Miss Amelia's shoulder. "The wedding's going to be ruined. I've worked so hard. Chet Easton's gonna be furious with me over this. I mean, how can he have his big wedding here when we got us a dead body?" She sobbed and Miss Amelia patted her back as she moaned on. "I'm gonna be ruined by all of this. I just know news will get to Houston. Chet Easton's a big, important newscaster. He's gonna hear about it." She threw back her curly head and moaned again. "I've got everything ordered. How could anybody do this to me?"

Bethany turned her streaked face up to Miss Amelia, who smiled as she got up, leaned the sobbing Bethany back against the cushions, and left the room.

She was back in ten minutes, coming down the hall from the kitchen with a platter of pecan cookies in her hands. Always prepared for "guests," Miss Amelia passed her cookies and took orders for "a nice, cold drink" from the gathered policemen until Mama, stretched tight, had enough and, from between clenched teeth, said, "Miss Amelia, let's not make our 'guests' too comfortable. That all right with you?"

I watched as Miss Amelia colored up and bent to make room for her platter at the center of the large, square coffee table in the middle of the room. She fussed with the framed Blanchard photos on the table, pushing us aside as she made room for her cookies.

We'd all given statements—as much as any of us knew. Mine took longer than the others because I was there, on the scene. Talking about it brought everything back—especially that plant stake with the number tag swinging gently. Number DC8700. I kept turning over that number in my head. It meant nothing, one picked at random from a pile I kept near the planting bins. I would never use that number again. In a dark moment, I wondered if maybe my work was going to end there, with that classification and that number.

Waiting for the sheriff and his men to leave the house and the grounds was like sitting still while acid slowly dripped on my head. There was nothing to distract me from thoughts swinging back and forth from my poor broken trees to a fire and a dead man.

"We'll be out of here soon, Miss Blanchard." Sheriff Higsby read my mind. He was back, just inside the room, big boots clamped hard on a small, woven rug, his hat pushed firmly down across his forehead. He bowed slightly to Mama. "Just a few things left to clear up."

Mama shrugged up at him, narrowing her red-rimmed eyes. "You understand, Sheriff. We knew Amos was back in town. He was at the Nut House today, just like I told you. But that's all any of us know about him. I sure hope you don't think somebody in my family had anything to do—"

"And you have to understand, Miss Emma. Everybody in town knows the trouble he's been . . ." The sheriff's voice dropped as he looked slowly toward Justin.

"Don't look at me, Sheriff." Justin was beyond being angry. I could see frustration and anger building across his wide, taut back and in his fists, clenched on his knees. "I told you everything I know. Heard sirens out in the grove, same as Mama here. And no, I'm not unhappy Amos is dead. But no, I didn't kill him. I was cleaning ditches with my men when I saw hogs coming in from the river and took off after 'em by myself. You ask my men. They'll tell you."

"And . . . you were by yourself, after hogs, for maybe an hour?"

"That's what I said. Got down there and stopped to clear some tall brush so those hogs couldn't hide."

"If I go talk to your men, that's what they'll tell me, too?"

"That's what I said. Sheriff, I'm not known as a liar and I don't like what you're—"

"Things I gotta ask, Justin."

"Well, I'd appreciate it if you and your boys would get moving, get on out of here, and go find whoever did this to Uncle Amos. Time you stopped concentrating on the Blanchards. Me and my family got a lot to talk about."

"Got my job, Justin. You know that."

"Sure like to see you doin' it." He squinted at the sheriff. "I'm beginning to think we maybe should get Ben Fordyce out here. Seems like a lawyer's gonna be needed if you boys don't get goin' on this."

Sheriff Higsby shook his head and looked around at Hunter, who stood with his hands folded and his head bowed.

"Wouldn't've taken long if you killed him, Justin. Amos over there fooling around, maybe at the fence, or something like that. Could've surprised him. Done him in 'cause you couldn't help yourself."

Miss Amelia let out an exasperated sound. She flounced off the hard chair she'd taken in a corner of the room and went to stand with her hand on Justin's back as he gave a harsh bark of a laugh. His dark eyes were shining with fury. I knew the look. The two of us had scrapped enough when we were kids. What I'd counted on back then was getting him so mad he'd end up sputtering.

"Yup, Sheriff," Justin said. "Then I went back to clearing ditches. All in a day's work. I'll give you this much, if I caught Amos in there, doin' what he was doing . . . maybe you'd've found him with a broken arm or two—but not dead. At least, not until he told me how he rigged my daddy's death on that mower to look like an accident."

Someone coming in the front door stopped the sheriff from answering. An officer, holding a plastic-wrapped object in his hands, walked over and showed the object to the sheriff, who nodded. The two went out into the front hall and consulted briefly in whispers before the sheriff was back, motioning for me to come out to the hall. He held the wrapped package out and asked me if I recognized it.

Through the doubled-over plastic I could make out a small hatchet.

Behind me, Justin, who'd followed us, spoke up. "Looks like any other hatchet. Where'd you find it?"

"Found tree fiber between the blade and the handle. It was layin' by Amos's body. Guess it's what he used on your grove, Lindy."

I made a face. "It looks like one I kept in the greenhouse. I had a hatchet, an ax—in case I needed it . . . you should find lots of tools. Of course there'll be tree fibers on all of them."

"Only thing is . . ." He turned to look around directly at me. "The tech says no fingerprints. Not on the handle and not on the blade. How'd you imagine Amos did all that damage and didn't leave a single fingerprint on the weapon? Not even yours, Lindy. Wiped clean."

He scratched at his shaggy head. "Wasn't wearing gloves when he got himself killed. No dirt on his hands. No dirt on his clothes, 'cept what was on his back from falling down in it. Tech said soil on the floor of the greenhouse was different from the dirt outside. You must use special stuff inside, that right?" He turned back to me.

I nodded. "My own mix."

"So," the sheriff went on, "how'd he do it, you imagine, all that damage? Anybody in this room can answer that one, well, you're a better man than I am."

Sheriff Higsby turned his hooded eyes back to me. "There're a couple more things, Lindy. Said they found your computer out beyond the fence. Smashed to pieces. Guess that killer didn't want to have to carry it. Or Amos stomped on it before going into the greenhouse. Sure gives you one more thing to hold against him."

I let the implication pass. There were more important things to worry about. My mind went to ways to get my files back. I had backup disks but they were probably somewhere in the ashes. My only hope was the computer in my apartment.

"Another question," Sheriff Higsby interrupted my thoughts. "That all the trees you had out there in back?"

I thought. "Sure. Every one of them . . ." I stopped when a thought hit me. "Well, maybe not. There were five in pots. I didn't see 'em . . ."

"Five in pots? So whoever did this could've taken those five. Like they wanted some of your stock."

I nodded. That was all I could do. Of course, the five best of all my trees. The five with the greatest promise. I hadn't even missed them.

"Heavy to cart away?"

I shook my head. "Not big trees yet. I carried them in and out easily."

"You think maybe somebody's after your work, Lindy? Maybe that's what happened out there? Now they got those five trees?"

I was too tired to think about it. Personally, I took this as good news. I could make up time—if I could find the missing trees.

He shut his notebook with a snap and slid it into a back pocket. "Sure hope we don't find those trees hid somewhere on this ranch. My men are searching now. Might take some time, but if you folks hid 'em . . . well, I'm gonna be thinkin' maybe the whole family's in on this and you're all tryin' to cover up a murder."

He looked slowly, and sadly, from one of us to the other.

"It's one thing to be mad, maybe even hate somebody. It's a whole other thing to take the law into your own hands."

"I want you and the rest of these men off my property." Justin got up and stood tall. When he spoke, his voice was colder than I'd ever heard it. "You got any more to say to us, you call Ben Fordyce. What you're saying, Sheriff, is that we murdered Amos. Far as I'm concerned, you're an enemy to our whole family and that's the last help we're givin' you . . ."

Bethany moaned and hugged a pillow. Miss Emma hurried over to stop Justin, but he waved her back. "From here on, we'll take care of this the way we've always taken care of threats against our family. We'll do it ourselves."

"I wouldn't be doin' anything rash, Justin. If you're right and none of you was involved in the killin', well, we'll find out . . ."

"Funny, Sheriff. That doesn't make me feel any better."

"One last question, Justin." The sheriff went on as if he were deaf. "You wear gloves out there when you're working? Cleaning out those ditches is dirty work . . ."

Justin said nothing. He eyed first one of the officers and then the other. He came to Hunter last. When he spoke, disappointment was thick in his voice. "Never thought we'd come to this, Hunter. We been friends since we were little. Now, you turning like this . . ."

Hunter shook his head. "I'm no enemy to the Blanchards," he said. "And you know I will never turn"—he looked around at me—"on any of your family. We'll get the truth. You all just hang in there and let us do our job."

On his way out the door, Hunter turned to me a last time. "Get somebody to protect your greenhouse, Lindy. You've got those seedlings that whoever did this didn't get to. Better have Martin Sanchez put a man on watch."

"They've got my best trees, Hunter. The rest don't mean a whole lot."

"Somebody murdered a man. Maybe it was all to get those trees, Lindy. I'd say everybody in this house better be careful from here on in."

I nodded. Hunter was right. It seemed we were all targets in one way or the other.

Chapter Eight

When the police left, the house around us seemed emptier than it had ever been. Empty and unfriendly. We sat huddled in the living room, wrapped in little bubbles of misery, each with no hope of tomorrow being any better than today.

It felt like the middle of the night, but when I checked, my watch said ten twenty-five. I thought it had stopped, or time had stopped. All that had happened to us, changed our lives—in the space of a few short hours.

Miss Amelia started fussing about no supper though everybody swore they couldn't eat a thing. True to who she was, my grandmother said that was nonsense and got up to go see what she could rustle up in the kitchen. Mama and Bethany followed, offering help, maybe needing to do something other than sit there feeling bad. It was kind of like I felt, my hands between my knees, my face certainly set and angry. I was unable to move or think of a way to stop everything from happening.

Lamps burned low on the tables around the room. They

cast trembling shadows on the ceiling. Justin and I sat across from each other, with me facing the big windows, where the black velvet of a Texas spring night beyond mirrored me and my brother and our misery.

We said nothing at first, letting the turmoil and anger and sorrow—all the emotions we'd been feeling—settle.

"The sheriff's got his mind made up. You know that, don't you, Lindy?" Justin looked up at me finally.

All I could do was shake my head. The weight I felt inside my chest was a mix of disappointment and fear and uncertainty. Might as well say our world was ending. Murder changed everything. For a split second, even I'd wondered if Justin caught Amos out there and flew into a killing rage. Maybe, deep inside, he thought the same about me. And who knew? If I'd come in on Amos destroying my trees, and another ax or hatchet had been around . . .

But damn it, I told myself. Not one of my plant stakes.

"What can we do?" I turned to Justin.

"All I know is that Higsby is looking straight at this house for his killer. Nowhere else. A lot easier to come after a Blanchard."

"We don't have the resources the police have. And, Justin, it could be dangerous. Some lunatic—"

"Yeah, well, I've got the feeling the sheriff's coming after me. Something about when Hunter came in that last time. I think they found something else . . ."

"What was there to find? You didn't—"

"Geez, Lindy." Disappointment. I shrugged.

"What I'm saying is that we know people. We know our story inside out. It's not one of us, so who could it be? What we've got to find out is who in town hated Uncle Amos more than we did. Then we've got to look at where he's been for the last two years. One thing Uncle Amos did really well was make enemies wherever he went."

I hated to say what I was going to say. "There's Martin. After Amos broke up with Jessie, and that woman went into the library and told Jessie she was pregnant by him, I don't think anybody hated Amos more than Martin did. Cheating on his only daughter like that."

"You saw Martin on the mower this afternoon."

I nodded. "But he could have done it before. If he saw Amos in my grove . . . well . . . you know how Martin feels about all of us. Daddy gave him a job to begin with and then made him foreman. He'd do anything . . . I swear it."

He shook his head. "Not Martin."

He added. "Gotta be somebody. You know I still don't believe that 'accident' stuff about Daddy. Never will. Turn a mower over—okay. But fall under the blades, get that many cuts to his spine?" He shrugged. "First place, Daddy wasn't dumb. He knew how to throw his body out of the way. Second—anybody ever check the cuts? See for sure a mower blade did the damage? Look at it that way, two Blanchards are dead."

"It was an accident," I said again, as I'd said so many times over the last two years.

"Lindy, you live with your head in those trees of yours. Life's not what you think it is. There are people out there who would kill for a few dollars. Maybe kill for a few hundred bucks."

"You mean, like a hired killer?"

He shrugged. "Who knows?"

I wasn't going there with him, like walking into a dark alley. I knew enough to let him alone once he turned back into his old, simmering hatred. He'd calm down, just needed time.

After a long, sad five minutes, I said, "I say we talk to people like Ethelred Tomroy. If anybody knows what's been going on in Riverville, it's Ethelred. Maybe Amos said something to somebody, or fought with somebody. She'll know."

"And Harry Conway—we gotta talk to him and Chastity. Amos had been livin' there for the last couple of weeks. And the twins out at the Chauncey ranch. Amos worked for them before he left town, after the big blowup the night of Daddy's funeral. I think Mama called and asked them to give him a job and keep an eye on him. Wouldn't put it past her. Maybe the girls would know where he went when he left town. Could be it's part of that—making enemies in some new place and they followed him back here."

"And I've got those five trees of mine to think about. The sheriff said he'd better not find them on our property—make it look even worse for us. Like I couldn't stand to kill off all my stock. Like we're in this together."

"What I was trying to say," I forged on. "That other woman was from over at the Barking Coyote Saloon. There was that boyfriend she threw over, hoping to get her nails into a Blanchard. Remember? He came to the house that one time, looking for Amos."

Justin nodded. "Somebody else who wouldn't want to see Amos back in town."

"The way I see it, Justin, is if it wasn't you and it wasn't me, and it sure wasn't Mama, then we gotta start looking into Amos's past and where he's been these last two years, just like you said."

"I know the sheriff's already got somebody going through his room at the Conways'."

"We should be looking, too."

"They'll get everything."

"What if there's something they won't recognize as being a part of Uncle Amos's death?"

"Like what?"

"I don't know. A book. A letter. Who knows? I think we should get over there and look for ourselves. Maybe we'd connect it up."

There wasn't much more to say. The thinking hard felt good. At least a path to take that didn't lead us straight to jail.

When the doorbell rang, I got up reluctantly. The last thing I wanted was any more company that night. Well, maybe not the last thing. Hunter Austen, standing on the porch, a laptop computer in his hands, was even worse.

"Lindy." Austen tipped his bare head. "We picked up your laptop at the Nut House. It's been dusted for fingerprints. Need you to give us your fingerprints in the morning. For comparison. Tech says looks like only one set, though. A few are smudged. Probably all yours." He shuffled his feet uncomfortably, then handed me the MacBook. "Morning's soon enough."

He hesitated. "I wanted to come back anyway, to talk to you. I . . ."

I opened the door wider. Without smiling, I took the laptop from him and nodded for him to come on in. He stepped into the foyer, looked over at Justin, tipped his head, then bent low to whisper toward me. "Could we talk somewhere . . ."

"I don't think so, Hunter," I said. "Your boss thinks one of us did that to Amos, and we know we didn't. So that kind of leaves us on very different sides of this fence."

He shook his head hard. "You know I don't believe what the sheriff's thinking. That's one of the reasons I came back tonight. Just wanted you to know I won't let anything happen to you. I asked to be put on this case full-time and the sheriff gave me the go-ahead. He sat me down first. He knows . . . um . . . what good friends we are. I told him I didn't think any of you Blanchards had anything to do with this but that I'd look at the facts just the way things played out." He shuffled his feet on the polished tile of the foyer. "I just wanted you to know."

Justin got up slowly from the small sofa where he'd been sitting and made his way over to lean against the archway. "I don't think we've got any options here, Hunter. In a way, we're enemies until this thing is settled."

"I'm not your enemy, Justin. Never will be. You know that."

"That's what I always thought."

"Well, you can keep thinkin' it. I swear, I'm going after who did this . . ."

Justin nodded. "Just to let you know—so are we. There's no chance I'm sitting still and waiting to go to jail for something I didn't do, though I'm still not sorry somebody did him in."

"Shouldn't talk that way . . . folks'll think—"

"Yeah, well, Hunter, that's where you and I are different. I don't care what folks think. I care about what really happened, and about whose got it in for my family."

Hunter frowned. "What do you mean, 'got it in for' your family? I don't see—"

"I know you don't. That's what worries me. I see somebody coming after Lindy's work. Then I see them killing a man who hates all of us, who's let it be known for years what he thinks of us. And who we hated, just as bad, right back. No secrets about the Blanchards in Riverville."

"I gotta work with what is."

Justin pulled in a deep breath. "That's what I'm afraid of."

Hunter put his head down. "I can't say I'll work with you, but I won't work against you."

He turned directly to face me. "This is murder, Lindy. Whoever did this won't stop at doing it again. If you get in his way . . ."

"I don't have a choice. Neither does Justin."

"Just give me your promise—don't get yourselves in so deep you're in trouble."

"We'll see," Justin said. "We'll be protecting our family first. Whatever that takes. But . . ." He looked hard at me, a slow kind of worry spreading into his eyes. "If it appears like we're on to something we can't handle, or if we need your help, I promise you, Hunter, we'll come to you."

Hunter was gone with only a single nod. Our roles in Amos Blanchard's murder were clear-cut now. Maybe our goal was the same, but it sure seemed the paths we had to take would be different.

Chapter Nine

We picked at platters of scrambled eggs and ham and thick toast, which Miss Amelia had set on the round table. Justin washed his eggs down with a very small shot of Garrison Brothers Texas Straight Bourbon Whiskey. I joined him, thinking if there ever was a time for courage in a bottle, this was it.

"Just for keepin' spirits up," Miss Amelia, who didn't believe in hard liquor—usually—had said when she set the bottle down in the middle of the table.

My trouble was whiskey made me sleepy, which I was thinking might be a good thing. I was staying the night in my old room, not willing to go back to the Nut House by myself, at least not in the dark. I started to get up, telling myself how tired I was and how I'd probably need a lot of strength for the morning, when another sharp ring of the doorbell sounded from the front hall.

Bethany, sitting across the table from me, tapping furiously at her computer, dropped her head lower and ignored the bell.

Justin wrote on sheet after sheet of a pad of paper as he shoveled food into his mouth, took small sips of the Garrison Brothers, and went on as if the doorbell didn't exist.

I'd logged on to the computer Hunter'd brought from my apartment with high hopes that all my files would be there. But there was nothing. I'd figured: two computers, backup hard copies, backup disks—that would handle any problem. What did I have to worry about?

Now I knew and felt more than bad. A totally blank screen. Not a single icon.

And I couldn't tell anybody. I looked around at the worried faces of my family and knew I had to keep this new disaster to myself.

I didn't want to register the sound of a bell ringing either. Not at eleven thirty at night. Maybe some reporter. We'd been getting phone calls all evening from newspapers as far away as Dallas. So we were going to be famous all over Texas. Us and the Alamo, I thought.

Perfectly rotten day and evening . . . and future.

And about to get worse.

Miss Amelia, who'd gone to answer the door, came back with her face a mass of warning smiles, leading the couple behind her, preceded by an ill wind of overpowering perfume and shaving lotion.

Chastity Conway burst into the kitchen with her hands in the air, shaking them like a sinner in church. Her bright red hair was electrified, a mass of charged fuses. The red cowgirl boots she wore tap, tap, tapped across the tile floor. At the table she bent forward and threw her arms around Mama, grabbing her from behind, pulling my surprised mother back into a generous pair of bosoms and hugging her. Mama's eyes got huge. She held herself still until the hold on her head was loosened.

"Lord! Lord! Lord!" Chastity wrung her hands together.

"Me and Harry know it's late, but we couldn't stay away. Not when our good neighbors are in trouble like you people are. Nope, couldn't just sit there in that big house of ours and think about all of you over here. Miserable. Saw your lights and figured we'd come on over and tell you . . ."

She smiled a wide, bright smile at each of us around the table. Red lips. Red cheeks. Red, dangling earrings. She jingled and she swished—her stiff cowgirl skirt brushing behind our chairs. Chastity was colorful and loud and smelled good.

"Well, if there's anything me and Harry can do . . ."

She reached a hand with long red nails around and pulled Harry up to stand at the table beside her. He'd been hanging back in the middle of the room, thumbs stuck in the wide leather belt he wore with a buckle on it the size of Houston. He nodded to each of us around the table. "Evening," he said, looking uncomfortable. "Sorry to come over so late, but it's like Chastity says. Just couldn't sit there and not be neighborly enough to offer a hand. Whatever y'all need."

Something about Harry's "y'all" always made my scalp itch. Harry and Chastity had come to Riverville only seven years before from someplace in the Midwest. They bought the neglected ranch next to ours, tore down the old ranch house, and built something that looked like a manor house: big stones and blocks of granite. People in town forgave them their otherness, though, when they got the pecan groves going again. My daddy was the one who got them into the Pecan Co-op and introduced them around. That made all Blanchards friends with the Conways—like it or not.

"This is just awful! Awful! Awful! Awful!" Chastity collapsed into an empty chair. "Our place is crawling with cops. Amos dead! Why, I can't bring myself to believe it. And right out there in your greenhouse, Lindy! Ain't this the most awful thing? And Harry here . . ."

The thing was, I liked Harry Conway. He'd stepped in after Daddy died, offering any help we needed out in the groves. He had extra men, he'd said. Even offered to fill in over at the co-op. Daddy'd been president and got Harry nominated to the board. He was there when we needed him.

I never warmed to Chastity though there wasn't anything about her I could point to as annoying—unless it was the phony cowgirl image, or that cloud of perfume she went around in—like Pig-Pen's cloud in the Peanuts comic strip. Or maybe because she tried too hard and the one thing Texans didn't care for was people pushing themselves forward the way she did.

Harry came over to put his hands on my shoulders and hug me. Next he moved to Bethany, who tried to pull away. Then it was Mama, then Justin. He turned to grab Miss Amelia but she'd been smart enough to arm herself with a tray of sweet teas.

"None for me, Miss Amelia." Harry threw his hands in the air. "Be up all night as it is. Me and Chastity talking about getting a new burglar alarm. After this, why, it seems none of us are safe in our beds."

"Harry's just been a wreck since he heard." Chastity took a glass of tea as she assured us again what a wreck Harry was. "I mean, if he didn't take in Amos like that, well, maybe Amos wouldn't've hung around Riverville and maybe he'd still be alive."

Harry sat down between Justin and me. "Hope y'all know I only did it to keep him out of your hair." He turned a worried face to Mama. "Thought I was helping."

Mama smiled a smile that fell somewhere between a grimace and a yawn.

"For Christmas' sakes, Lindy." Chastity wriggled in her seat, turning to me. "Heard about your trees. All that work up in smoke. Well, you never know . . ." She leaned across Mama and patted my knee. "Heard they took off with five of 'em trees. That right?"

I nodded, miserable again at the thought of my trees in enemy hands.

"Why'd anybody do such a thing? You got any idea? Seems kind of . . . odd."

"Not the only thing odd," Justin muttered, reaching the very limit of his patience.

"What I'm saying is, why take any of 'em?" She turned back to me. "Think your trees got a chance of living? Special, is what I heard. Like you was coming up with something new any rancher would give her eyeteeth to have. Lucky you . . . but, oh my, now they're gone."

Bethany spoke up. "Sheriff says if he finds Lindy's trees around here, it'll look even more like one of us did that awful thing to Uncle Amos." She shuddered.

"If they get the right water and whatever it is you give them, maybe they'll still be okay when they catch this man," Harry said.

I sighed. "Maybe."

"Hope they get who did this pretty fast," Harry said. "By tomorrow morning Riverville's gonna be up in arms."

"Me, too," Chastity spouted, flouncing in her chair again, the smell of her mega-strength perfume wafting around the table. "That's just how I feel. Murder, right next door to us. Maybe somebody's got it in for all us ranchers. Harry, here, says there's nothing to worry about but you know Harry. Ain't been around Texas that long." She poked at that enormous pile of unmoving hair. "'Course, Amos coulda brought this back with him from wherever it was he went away to. Don't need to tell you folks about Amos's temper."

Bethany looked up from her laptop, blond hair springing out into a curly halo. "I'm sure hopin' the news doesn't travel all the way to Houston."

"What's going on in Houston, hon?" Chastity asked.

"I've got a huge wedding planned for here. Two weeks. Don't want him canceling on me."

"Who you got, honey?" Chastity asked, giving Bethany a sweet smile.

Bethany hesitated. She knew better than to give out too much. Though the Conways were good family friends, Chastity was putting up an event tent of her own and they'd soon be competitors. Beth, the youngest in our family, was proud of the niche she was carving out—big, expensive weddings and maybe a few political events. I watched her figure the angles and then smile sweetly at Chastity, as if she didn't understand the question.

"Somebody from around here?" Chastity pushed.

Bethany shook her head.

"How many you got comin'?" Chastity zeroed in.

"Not many."

"You getting doves and all that stuff? I'm getting doves for my weddings. I should be up and running by next week. You need to move your wedding 'cause of this murder, don't forget about my place."

"Things'll be fine by then. And yes, Chastity, I am getting doves and the biggest cake ever. My newscaster wants the best of everything."

"Newscaster?" Chastity's eyes lit up. "From Houston? Must be important."

Bethany shrugged, hugging her secrets to herself, though her face lighted briefly at the thought of the doves she had already ordered, and the cake looking like that TV station in Houston. And many, many flowers.

"Well, I truly hope he don't cancel on you. You call 'im

since this happened? Saw it on the eleven o'clock news. As I say, Bethany, you can always send 'im over to me, it comes to that. I mean, if the couple don't like the idea of a murder right where they're getting married."

Bethany bit down on her bottom lip. She looked to Miss Amelia for help.

"I don't think Bethany's up to talking business right now, Chastity." Miss Amelia cleared her throat and snatched Chastity's tea glass from the table. She was giving the signal it was time to leave.

"Well," Chastity finally said as Miss Amelia stood at the middle of the room, waiting to usher them out. "Me and Harry didn't come over here to add to your family's misery. Last thing we want is more strain on you. I can see yer all tired out. Especially you, Miss Amelia. If I was you, I'd close that Nut House down tight 'til this was all over. How much can a woman of your years be expected to take, I'd like to know?"

Miss Amelia's eyes went dark, almost like shutters coming down. I knew that face and squirmed just seeing it come over her. She drew her mouth into a tight line. "Well, bless yer heart for worrying about me, Chastity. But I'm doing just fine."

I knew Meemaw's "Well, bless yer heart." Four little words that could barely hide the knife of steel at their center. A few more minutes of Chastity and my grandmother was going to have steam coming out of her ears.

I stood before my grandmother went after the woman and "snatched her bald-headed," as Meemaw liked to warn, when her patience was tried beyond her ability to maintain the cool look she turned on most people. "I'll say good night," I said. "It's been a rough day. I'm sure you and Chastity understand . . ."

I waited expectantly in the archway leading to the living room and out the front door.

"Sure thing." Harry motioned for Chastity to get moving. "Not a night for chitchatting anyway."

"Remember, Bethany." Chastity leaned back from the doorway. "You need to send your wedding to me, I'll be ready. Gettin' my flyers printed now. Gonna be a beautiful place. Not that yers isn't. Just that mine's newer, you know."

Bethany didn't look up, just bit down hard on her full bottom lip. Justin was on his feet, pushed beyond his endurance. "Ya don't mind, we gotta get to bed," he said.

"And thanks for coming over," Miss Amelia threw in for good measure as she put a hand on Chastity's back and steered her down the hall.

They were gone. We listened for the outer door to close, then all sighed our gratitude.

Miss Amelia finally rubbed at her nose with a finger. "I think Chastity's lost her sense of smell. All that perfume. Skunks can't smell themselves either. You know that?"

She looked around the table, from one to the other of us, as we burst into laughter.

"That's not true, Meemaw," I said when I could talk. "Skunks hate the smell of skunk oil."

"Well"—she waved a dismissive hand in the air—"you take my point."

Chapter Ten

The doorbell rang again at eight o'clock the next morning.
I felt as if I had just shut my eyes. My bedside clock was
blurry. The bell rang again. I groaned and threw an arm
across my eyes. "Go away," I moaned.

It all hit me. All the horror ahead of us. *My poor trees . . .*
I wished I'd been smarter, put chips in all my trees, the way
they did in dogs. But when would I ever have expected my
trees to be stolen—let alone destroyed? Awful.

"Lindy!"

Meemaw called me from downstairs. If I ignored her, I
wouldn't have to get up and I wouldn't have to face whatever
it was we were going to have to face again today. Something
awful . . .

"Lindy! Get down here. The sheriff's come to arrest your
brother."

I was out of bed and throwing a ratty old bathrobe on,
then down the stairs and into chaos. Mama was yelling at
the sheriff through the screen.

"You get out of here." Her voice was filled with anger. "Yer not taking Justin anywhere."

Miss Amelia tried to calm Mama with a hand on her arm. Bethany stood against a wall, both fists knotted at her mouth, eyes panicked. Justin stumbled down the stairs from the back of the house, behind me. When Mama saw him, she yelled for him to get back upstairs. "Call Ben!" she hollered. "Don't come down here, Justin."

But of course, Justin did just that. Straight to the front door, where he held it open for Sheriff Higsby to come in.

"Sheriff." He nodded to the man. "What can we do for you? Kinda early to come calling, isn't it?"

I didn't know what was going on though I figured Mama was all upset about something bad happening. Miss Amelia frowned hard at the sheriff, who took up a lot of space in the front hall, with his guns and big chest and badge and belt and shoes that looked like the feet on a statue over in the park.

Sheriff Higsby shoved his large sunglasses up on his wide forehead. His broad face was set and official looking. Hunter was behind him, looking off toward the groves turning golden in the first light. From Hunter's set and unhappy face, I knew whatever was ahead wasn't going to be pleasant.

Sheriff Higsby dipped his head, greeting us solemnly one by one. His sunglasses fell down his nose, which disconcerted him and his official dignity. He fumbled them back up to the top of his head.

"Justin Blanchard," the sheriff said, looking over Justin's head, avoiding looking at any of us.

"Right here, Sheriff," he said, pushing his arms into a white cotton T-shirt as he spoke. His hair stuck up, uncombed. His belt hung half in and half out of the pant loops.

"Would you step out to the verandah, Justin?"

"I'm not even . . . well . . . could I finish getting my clothes on?"

"No need. This isn't a social call."

"You arresting me, Sheriff?"

Sheriff Higsby took a deep breath and looked away again. How uncomfortable we all were. All this official business nobody wanted to be a part of. I looked out at Hunter, who was avoiding me. Sheriff Higsby's face had gone bright red. Mama was quiet now, tears running down her cheeks. Miss Amelia'd turned to solid rock. Bethany cried. I stood there feeling betrayed and mad and bursting with pent-up fear with no place to go with it.

"Hunter here's gonna read you your rights."

Miss Amelia shook herself and put her arms around Mama. "What the devil do you think you're doin,' Willard?" she demanded of the sheriff, this grown man she'd known since he was in his teens, a man she'd stood up for when he'd once been arrested for drunk driving after his wife, Dora, died.

"Sorry, Miss Amelia. Gotta do my job."

"You, too, Hunter?" I eyed my friend. Hunter's face flamed up into his hairline. He said nothing.

"What're you arresting me for?" Justin demanded.

"First-degree murder," the sheriff said. "The murder of Amos Blanchard."

"That's crazy! I didn't murder Uncle Amos and you know it. I wasn't even there . . ."

"Stand still." The sheriff turned Justin and cuffed him as Hunter, in a low, sad voice, read his friend his rights.

We closed in tighter around Justin, who stood with his hands cuffed behind his back as his old friend intoned his legal rights.

"Damn right he's getting an attorney." Mama spoke up, her hand on her boy's shoulder. "I'm callin' Ben Fordyce right now. He'll have 'im outta there before you get him locked up."

Sheriff Higsby lowered his head. "You do what you have to do, ma'am. I'm doing what I have to do, too. Doubt it'll do much good. Murder one means no bond 'til there's a hearing. Judge'll decide."

"Least let the boy get his boots," Miss Amelia demanded, freezing the men in place with a voice everyone who'd ever had a grandmother recognized. Bethany ran back into the house and brought Justin his boots.

"Hunter?" I looked out at him. I saw him swallow hard before he turned to face me. "What's going on? You know Justin didn't do that to Amos."

Hunter opened his mouth a time or two then shook his head and went off beside Justin, leading him carefully out to the waiting police car.

"You should be ashamed of yourself, Sheriff," Miss Amelia yelled after the man. "How long you known the Blanchards? All your life?"

She threw her hands in the air, wordless, tears running down her wrinkled cheeks. Bethany put her arms around Meemaw and held on tight while I stood apart, separate from the women in my family. They were suffering. They were good women. All I felt was rage, and a need to do something, anything. Most of all, I wanted to get my hands on whoever was trying to destroy our family. At that moment, all I wanted to do was hurt somebody.

Chapter Eleven

"Being processed," Reggie Crystal, the officer behind the high mahogany counter at the Riverville Police, told us when we got into town, a half hour behind the sheriff and Justin.

"You all wait over there." Reggie pointed to a row of hard folding chairs set against the far wall. "Don't know if you can see him or not. Interrogation takes a lot of time."

That word "interrogation" froze my skin. It sounded like a bad murder movie, or one of those true crime TV shows where the suspect is left alone for a while to beat his head on the table, then confess, and sign anything.

"We'll wait all right." Miss Amelia shook her finger at Reggie, who looked down at his computer like a chastised kid. "And you boys better just hurry it up. We got a right to see Justin. Go tell that to the sheriff."

She made a scoot motion with her hand and Reggie was out of his chair and through a swinging door to the inner offices and cells like a man on a sacred mission.

He was back pretty fast, a hangdog look on his face.

"Sorry, Miss Amelia. Like I said, takes time. The sheriff'll be out . . ."

Ben Fordyce came striding in like a lone cowboy riding to the rescue in his custom-made cowboy hat, custom-made boots that must have cost a fortune, and an Eastern business suit caught somewhere in the middle of all that pure Texas.

Ben Fordyce had been the family attorney for the last ten years. Ever since he came to Riverville, after a bad marriage and a worse breakup with his partners in a New York law firm. He'd come to town right after my grandfather's best friend and family attorney for more years than I could count, Harold Marshall, died. New lawyers in Riverville don't get much business at first. It was that thing about being an old resident; that thing about taking thirty or more years to be trusted by the town folk. But after Ben helped Daddy with a land grant problem, they became friends and Ben became the family lawyer. With Daddy behind him, Ben started doing better than most lawyers could expect in twenty-five years or more. It was Daddy's backing that got even the Pecan Co-op to bring their legal work to Ben.

He was a thin man with a fringe of graying blond hair sticking out from under his white hat. He took off the hat and nodded to each of us, saying a "Good morning" before pulling a chair up next to Mama, setting his briefcase down beside him, and looking sadly at each of us in turn. "Sorry for your troubles," he said, meaning it. "Good thing your Father's not here to see this. He'd be tearing this building apart, brick by brick, arresting Justin the way they did."

"Can't you get him out of here, Ben?" Mama begged, her face wet with tears. She took a swipe at her nose with her sleeve. Miss Amelia pulled out a tissue and handed it to her.

"It's gonna take a little patience, Emma," Ben said, his gentle face saying how sorry he was for not bringing better news. "Let me get inside there and talk to the sheriff. I'll see what's happening."

He got up and went over to talk to Reggie. There were a few heated words before Ben blustered on past him, through the swinging doors, and into the back toward the cells.

I felt something like relief. Ben was our cavalry. After Daddy died, he'd been at the ranch every day being Mama's champion, and hugging the rest of us when the trying to be brave got to be too much.

The fifteen minutes Ben was gone felt like an hour. He came out and sat back down. He leaned in close, whispering, "Doubt if they'll be keeping Justin long. At least not here. Probably go over to Columbus. Court's there. I'd like to get him out on bail before then, but to tell you the truth . . ." He looked hard at Mama and the rest of us, as if assessing how much we could take. "Well, let me do my best. But if he's moved, don't worry. It's about process from here on in. Like gettin' caught up in a washin' machine—can't get out until it's done. Might be just as well anyway, havin' Justin outta Riverville. People get worked up and they don't know a thing about what's happened and then they get talkin', and before you know it, you got hotheaded fools deciding they know more about justice . . ."

"People won't believe Justin did this." Miss Amelia looked shocked. "At least I hope our friends won't."

"I want him out of jail," Mama said through tight lips. "You understand, Ben? I want my son out of here and I want this settled."

"Means we gotta find out who did that to Amos, Emma. Doubt the sheriff here is gonna put too much effort into looking, now that he's got Justin."

"Hunter won't be a part of anything like that," I said as I tried to keep a lid on my festering anger. "He'll keep goin' . . ."

"Wasn't he there this morning, Lindy?" Mama turned on me, her eyes flashing. "Wasn't he the one read Justin his rights?"

"That's his job, Mama."

Miss Amelia bent forward, her back stiff. "What I'm thinking is, we've gotta get a plan together. Just us." She dropped her voice into ice water. "If you can't rely on family, you got nobody."

Ben stood. "I'll be busy here awhile. Seems they found some evidence near Amos's body. Something that implicates Justin. That's all the sheriff would tell me."

"Oh, Lord." Mama leaned toward her mother. "That's not even possible."

Ben nodded hard at her. "Let me get going on filing papers and talkin' to Justin. Are you waiting here? Or do you want me to call later at the house?"

"What do you think?" Mama pulled her leather shoulder bag around to the front of her. "I'm not going anywhere 'til they let me see my son."

Ben turned to me. "And, Lindy, I'd say trust Hunter to be fair. No matter what it looks like, I think Hunter Austen is on our side. Probably—if push comes to shove—he'd put you before his job. Just try not to push him too far, Lindy. He loves law enforcement, but a woman can have a strange hold on a man. Remember that. It's a power some women know all too well. Just don't judge him harshly, and don't ask for more than he can give."

I took that in and was ready to go after Ben. "I'm going to do whatever I have to do to find out who did that to Uncle Amos. Don't tell me not to judge a man who's been a friend all my life. If Hunter turns against us, well—if it's true a woman's got power over a man, then I'm using that power. Using it to get my brother out of here. Nothing's going to stop me asking for Hunter's help. And nothing will ever make me forgive him if he turns me down."

Ben, bowed a little in the face of my outrage, got up and walked toward Sheriff Higsby, who'd just come through the swinging doors.

Chapter Twelve

We sat in that dreary place right into the afternoon. It was close to three o'clock when Reggie finally told Mama she could go back to see Justin, but only for a few minutes.

When she came out, she wasn't crying anymore, just looking resolute. "Justin wants to see you for a minute," she said to Miss Amelia. "The sheriff said it's okay."

Emma pushed her short hair back from her tired face and laid a callused hand against her cheek. "Justin wants me to stop by Martin's house. He'll be running the whole ranch until this is over."

She thought a minute, closed her eyes, and took a long breath. "Something about Martin doing a special job for him—if I can find out anything. Guess that's about the fences those hogs tore up. Anyway I'm going on home. Anybody coming with me?"

Miss Amelia went back to see Justin. Bethany, saying it would be best to make the dreaded phone call to her newsman from home, went with Mama. I'd come to town with

Miss Amelia, who wanted to get over to the Nut House, so I hung around to wait for her.

Miss Amelia was back in twenty minutes, not saying a word, only motioning for me to get up and follow her outside. We were in my pickup before she said a word. And then it was only an order to get over to the Nut House.

"Folks'll be wondering why the store's closed," she said. "A Saturday, after all. One of my busiest days."

"Don't worry, Meemaw. They all know why by now." I waited only a minute before asking, "What did Justin want?"

"I gotta think," she said, snapping at me.

I knew when to leave my grandmother alone so I kept quiet, turned the corner, and parked in front of the Nut House. The two green and white flags with the family crest still flew in front of the building. Nobody'd remembered to take the flags down the night before, and anyway it looked right, like saying to Riverville: Don't count the Blanchards out.

We sat looking at the store for a good five minutes.

"Why don't you just go ahead and close it up today?" I said after a while.

She nodded, then nodded again. "Got a death in the family anyway. Think that's only the right thing to do."

She went on sitting. "Need a sign up on the door," she said after a couple of long sighs. "Think I'll call Treenie about baking off the cookies on Monday and opening up. But no pies. Not one damned pie. People sayin' my baked goods don't taste like they used to . . . well, let 'em put up with that mediocre stuff they sell down at the Pick and Run, or go askin' Ethelred to bake 'em one—she thinks she's so good."

Miss Amelia was mad about everything at once. I didn't blame her and got out of the truck as fast as she did, up the steps of the wide front porch, key in the lock, and into the shop.

"Anyway." She turned once we were inside, blinking as

if surprised to find me still behind her. "You and me have things to talk about. I made a list with Justin—people we got to go see. He's been doing nothing but thinking . . ."

"You mean, like talking to Ethelred and the Chauncey girls and getting over to the Barking Coyote? I've got some ideas of my own. But, Meemaw, are you sure you're up to taking on something like this?"

I got the most cutting, the most withering look my grandmother ever gave me. I wanted to disappear right down inside my white T-shirt.

"You hear news of my death yet?"

I shook my head, knowing better than to say one word.

She waited, fixing me with a look meant to reduce me to the size of a peanut. "Then I guess we're all set. Gotta go after who did this to Amos. I just know in my heart it's tied up to your experiments somehow, but who'd want to go after your trees? What you're doing out there is supposed to benefit everybody, all the ranchers. That's what you always said. So maybe not a rancher at all. Can't figure that one. And what was Amos doin' out at your greenhouse in the first place? If it wasn't one of us who came on him in there, then it was Amos who came on somebody and died trying to stop them from ruining your experiments. How's that sound to you?"

I thought a minute. "Or maybe he was meeting somebody there."

"Why? He knew he wasn't exactly the prodigal son coming home."

"Maybe he was in on it with the person destroying my trees. I don't know. If anybody wanted to see us fail, well, I'd say that person was Uncle Amos." I shook my head hard, as if ideas could be made to line up better.

"When he came in the store earlier, I wouldn't say he was belligerent, would you? He had that letter he wanted to give Emma. You think maybe he came out to see you about that?"

"Why didn't he stop at the house and see Mama directly?"

She headed toward the front counter, straightening a tipped gift box here, a package of pecan turtles there. "This whole thing's a mess," she said over her shoulder. "Usually I can see a true path through things that happen. You know, the past leading right up to the present. Old hatreds and hurts are behind bad things most of the time. And there's plenty of that here—with all Amos's old rantings and ravings. I'm just not seeing a high road through what's happened."

"Don't you think we've got to find out where Amos has been for the last two years? Seems like that's got to come into this."

She nodded as she rummaged through the drawers behind the counter, pulling out a pad of paper and a pen. "So what we've gotta do is talk to everybody. Wherever he went, maybe this was a plan he'd hatched to get even with us, brought somebody in on it with him."

I nodded. "Maybe they had a falling-out. Sounds most logical."

She nodded. "So let me get this note on the door and we'll get going."

"Where?"

"Why, over to the Conways'. That's where he was staying."

"The sheriff and Hunter were already there. Remember? Last night Chastity said they were still there, going through Amos's things?"

"Aren't we Amos's kin? You're his grieving niece."

"What about the sheriff?"

She made a derisive sound. "That man? You think Willard Higsby wants to come against me? I don't think so." She stopped, looked around, then went over to straighten drooping packs of spiced pecans in the cardboard dumps set off against the wall. "I don't have a thing against him, mind you.

But since Dora died, he's lost a lot of his . . . what would you call it? Flexibility? So straitlaced and tight. People sayin' he's a real lawman now: The Law's the Law, and all of that. I say you got a man like that, you're buying misery."

I nodded. "You're right. But—"

"Hell's bells and panther tracks, girl," Miss Amelia chided. "I'd rather curl up in a corner and die right now than give in to somebody trying to hurt one of my kin. I don't care if it's the sheriff, a murderer, or some plant hater come to put an end to your evil messing with nature."

I opened my mouth but knew enough to snap it shut again.

"And I'll tell you something else, Lindy. Maybe you think I'm too old 'cause you don't see me out running marathons. But the thing about getting old is you learn to use your head instead of throwing your body at things. You learn to look at people and figure them out. And if anybody knows the people in this town, it's me. You got your mean ones, like Willy Shuck. That man hates people and dogs and all species in between. Willy brings me back cookie packages with one cookie left and demands his money back. Tells me they weren't any good. I know what old Willy's capable of, and I know what he's not capable of. Then I know the nice people with nothing but good things to say about my pies. The Chauncey sisters are like that." She hesitated. "Maybe I can't go running down Carya Street after some bad guy. Not like I once coulda done. But I'll do my share of asking questions and dropping in to visit folks who might help us. I'll do my part, Lindy. Don't you worry about that."

She put up a hand, stopping me as I dared open my mouth. "And we're gonna trust Hunter. So don't go spouting off on me. I know it and you know it, too—he's the best friend you've ever had and he'll be there when you need him. What we gotta do is start digging into Amos's past and those years he was gone. Then we gotta look into who he's been seeing since he came back. Could be old enemies and could be new ones."

"So like you said, we gotta get over to the Conway place."

"That's my girl. Now you got that overeducated head of yours thinking in the right direction."

"Granny, whatever it takes. Let's saddle up."

She sniffed. Frowned at me and then laughed. "Now I got this picture in my head. Me on Old Paint, struggling out through the sagebrush, waving my empty gun at the long-gone back of a cattle thief."

I laughed with her because the picture I had in my head, of me trying to stay on that horse, wasn't much better than hers.

Laughing was a lot better than crying.

Chapter Thirteen

Before we left the store, Miss Amelia called Treenie Menendez, who said she'd be right in to bake off the cookies. "But no pies," I heard Miss Amelia telling her. "You tell 'em go someplace else for a pecan pie as good as mine."

Treenie must have been laughing on the other end of the phone.

"Sure I'm getting even, Treenie. Never said I didn't have a little darkness in my soul. Let's see what they'll be saying about me after a week or so eating Ethelred Tomroy's pecan pies."

On our way, Miss Amelia took time to post her sign.

Outside, standing in the heat of bright sunshine filtering down through the pecan trees and live oaks lining Carya Street, I turned back to read the handwritten cardboard sign that made Miss Amelia smile:

> NO PECAN PIES FOR THE
> FORSEEABLE FUTURE DUE
> TO A VERY SAD DEATH IN

THE BLANCHARD FAMILY.
IF YOUR NEED FOR A PIE IS
GREAT, CALL ETHELRED TOMROY.
SHE MIGHT BE ABLE TO HELP YOU.

After shaking my head at my grandmother's duplicity, I took a minute, while she stepped back and folded her hands in front of her, admiring her handiwork, to cover my eyes against the sun and check the street to see who was watching us. Freda Cromwell, the queen of Riverville gossips, hailed us from across the street, hand up and waving hard as if she needed to talk. Miss Amelia signaled me from the corners of her eyes, then waved back as she whispered, "Let's get outta here."

With the bent woman still waving and bumbling across the street, we got in the car and drove off, leaving a wake of dust and a frustrated old lady behind us.

Leaving town, I sped up where the road widened flat and dead-on. Tiny heat waves, like a faint mirage, played across the pavement. I was hot and wanted to put on the air-conditioning, but Miss Amelia frowned on air-conditioning unless the thermometer read at least one hundred and one. We had the windows down, my limp ponytail flapping against my damp back, sweat pouring down my face, while Miss Amelia sat beside me, cool and untouched by the hot sun or the cloudless sky or much of anything beyond her own deep thoughts.

"As I was telling you before," she said after a while, "there's the mean ones and the kind ones and there's the liars and there's people so poor they come in for one pecan sandy though most of the time I make it at least two, telling them I got a special going. And there's rich people with a hundred-dollar saddle on a ten-dollar horse; don't pay their bills on time begging me for credit, which, as you know, is against everything I believe in."

She thumped her hands in her lap. "And I know who's having a little too much fun with another man's wife, and I know the lady who comes into the store smelling like whiskey at ten in the morning. I know who's having a fight with this one or that one 'cause they can never learn to keep their mouths shut. You just wouldn't believe the things you learn about people when you run a store, Lindy. There's that Tommy Johns, you know, the boy living down by the river in town with his daddy who's so sick. Comes in asking for work all the time. Give him what I can. And that Wright boy from over by the old railroad tracks working three jobs to get himself to college. That one girl pregnant . . . I'm not saying any names. Why, baking pies for people seems to come with a kind of trust you don't usually get from human beings." She nodded hard along with her own words.

"And I can tell you other things. Like about those cheaters at the county fair, wanting to take home the pecan pie prize so bad you just wouldn't believe what they'd do to win. And then I had thieves—well, one, who will remain nameless—trying to steal my recipes. Caught her back in the kitchen at the store one day. Riffling through my recipe boxes and telling me she was only looking for a blank card 'cause she had to write something down right then. And her bragging all over town that her pecan pie's just as good as mine."

I had to smile, knowing my grandmother's continuing feud with Ethelred Tomroy, even though they'd been friends since the first day Miss Amelia came to the ranch.

"You'd just be surprised at what pie envy brings out in people," Miss Amelia said, talking almost to herself.

"One thing I learned, though, is you don't judge too harshly. Everybody's got their story, you know. Wish you coulda known your grandfather. Darnell Hastings. A fine man. Would've made a great governor of this state. He believed in Texas values. The real values—like taking care of your family and yourself and still sharing this country with others. My Darnell would never've stood for the kind of raw violence some of these politicians stand for today." Miss Amelia took a long breath. "The man died way too young. Then there's your daddy Jake's death and Justin so sure somebody killed him. After a while you get so you don't feel sorry for yourself so much as you just get plain mad at the world. That's what I'm feeling right now . . . so gosh darned mad."

She paused, took a deep breath, and sat up even straighter. "So I'm saying the two of us can take on anything. We got you with your college smarts and me with my people smarts. Good combination, I'd say, for finding a murderer."

She glanced over, catching the big grin on my face. For maybe the first time, I had a true picture of the young woman behind the tired, older face. I recognized this different woman, one who could be a friend, not only a grandmother. I reached over and squeezed her hand.

"So, to Rancho Conway?"

Miss Amelia nodded. "Giddy up," she said. "Time's a wastin'."

I turned in under the huge, square sign spelling RANCHO CONWAY and slowed to drive up the long paved road to the Conway house, bigger than our house. Actually bigger than anybody's house. A real showplace. Like something straight out of the English countryside. Not exactly Texas, but surrounded with old pecan trees, branches lazily swaying in the hot afternoon breeze.

There was a white swing on the lawn and white wicker rockers with bright chintz cushions. This part of what they'd done with the place looked Southern, a place for ladies in long dresses and big bonnets to gather of a hot afternoon and sip their mint juleps while gossiping about their neighbors and declaring they hoped Davy Crockett was doing all right for himself over there at that Alamo.

The neatly trimmed lawn swept around the house and down toward the Colorado on one side, back to brand-new barns on the other.

I rang the bell, listening to a big gong sound inside the house. Chastity answered the door looking from me to Miss Amelia as if bowled over at the sight of us.

"Well, well, well. What do you know? I never expected Blanchards at my door this morning."

She made it sound as if Miss Amelia and I were a pair of twos in a high-stakes poker game, but then I wasn't happy either, coming here.

She stepped back and gestured grandly, inviting us into the high-ceilinged front hall with a huge crystal chandelier overhead.

"Harry's out. You know, business, business, business. But why am I tellin' Blanchards about that? You folks been here how long? Hundred years or so? Seen all kinds of things come and go, I'll bet. Like Harry says, if it ain't drought, it's scab or some other leaf-browning thing."

"That's pecan ranching, Chastity." Miss Amelia smiled and tipped her head to one side as she stepped across the grand foyer, in a hurry to get on about business. She held her hands together at her chest, giving the impression of a spritely old lady just dying to talk ranching with this woman who came from who knew where . . . but with so much on her mind . . .

"Well, don't I know it?" Chastity threw her hands in the air as she led us from the white-tiled front hall into a cold and darkly paneled living room with the windows firmly shut and covered by gold drapes. Lights burned everywhere and air-conditioned air blew hard enough to ruffle the frilly doilies on every table. "Now we got us this drought. Harry's so worried. If we don't get rain soon . . ."

She interrupted herself to see to her hostess duties. "You two have a seat here and I'll go get Bessie to bring us some sweet tea . . ." She turned in her high-heeled, nail-studded boots, to make her way out to the kitchen. "It's about time the three of us sat down and had us a good chat."

"Bless your heart, Chastity," she called after the woman. "Me and Lindy don't need a single thing. We just came to take a look through Amos's possessions. I'm still so distraught . . ."

Miss Amelia put a hand up, toward the direction of her forehead, then stopped and let the hand fall languidly to her side. "I'm sure you understand, Chastity. Some other day we'll drop by and spend hours chitchattin' . . ."

"Well, I don't know." The woman hesitated. "Harry's not here. Maybe I shouldn't let you go back there. It's out in the big barn. That's where he stayed. I woulda had him here in the house but Harry thought . . . well, since Amos was just a worker . . ."

I heard a rumble starting in Miss Amelia's throat, and I hurried to step in. "Still, the man's our kin." I pulled out my best drawl. "You understand. Me and my meemaw here, why, all we want to do is see where our Amos was livin' here at the last."

Chastity stayed confused a minute more, before giving in. "I guess there's nothing wrong with you two going out there. Family's something I understand, coming from a fine Texas family myself. If y'all just follow me . . ."

We were off, out through the large, unused kitchen, where a uniformed woman stood watching TV, and out the back door into heat like liquid fuel. Once we were through the clipped-short grass of a yard filled with lounges and tiny white tables, and out under the tall trees, Miss Amelia gave a sigh of relief, which I understood.

The Conways' barns were bigger than ours, and newer, and surprisingly empty. Even off-season, when we weren't packing, our barns were filled with mowers and sprayers and tractors and workers preparing for the picking and packing and shipping season in November. Here, Harry's pecan bins looked almost untouched. All neatly lined in rows, the wood pale and unused.

"Wow." I couldn't help myself.

Chastity preened at what she took to be a compliment. "Whole place is like that. Harry just came in and tore down all that old stuff. Took him one winter to go through everything. Now he's got the heavy equipment back in the old barn. Wants to keep this one so visitors can see the kind of clean operation he's running. A really tight ship. Not like some. You know." She smirked. "These old ranches with everything looking so rundown and all."

I watched Miss Amelia, one of those "old" ranchers herself, bite her tongue.

"Well, you've got a nice clean business going," I said. "I suppose you'll be packing this year. Trees okay?"

Chastity shrugged. "Well, of course they are. But that's Harry's department. I keep my hands off the nuts. I'm more interested in our new pavilion. You gotta come see it. I'll be handling the social side of things. You know, like your Bethany does. Weddings and such. Then we're thinking of opening a store of our own just like yours only right down by the road, not in town. We won't be in competition with you folks, or anything like that."

She stopped talking and turned her large, black-ringed eyes to us. "Not that I'd be much competition for you all anyway. Why, you're known just everywhere in Texas. I mentioned your name once at a big 'do' in Houston and a man said he heard good things about you."

"Could we see Amos's . . ." I decided I'd better break in or we'd be standing there in that big empty building forever. "We've got so much to do today . . ."

"I heard. Me and Harry were thunderstruck. The sheriff went ahead and arrested Justin! Now what led the man to do a thing like that? You got any idea?"

She peered closely at me.

"Not a clue. Probably be just a short time. Ben Fordyce is working on it. Some mix-up. The sheriff's got to do what he's got to do, but he made a mistake. It'll all be straightened out soon. Now . . ." I looked around like Amos's room was going to appear out of nowhere.

"Well, me and Harry said, when we heard, what a shame it is. And we're both just hoping against hope he didn't really do what people are sayin' he did." She stopped to give me a look then stepped over very close. "Harry was saying . . . about Ben Fordyce. You'd better watch 'im. Got a kind of past with Amos himself, is what we heard."

Miss Amelia moved up beside me. I recognized the icy smile and stayed back, out of her way. "Can we please see Amos's room?" she asked.

Chastity, looking as though she had more to say on the subject, hesitated only a few seconds more before leading us out through another door in the barn, to a back lean-to.

The room wasn't large. The roof sloped overhead. Everything in there was old and well used. A rickety cot, set along the inside wall, was piled haphazardly with underwear and socks, all dumped on top of a faded quilt. A brown folding table, set up at the middle of the room, held a few bowls and cereal boxes, along with a can of black pepper and a box of salt. The rest of the table was piled with books, some fallen to the floor, splayed open, spines cracked.

Manila envelopes had been emptied by the sheriff's men, I figured, and thrown to the floor near an old three-drawer bureau. The bureau drawers hung open. Empty. A small TV sat on top of the bureau.

"My, my." Chastity looked around the room. "Look at the mess those men left for me to clean up. Think I'm sending them a bill."

Her hands were on her ample hips. "Didn't look this bad when Amos stayed here. I can assure you of that. Not what he was used to, being a Blanchard and all, but he said he was grateful we gave him a job. Just wanted a chance, was what he said to Harry."

I looked over at a tiny kitchen area with a sink, an under-counter refrigerator, and a hot plate, where a blackened aluminum coffeepot sat. Above the sink, a single cupboard hung open, showing a couple of dented and scorched pots, a frying pan, a drinking glass, a cup, and a few groceries.

All I could think was, What the heck was Amos doing in a place like this? Almost made me feel sorry for him.

I checked and found cornmeal and flour and sugar, along with a half box of toothpicks in the cupboard, while Miss Amelia kept Chastity busy with questions about Amos's job there on their ranch.

Open cardboard boxes had been dragged from a narrow closet and overturned, the contents gone through and scattered.

Chastity frowned, breaking into what Miss Amelia was saying as if she wasn't listening. Lines around her red mouth pulled into a pucker. "I don't know if I should leave you two . . ." She thought awhile. "Ya know, the sheriff and all . . ."

I put on my saddest face. "Hope you understand. We'd like a minute alone, if you don't mind. This has been a great shock to all of us."

Miss Amelia immediately put a shaking finger to the corner of her eye and wiped away an invisible tear.

"Well." Chastity frowned. "I suppose . . ."

I took Chastity's arm and walked her to the door, talking all the way about how grateful we were for her cooperation at this terrible time in our family's life . . . and on and on until the woman was back in the big barn and I closed the door between us firmly in her face.

Chapter Fourteen

When I was sure Chastity was gone, I turned to Meemaw. "Where do we start? The sheriff's been through everything."

Miss Amelia looked at the clutter. "Well, now, I don't know. You got any thoughts?"

"Anything that'll tell us where he's been and who had it in for him or was so afraid of him he needed to be killed."

Miss Amelia nodded, looking hard around the room. "I'm hoping trouble followed him back here from wherever he'd got to. Silly, I suppose, but I don't like thinking anybody in Riverville could do what was done to Amos."

"So let's keep all scenarios in mind," I said. "Somebody he was in league with against us and they had a falling-out. Or maybe an old enemy who didn't want him back here. Or somebody who followed him from wherever he was."

"Think we can say it wasn't somebody new he met here in town? Only a couple of weeks, after all. Still, you know your uncle Amos. Coulda got himself into some kind of woman trouble."

"If this was really about our family and he was back to make more trouble, I'd say there'd have to be papers, court records, legal documents. Let's look for any of that. Unless the sheriff got it." I opened the door to the little closet, where I found a row of hanging shirts and pants and a single pair of old cowboy boots, well cracked over the turned-up toes, tops hanging over like they were shot.

"Things like that might make it look worse for Justin. Protecting the ranch, and all. Along with whatever it was they found by Amos's body. That's something else we need to know. What do you imagine it could be, pointing straight to Justin?"

Miss Amelia opened the small refrigerator, moved a quart of milk to one side, checked a dish covered with aluminum foil to find half a stick of butter, then stood back, frowning at the contents. "You think you can get Hunter to tell you what that thing was?"

"I don't really want to talk to him just yet." I knelt to go through a stack of papers dumped on the floor. Bills. Articles cut from newspapers. The articles were all about pecan ranching. Most were old and yellowed, the newsprint faded.

"Looks like Uncle Amos never lost his interest in pecans," I said. "Lots of reading material here. Mostly about diseases and stuff. Out of date, from what I can see."

"And a lot of these books are about ranching, too." Miss Amelia lifted book after book, checked the titles on the spines, then set the books down, neatening them so no more fell to the floor.

"Here's one of those Alcoholics Anonymous handbooks." She held the blue book up to show me. "You know, about taking steps to help yourself get off the drink. Well, I'm glad to see he was doing something for himself after all. Maybe while he was away, he was at one of those rehab places."

"Or he could have just been going to meetings. But that's a good thing, too. You think we could find out where he went?"

"I don't think the organization would tell us anything. That's what the 'anonymous' part's all about, you know."

"But it's something."

"Yup, something. And it goes along with what I've been noticing. Not a single liquor bottle in here, Lindy. No Jameson's. No Garrison's. Not so much as one bottle of beer."

I bent over to go through the manila envelopes and other papers strewn around when I heard Miss Amelia give a loud gasp. I turned to see her standing at the middle of the room, a hand over her mouth, pale eyes wide.

"What is it?" I demanded as I got up and hurried to where she stood.

"What on earth's wrong with me?" she asked herself, hands now at either side of her head. "Oh dear, oh dear. My brain's not working right. Amos came in to give something to Emma. Remember? I wouldn't take it from him, and the next thing we know, Amos is dead."

"I forgot, too, Meemaw. It's not just you. Too much going on is all. So that's another thing we've got to look for. You said it was a paper or something he was pulling from his shirt when you stopped him?"

Miss Amelia nodded. "I'm guessing it was a paper because it was flat. Nothing bigger than a letter, I'd say. Or as I said before, I thought it was a legal thing. But, Lindy, how do we know the police don't have it already?"

"If they've got it, we'll know soon enough. If they don't, he stashed it somewhere and we need to find it."

"So I guess we got our path pretty well cut out for us . . ." She hesitated, looking helplessly around the room. "Maybe first we gotta go talk to Melody and Miranda Chauncey. If anybody would know where he went and what he was up to, it would be those girls. Why, for the last eighty years they've been a part of every single thing that's happened in Riverville. If they don't know something for themselves, they sure as shooting know who to go ask."

We went back to searching a last time through everything in the room. I tested the floorboards, seeing if one was loose, if I could get my fingers between a couple of them. Miss Amelia went through every single paper a second time, sitting in the middle of the floor, her legs stuck straight out in front of her.

I pulled the empty bureau drawers out though they stuck from the heat and humidity in the room, and had to be yanked hard again and again. I turned over each drawer, checking the bottoms for something taped there. Nothing.

Then I turned over the bureau itself, checking for anything he might have stuck to the bottom side. Nothing.

In the closet, I found an old Samsonite suitcase that looked as if it hadn't been moved by the sheriff. It was empty. I went through every shirt and pants pocket of the hanging clothes, then bent to the old boots that looked like they'd been worn forever.

I slid my hand in one boot, even pulling out the lining to see if anything had been pushed up inside. Nothing.

I did the same in the other boot, sticking my hand down to the toe. It seemed there was less toe space in this one. I felt around until I could pull the sole away from the upper part of the boot and stick my finger through a hole in between the lining and the sole. The material came away slowly, as if it had been glued down, but not the way Texas boot makers usually glued or sewed things—to stay.

With the material came something thick against my fingers. I pulled until the lining was away at the heel and a smudged sheet of paper lay against the sole of the boot. I pulled the paper out and unfolded it.

A letter. A single page. No address. No date. Handwritten and a little hard to read, except it read:

Dear Amos. I got the package and will keep it until you tell me what to do with it. Just the way you said, I won't give it to anybody but you, unless the police or some official comes asking and proves to me you are dead. I hope you're sticking with the program the way you promised everybody here. It's never easy, going back into an old life the way you are, but we're all pulling for you to make it okay. I just have to say, Amos, that what you said to me in your letter goes for me, too. Maybe we can still have our day together. So much baggage we keep carrying around. I'm doing my best on this end. I hope you're having luck on yours.

The letter was signed simply, *Virginia*.

I read the letter to Miss Amelia, who listened hard then asked me to read it again.

"So?" I asked. "What do you think it means?"

Miss Amelia thought awhile. "I think we gotta get over to the Chauncey girls' place and see if we can find out where he went. Sounds like he was in AA, doesn't it? But what's this package the woman's talking about? Who is she? Where's she live? We've got to find her. And what's all of this got to do with what Amos wanted to give to Emma? Or maybe it's all nothing. Could be he sent this Virginia stuff about us. About our family. More proof we stole the ranch from him. Who knows?"

"Looks like this path we're on just got a little longer," I said, shaking my head as I folded the letter and shoved it in my pocket.

We made our way back through the silent barn, then walked toward the edge of the property. Without a word to each other, we found my truck in the front driveway and got in, avoiding Chastity altogether.

Chapter Fifteen

I wanted to go straight back home, but Miss Amelia insisted we head to town to check on Treenie at the Nut House. I had a sneaking suspicion it was really to check out how many disappointed customers had come in for pies, but I drove past our ranch and into town, pulled over, parked, and followed her up on the porch. Her sign was gone from the door.

Inside, Treenie Menendez stood behind the counter, handing over a logoed shopping bag to a pair of tourists in plaid shorts. She eyed the two of us through narrowed dark slits and crossed her arms over her abundant chest.

"Well, well, well." She shook her head at us. "Cowards, the both of you. You know how many people read that sign you put up out there and come on in anyway, just to complain about having no pecan pie for their Sunday dinner? I thought to myself, might just as well open up the place. No use having all our goods go bad."

Miss Amelia smirked. "So you got a couple people wantin' pies?"

"Couple! Why, Miss Amelia, you don't know. And some calling—trying to act like they don't know about no pies bein' made and ordered three and four pies." She stopped to sniff an unhappy sniff. "All I heard for the last couple of hours: 'What! No pecan pies! What's this world coming to?'"

Her round face broke into a wide smile. She giggled and Miss Amelia giggled with her, then stopped herself, pretending her giggles were really clucks of unhappiness.

"Guess not everybody in this town thinks you're too old to keep baking, eh, Miss Amelia? Guess your baking's up to somebody's high standards." Treenie's sly look was transparent.

Miss Amelia pursed her lips as if she was going to chide Treenie, but didn't. "Always better to show somebody a fact than just tell 'em."

"I think some people in this town are learning a few hard truths today. One of them: how dumb Sheriff Higsby is. Heard about Justin. Why—"

"Not even out looking for who really killed Uncle Amos," I added, fueling Treenie's fire.

"He's doing his job by the book," Miss Amelia agreed. "Means no imagination. Sometimes a heavy dose of imagination is what's needed. Like imagining who would need to kill Amos; what would drive a man to do such a horrible thing? Or imagining why anybody would want to go after Lindy's trees."

Treenie shrugged.

"A lot to look at." Miss Amelia nodded. "Like the truth's hidden behind this big pile of trash and you gotta dig through a lot of smelly stuff to get at it. It's like back in Dallas. There was this sheriff picked up a woman for shoplifting a dress and took her right to jail. That woman was an old friend of my mother's so I went down there and told him he was making a bad mistake. That man looked at me like I was dumb as a stump until their family attorney came in. Biggest lawyer in Dallas. Sylvia was from one of the wealthiest families in town, just like I told the sheriff. In fact, wealthiest in the whole of Texas. I mean big oil money. She didn't need to shoplift anything—it was just that she was old then, and getting forgetful, and walked out of a store she'd never been to with a dress for her granddaughter's wedding. Didn't give it a second thought. No malice. Then that sheriff thought he was being pushed around by rich folks and persisted, taking the case to the district attorney, who shook his head at the man and threw it out. Just goes to show you. Sometimes, even over silly things, a man can get stuck for reasons having nothing to do with the facts. I think some men with a little power forget they're dealing with human beings and not numbers."

"I never thought Sheriff Higsby would be like that," I said.

Miss Amelia shrugged. "A man can't conduct his life by the letter of some penal code alone, you know. Not and stay his own man."

"If we only knew what it was of Justin's they found near the body," I said, moving on to what I had a chance of understanding. "We could fight that. It's this . . . nothing stuff that's driving me crazy."

"Like that gossip about Miss Amelia," Treenie said. "I'm gonna go back and say a few words to that Freda Cromwell. She's the one said it to me. Finger over her lips like it was some big secret."

"She tell you who it was said it to her?" I asked. "You know Freda doesn't come up with stuff by herself."

Treenie shook her head. "You think I wanted to hear any more? Not on your life. Like a rat with a ham shank, that's Freda with a bit of news. She just had to pull me aside over at the market and ask me if I heard what people were saying and did I agree, since I was right there 'on the front lines' with you. Well." She drew her short and square body up as tall as she could get it. "I told her what I thought of talk like that—about a friend of mine and a woman who can outwork any twenty-year-old in this town. She started squealing but I told her what I thought of lazy gossips with nothing to do but sit around all day drinking sweet tea and spreading stories about hardworking folks."

"Whew!" I was impressed. "I'll bet that stopped her in her tracks."

"Not much, I don't imagine," Treenie said with a final shake of her head. "Mean is mean."

"Looks like there's another one we've got to talk to," I said to Miss Amelia, leading her to give me a weary look. "I mean, time we stood up against this stuff they're spreading. Seems like just more folks wanting to hurt us."

"I been thinking while you two were carrying on," Miss Amelia said. "I'm wondering if the sheriff didn't arrest Justin for his own good. Ben was saying something like that. You can see somebody wants him blamed for killing Amos, and if that doesn't work, why, they just might try to hurt him themselves."

I stepped back and gave my grandmother a hard look. "Woman, you can change on a dime. One minute the sheriff's a soulless man. The next he's God's gift to the Blanchards."

"Now, Lindy. Let's worry about being fair here."

I think I snorted. "Fair! First you get me mad as hell. Next you're telling me why I'm wrong. They've got a name for that kind of thing, Miss Amelia . . ."

"For goodness' sakes, Lindy. Calm yourself down. If I'm right, isn't it better he's in the safest place? The local jail? Or—if I was right in the first place, and the sheriff really is that dumb, then we're already ahead of him, knowing what we know and what we've got to do. And we'll get it taken care of without falling over the sheriff everywhere we go."

"Hunter will still be everywhere we go." I said the words and knew they had to be true. I couldn't discount Hunter as a smarter enemy. "If I could just talk to him, maybe he'd tell me what they found on Amos's body."

"I'm wondering if it was that letter Amos wanted Emma to have. Seems like the most likely thing. Couldn't have been anything good. Not from Amos," she said.

"Crap!" I used one of my stronger swear words. But in my head things were going around and around. Maybe Miss Amelia and I were just spinning our wheels. Maybe they did have evidence that would convict my brother. And maybe Hunter was staying away from me because he couldn't bring himself to tell me Justin would be convicted of murder, would spend the rest of his days sitting on death row, all because his uncle hated him the way he'd hated the rest of us.

"Oh, almost forgot." Treenie turned back from checking the tins of pecans on the counter. "Speaking of old biddies, Ethelred Tomroy called maybe half an hour ago. Said for you to call her as soon as you got back or drop by after church in the morning. She's got something she needs to talk to you about."

"Wonder what she wants now." Miss Amelia sighed.

Treenie shook her head. "Maybe she's swamped with pie orders."

She laughed at her joke as the Carya Street door opened and a busload of tourists, bent on buying everything pecan, trooped in.

Chapter Sixteen

I picked up Miss Amelia after church service the next morning. It was close to eleven thirty. The good folks were a little late coming out of the church. I waited in the parking lot for almost half an hour, then honked when I saw her on the church steps, visiting with friends and the minister, taking her own sweet time.

I had to endure her scowl when she climbed up into the truck, saying I'd embarrassed her. "Honking like that."

Miss Amelia was no more a fashion maven than the rest of us. Still, she looked neat and comfortable in white pants that weren't ancient elastic-waist jeans. She had on a pretty pink-flowered loose top over the white pants. Instead of her worn sneakers, she wore comfortable looking slip-ons. Topping off the outfit was a gold filigreed clip in her gray hair.

Our agreement had been that I'd drop her off at the small chapel on my way into town to see Justin. Of course, I now got guff handed to me about the state of my mortal soul, but when she saw she wasn't getting far with it, she dropped the complaint and asked about Justin.

"Says hello," I told her.

"How's he holding up?"

"How'd anybody be holding up sitting in jail?"

She ignored my remark.

"Some of the ladies were asking for you." Oh, and I thought we'd moved past that topic.

"All so sad about Amos, and now Justin." She clucked. "If you weren't so stubborn, we could've gone to see Justin together. Hope you told him I'd be there later. Think I'll bake him one of my 'special' pies. Deserves it, where he is."

"See Ethelred? You tell her we're coming over to talk to her?"

She shook her head. "Probably stayed home to clean her house and bake one of those awful pies of hers. She thinks she's rubbing my nose in how she's still baking while I'm too old and feeble to put a pie together anymore. That's what she'd like to believe."

"Come on, Meemaw. You two have been friends forever."

She made a noise. "Sometimes it takes all the fortitude I can muster to be a friend to Ethelred."

She looked out her window and commented on how dry everything was getting.

I didn't answer because there was no answer when you waited day to day for the rain to come and nothing was happening.

"People at church do any praying for rain?" I asked. "Sure could use it."

"Of course we did. Prayed for rain. And the state of your soul." She looked over and gave me a merry—*I got the last word*—smile.

"And they had a lot to say about there being no pies at the Nut House. Mostly, they were telling me how bad they feel for all of us. Nice folks. Sorry for our trouble, everybody. Leaning in close to say how the sheriff had the wrong man. True to Rivervillians, they had a few disparaging words for Sheriff Higsby, and then a couple of tongue clucks and saying it was all because of Dora's death. These folks just don't know how to stay on one side or the other of a discussion."

Ethelred Tomroy's house sat in the middle of a few acres of old trees and a few more acres of tall grass. Over the small brown wooden house, a pair of ancient live oaks bent so far as to almost touch the dark roof. Her Buick stood in the beaten earth circular driveway.

I pulled in the dusty drive and parked behind her. We climbed Ethelred's three concrete steps and Miss Amelia rang the bell. I could hear it far off, making a deep, grandfather clock sound.

When Ethelred answered, there was a worried look on her long face. With almost no greeting to either of us, she pushed the screen door open and let us in.

"Heard you didn't go to church this morning, Lindy. Never a better time to be going to services. What with Amos dead and your family lookin' like there's more trouble ahead."

"Heard you weren't there either, Miss Ethelred." I couldn't help myself. When you lived all your life in a town like Riverville, everybody thought they had a right to comment on what you did and who your friends were and how your moral character was developing. I thought my moral character was doing just fine, and anyway—I figured the Blanchards had other things to think about that morning.

Amelia brushed our bickering aside. "Treenie said you wanted to talk to me, Ethelred. If you're getting orders for pies, I'd better explain . . ."

The woman's dark eyes lighted. "What do you mean, 'orders for pies'? Nobody's been calling me. Heard you stopped making yours, though."

"Well, you see, due to the circumstances . . . with Amos's death and all . . ."

"And a grandson in jail."

"With Amos's death and all . . ." Miss Amelia repeated, ignoring the gloating woman. "I won't be making my pies for a few days."

Ethelred thought a minute. "Aren't you afraid they won't come back to yours if they start ordering mine?"

I wanted to step in but Miss Amelia only smiled a self-satisfied smile. "Well, I think my county fair ribbons tell who's got the best pie, Ethelred. Whether you want to hear it or not. And no, I'm not worried. You pick up a customer or two, well, that's fine. Plenty of room in this world for all of us, don't you think?"

Ethelred decided to say nothing more. She pointed off toward a living room filled with dusty antique furniture. "Come on in and take a chair. I'll get you something to drink in a minute. I just gotta come out with what I called you about first."

I waved off the chair and stood, hoping we wouldn't be there long.

Miss Amelia planted her feet where she was. "That's what we came about."

"Suit yourselves," Ethelred said, looking relieved at not having to provide greater hospitality than a place to stand. "I got to get something off my chest."

She straightened her back and clasped her hands together in front of her. "Just wanted you to know, if one of you Blanchards did it, well—you know, finished off Amos like that . . . well, don't think the whole town won't be behind you. We all know . . ."

Here she stopped talking and started nodding.

"So you mean you won't be cheering when they shoot one of us with a lethal injection there at Huntsville?" I said, then turned away, disgusted with the woman who thought she was showing her support.

"Now, young lady, don't you go twisting my words. You know darned well what I'm talking about. But there's something else I've got on my mind. I didn't want to go to the sheriff before talking to you both. I don't know if you remember a couple years back, Amelia."

"I've got a good memory, Ethelred. Despite what some people say. What are you referring to?"

"Been thinking. I'm only trying to help your boy out here, you understand. Sure looks bad for him, the way he blamed Amos for Jake's accident and all. I mean, and everybody's saying the sheriff found something right there at the scene that shows Justin did it . . . still . . ." She hesitated, then glanced at Miss Amelia's darkening face. "Now, don't get mad. Just listen to me. Might just be a way to get your boy outta jail. Remember, back before Amos left town, when he had something going with Jessie Sanchez, Martin's daughter? What I heard was that they were near announcing their engagement when Amos dumped her. You know Jessie's getting on. 'Bout your age, wouldn't you say, Lindy? Probably worrying about being an old maid, too. Anyway, from what people said, Jessie was all broken up. Over at the library, I heard she was crying so hard one day she had to go home. So"—she cleared her throat—"what I'm thinking is her father, Martin, had plenty of reason not to want Amos back in this town. Amos was a lot older than Jessie, but still a man like Martin's likely to get fighting mad over somebody breaking his daughter's heart. Wouldn't you say that gives him as much reason to do Amos in as Justin?"

She seemed very pleased with herself as she settled back on the heels of her oxfords.

Miss Amelia and I exchanged glances before saying

anything. Finally I couldn't contain myself. "So what you're saying, Miss Ethelred, is that you think we should hand Martin Sanchez to the sheriff to take suspicion off Justin. That right?"

The woman smiled and nodded. "Thought you'd be pleased. Me coming up with a different suspect. You never know with the law, which way it's gonna go, so you want to kind of muddy the waters. That's what I learned from that *CSI* program on the TV."

"You're thinking we should throw Martin, a man who's been loyal to our family all these years, and his daughter, and maybe even his wife, to the dogs to protect Justin? That what you would do?" Miss Amelia asked.

Ethelred nodded hard. "Sure would. I'd do anything to get my own grandson outta jail."

"You'd be hurting an innocent family, Ethelred."

Ethelred thought awhile. "Who says they're innocent? Like I said, just muddy the waters a little. If you want, I'll go right over and talk to Sheriff Higsby for you. Start the ball rolling. Least it'll give the sheriff something to think about."

I reached for the doorknob behind me, not able to get out of the woman's house fast enough.

"I wouldn't say a thing to anybody, Ethelred." Miss Amelia pushed at my back to get me moving faster. "Martin Sanchez was out mowing, surrounded by other workers, that day. Got a big fat alibi."

"Then how about Jessie herself?" Ethelred added, hurrying to have her say before we escaped. "Seems you could make a case for her doing that to Amos. I mean, after all, nothin' like a woman scorned, as they say."

Miss Amelia pushed at me again, then followed me out of the house, stopping at the bottom of the steps to take a deep breath. "You go to the sheriff with your nonsense, Ethelred, and you're going to look like the biggest fool on earth. If I were you, I'd say nothing to nobody."

"Well, somebody's got to look into this and I'm probably the most knowledgeable . . ." Ethelred Tomroy stood with her arms crossed.

"Gossip and knowledge are two different things." Miss Amelia narrowed her eyes at her old friend. "We've known each other a long, long time. I appreciate that you want to help my grandson. That's a commendable thing. But not by sacrificing the Sanchez family."

Ethelred frowned and crossed her hands hard against the pink smock she wore over green polyester pants. "Why, shame on you, Amelia Hastings. If it was me, I'd snatch at anything that would get my grandson out of jail. What kind of grandmother are you anyway?"

"The kind that teaches her children right from wrong, Ethelred. I'm truly grateful for your concern, but we know Justin had nothing to do with his uncle's death. Me and Lindy intend to find the person who did. The real person." Miss Amelia nodded her head hard a couple of times.

"What in heaven's name do you mean, 'Me and Lindy'? Why, that's nothing but playin' police games. I never heard of anything so ridiculous. And at your age, Amelia. Shame on you . . ."

"About that . . ." I stepped in closer and looked up at Ethelred. "Yesterday, at the Nut House, you were saying something about Miss Amelia. Something about people here in town saying she was too old to be working so hard . . ."

Miss Tomroy frowned at me as if she'd forgotten I was there. She waved a hand toward me. "Just what you'd expect people would be sayin', you Blanchards making her work over there at the Nut House. All that baking and stuff while you girls, who should be helping her, go flying off playing with that genetics stuff and planning weddings." She leaned back to stare. I stared back just as hard. "Seems, if you love your grandmother, you'd want to be there in the store helping her . . ."

As I sputtered, Miss Amelia stepped in. "What Lindy was asking, Ethelred, was who, besides Freda Cromwell, would be talking about me like that? We were wondering who in town is so worried about my health. Awfully kind of that person, still I'd hate it if people really were thinking such a thing. Why, too old . . ." She shook her head. "We're the same age and I don't hear people saying such a thing about you."

"Better not either. But then I'm solid Riverville stock. Not like you, Amelia. I mean a transplant from Dallas, after all. I'm rugged as one of our famous pecan trees, you could say. That's me."

"Heard about Freda gossiping about me." Miss Amelia ignored her. "But we all know about the noise an empty bucket can make. I was just wondering where she got it from. Somebody had to've set her off."

Ethelred narrowed her eyes. "She didn't say. I figured it was just general talk. Maybe folks only trying to make you open your eyes and stop letting yourself be taken advantage of."

Miss Amelia reached over and touched my tensing arm.

"Why, bless yer heart," Miss Amelia said with one of her broad, killer smiles. "It's just that I'd like to thank whoever it was . . ."

"No need for thanks, I'd say. You know me, I don't like to gossip. I just stay away from people like that most of the time."

"As well you should," Miss Amelia called over her shoulder. "As well you should. And the sheriff, too. I'd stay away from him. Never know what can of worms you're opening.

I mean, I remember that dispute you had with some antique store in Columbus. You remember how wrong that store owner was about you not paying what you said you'd pay and Sheriff Higsby had to come out to talk to you?"

"Why, Amelia! How could you—"

"It's just that I appreciate how much you want to help, Ethelred, but I don't want you stirring up anything that could bring misery down on all of us."

Ethelred's mouth dropped open a good inch. She appeared to be mulling things over in her head. "Well, all right. But I got something else you maybe don't know about. It was Finula Prentiss, over to the Barking Coyote Saloon, Amos got involved with. Heard she was telling people she was pregnant by Amos. He left town and no baby ever appeared. Which leads you to wonder . . . Anyway, heard her boyfriend wasn't any too pleased about the whole thing. You against turning the sheriff in that direction, too?"

"Nope. You go right ahead and tell the sheriff. Bet he knows all about it, though. Still, you go right on ahead, Ethelred. More power to you."

Miss Amelia got in the truck fast and slammed the door shut behind her. I drove around Ethelred's old Buick station wagon, a cloud of dust flying up behind me.

"She means well." Miss Amelia looked over at me eventually as I worked my way back toward town.

"At least we know the name of the girlfriend," I said.

"Yes, we do. Knew it already. Asked Justin yesterday. But Ethelred's a fount of information, don't you think? Just a fount of information."

I did.

Chapter Seventeen

A stop at The Squirrel Diner was long overdue. I'd grabbed a piece of toast and slapped some pecan butter on it that morning. Miss Amelia said she'd had nothing. We were both starving and Cecil Darling, the Englishman who owned The Squirrel, through what process of emigration I couldn't imagine, was happy to set us up with tall sweet teas and overly large menus that could be exhausting to read.

Our orders were simple, which always disappointed Cecil, who thought little of Rivervillian taste and faced constant disappointment when he pushed the black pudding and coddled eggs. I ordered scrambled eggs and whole-wheat toast. My grandmother asked for a tuna sandwich. Cecil, a tiny man with a small, round face, hid his distaste at our plebian ways but included a free dish of lemon curd with a sugar cookie when he brought our food. "Gratis," he sniffed at us. "I'm giving all of you a second chance."

"About Ethelred," Miss Amelia said over her sandwich, delicately cut into four pieces. "People who think the least about themselves are the first to criticize others. Especially if they can get at you while you're down. I remember . . ."

I pushed my plate away and settled back to listen.

"There was this one time. It was a Pearl Thompson. Came to me with a story about my husband, Darnell. She said he was having an affair with somebody in the office. Had it on good authority. Her husband, Frank, told her it was Darnell and he was going to put a stop to it. She heard because she got an anonymous note about the woman coming on to any man she saw, especially Darnell.

"Well, I went right to Darnell and he marched me over to Frank's office, shut the door behind us, and sat me down. Wasn't long before Frank was crying his eyes out. He didn't mean to hurt Pearl but she was getting wind of . . . well . . . what he called a 'dalliance'? He thought that letter, blaming it on somebody else, would put the whole thing to rest.

"Me and Darnell promised to take it no further, if he wouldn't go blaming Darnell for what he was doing and if he'd get himself out of the affair.

"Never heard another word after that. Pearl was off the warpath and happy how well her marriage was going.

"So you see, Lindy. People in trouble try anything to get themselves out. Maybe Ethelred's got a couple of sins on her own conscience. Like maybe she's the one told Freda I was going to that doctor in Columbus when I never did any such thing. Wouldn't put it past her. And you take this whole problem with Amos dying. I'm beginning to think Amos was on to something he wanted Emma to know about. Then somebody stopped him."

"Or he coulda been over there to hurt us—like he always said he would. Maybe somebody followed him over there. That makes his death still about somebody mad as hell at him and not me."

"Well, you think what you want to think. I'm going on human nature. Let's see who comes out right."

Church people, lingering over their midday meal, finished eating and came over to express their condolences to us. Most of them had the good grace to look embarrassed by the whole thing and get on their way. A few, the nosy ones, hung around like they'd get a piece of fresh news they could spend the afternoon sharing with others.

We left as soon as we finished eating, getting a curt nod from Cecil Darling because we left the lemon curd untouched though I waved my sugar cookie at him before going out the door.

"Savages," he called after us.

I was driving the long, winding dirt road into the Chauncey twins' ranch when my phone rang unexpectedly. It surprised me that I got cell service so far out of town. It was Mama.

"I stopped over to see Martin Sanchez last night and he wasn't home. Jessie said he got a call. Personal business, is what I thought. Though, to tell the truth, Lindy, I was surprised he'd go off like that, what with Justin in jail and the trees needing seeing to. I called back there today, just to see. He's not home yet. I'm picking up something in Jessie's voice that's worrying me."

"We're out here at the Chaunceys' ranch right now, Mama. I'll call Jessie on the way back. Maybe Martin planned on being away this weekend. Lots of relatives down on the border."

"You wouldn't think . . . What with Justin in . . ."

She didn't have to finish. She was right. The Sanchezes' house was next on our list.

Before I hung up, I asked how Bethany was doing. She'd been a sad wreck when I saw her that morning, after a phone call from her newscaster, informing her that he and his fiancée were "thinking it over, whether to have the wedding there or not."

News of Amos's death was all over Texas, I figured.

"But he didn't cancel, Lindy," Mama said. "She's still got hope he'll go through with it. You know Bethany—so much drama. All I'm hearing about is those doves . . ."

I narrowed my eyes at Meemaw and mouthed "Bethany" to her. She threw her hands in the air and rolled her eyes heavenward.

"Mama. Know what?" I said. "I've heard all I want to hear about those doves. My professional life's at stake here, you realize. All my trees . . ."

I didn't go on. Mama had enough on her mind. Bethany was her baby, and new to running the pavilion; with her first big wedding . . .

I hung up and pushed my sweating back against the fabric seat. I took a couple of deep breaths. The wind coming in the window, straight at my face, was hot and dry. I didn't say a word to Miss Amelia about the Sanchezes. Better to wait. First we had to talk to the Chaunceys. After that, I'd let other worries back into my head.

I drove through an opening in a fence, where the only sign posted was on a couple of boards painted with big red letters:

KEEP OUT.
THIS MEANS YOU.
ATTACK COYOTES ON GUARD.

The unpaved road ahead wove through flat, empty land, strung across by bone-dry arroyos. The road ran straight, leading back to a stand of pecan trees ringing a small lake that was way down in its banks. Beyond the ranch were small, rolling hills that seemed to go on forever.

"Creek's down," Miss Amelia said, pointing out her window to the creek that fed the lake. "Rain's gotta come pretty soon."

"Say that again. No rain. No pecans."

"Poor Emma. As if her plate wasn't full enough. Sometimes I wish my daughter would sell the ranch and take life easy for a change."

I looked over at her, knowing she didn't mean it. "It's in our blood."

"Nuts in our blood and in our head. Terrible hard way to make a living, you ask me."

"Be easier if I could've finished my work with the trees . . ."

"You were getting that close?"

I nodded. "I think so. A new strain I crossed with the old trees. Almost there."

"Why would anybody want to stop you? Unless there are folks who'd like to see us ranchers fail. Can't think who that'd be."

"I'd hate to think it," I said.

Miss Amelia squinted out the front window then pointed to two elderly women on horseback riding slowly toward us up the dusty road, the bright afternoon sun shimmering like gold dust around them as they bounced in identical cutter saddles.

"Think they got their twenty-twos on them?" I asked as I pulled to the side of the road.

"They'll know us from rattlers," Miss Amelia said and

opened her door, climbing down to stand in the dirt, hands over her eyes, calling out to the twins approaching cautiously on horseback. "Hello there, Melody and Miranda. It's me, Amelia Blanchard. Lindy and me come out to see you. How you girls doing on this fine Sunday afternoon?"

The Chauncey sisters, both in their late eighties, reined in their horses and stopped next to where we stood in the road.

Melody, who looked exactly like her twin sister in her faded plaid shirt and buckskin pants, wore a Stetson hat about as old as she was. Her old, scarred boots had only a little life left in them. Both women's faces were wizened from eighty and more years of looking up into the brutal Texas sun, and the way they stared out from under the brims of their hats was awfully close to Clint Eastwood, squinting down at a man he was about to shoot.

Melody leaned down from her horse to take Miss Amelia's hand and give it a shake.

"Well, what do you know? Ain't seen you in a coon's age, 'Melia."

Miranda Chauncey, a little quieter than her sister, a little grumpier, stayed up on her horse, too, twenty-two rifle held in one hand. She bent down to stare hard at us, her plain face unsmiling. "You, too, Lindy. What brings you out this far?"

"Not that we ain't glad to see the both of you," Melody Chauncey hurried to add, fearing her sister wasn't hospitable enough. She shot Miranda a dark look then slipped easily from her horse's back. "Don't want the women thinking we don't want company, Miranda."

"I didn't say we didn't, Melody. Don't have to go jumping on me for asking . . ."

"Well, it's your manners, Miranda. And no need to go snapping at people just for pointing out . . ."

The women got caught up in their ages-old bickering.

They'd been going at it since they were little girls living in the handmade, low-roofed house their father built a hundred years before. The house was as worn and weathered as the land around them. Worn and weathered as the girls themselves.

They wound down their argument, then let it slip away like an old story with no ending.

"What you think about rain?" Lindy asked to get the conversation going.

Miranda shrugged and squinted skyward. "Don't know. Ain't had a turd floater since maybe last year sometime. Emma worried about the pecans?"

"'Course she's worried." Melody jumped on her sister. "Drought's drought. We're all going to suffer from it."

In unison, the girls looked off at the rising horizon. Melody toed the dry earth.

"Bet you're here to talk to us about Amos." Miranda gave Miss Amelia a one-eyed look.

"We heard what happened there at your ranch." She reached down to awkwardly pat Miss Amelia's back, pulling her horse around fast before he stepped on my grandmother's foot.

"Miranda's got no sense when to bring a thing up," Melody complained. "Sorry for your trouble, is what she means to say."

"Know what I'm saying. Word gets around fast."

"Awful about Amos," Melody added.

"Awful about Justin, I'd say," Miranda put in. "Amos. Liked him all right, but when he was drinkin', had a mouth on him could scare a water moccasin."

"Well, of course," Melody sniffed. "But Amos is the dead one. Don't you think that's a sad thing." She turned to Miss Amelia and me. "I mean, being dead's forever, you know, and Justin, well, anybody with a brain knows he didn't kill his uncle and he'll be out of jail before you know it."

"Terrible, you ask me," Miranda put in, her tone more querulous. "Not meaning any disrespect for the dead but you take Amos now. There was a man looking for trouble since he was a boy."

"That's why we came out to see you," Miss Amelia said, shuffling her feet in the dry dirt. "About Amos."

"You don't say?" Miranda, intrigued now, slid easily from her horse and wrapped the reins around one leather-gloved hand. She stood in the road with her legs spread, as if she were still astride her horse. She'd lifted her rifle in the air as she slipped off the horse. A canvas bag, tied to the saddle, hung loose at the horse's side. "But we ain't seen Amos in about two years. Just up and left. Right when we were spreading fertilizer. Nothing from him since."

"He tell you where he was going?" Miss Amelia asked. "That's what we're after right now: where he got to after leaving here, where he was going and why."

"You thinking somebody from wherever he went came back to kill him?" Melody asked, catching on fast.

Miss Amelia shrugged. "Could be."

"Heard your trees got destroyed." Miranda turned to scowl at me. "I can see killing a man, he do you enough harm. But hurting trees? Why, there's no call for a thing like that."

I shrugged, agreeing with Miranda—somewhat.

"Not being too Christian, are you." Melody was shocked at her sister. "Like a man's life ain't as important as a tree. Fer heaven's sakes, Miranda. Watch what yer sayin'."

Miranda slowly turned to grin at Melody. "How many men been keeping us our whole life long, I'd like to know? And now you count up the trees we been living off—"

"That's not a way to look at things. I'd say—"

"Did Amos say anything when he left here? Maybe some small thing?" I interrupted, knowing the girls' battles could go on for hours and get so entwined nobody knew what anybody was saying.

The two women stopped arguing to think deeply, looking straight into each other's eyes, as if probing one brain.

Miranda was the first to shake her head. "He just left. We was counting on him and then he was gone. Not a word. And to tell you the truth, we still owe him some back pay. He didn't wait for the money, takin' off like he did."

Melody nodded, making a face. "We went out to the bunkhouse and it was clean as a whistle . . ."

"There was a letter came after he left us," Miranda put in.

"Oh, that's right," Melody agreed. "I remember now. What'd you do with that letter, Miranda?"

"Me!" Miranda stepped back, as if struck by a bolt of lightning. "I didn't do nothing with it. You said you'd put it away, since he didn't leave a forwarding address."

"I did not!"

"Yes, you did. 'Put it in a safe place,' that's what you said."

"Well, Miranda Chauncey, I never said such a thing. The way I remember, you took it out of the mailbox, tucked it in your pants, and that was the last I saw it."

"You sayin' I don't remember right?" An indignant Miranda fell back two more steps. Miss Amelia looked off, at the low, dry hills.

"Not a bit of it. What I'm sayin' is I never put a hand on that letter . . ."

I had to step in or we'd be there forever. The letter was too important a fact to get lost in one of the girls' endless arguments. "Could you find it, do you think?"

The women stopped talking to think deeply, frown, look at each other, and then nod in unison.

"Don't see why not," Miranda said. "Never threw a thing away in my life. Still got the blanket the stork brought me

in. That letter'll be somewhere in the house. Official looking, as I remember."

Melody nodded. "Not the IRS or anything like that. Just . . ."
She concentrated hard then gave up. "Well now, just give us a
little time, we'll find it for you. Got to be there somewhere."

"Could you call me?" Miss Amelia asked. "When you
find it?"

"'Course." Miranda nodded, then stepped back and froze,
her fierce eyes focused on the ground near my foot. She put
one hand on the stock of her gun; the other went up into the
air, warning me not to move. "Stay where you are, Lindy.
Rattler at two o'clock."

A single shot rang out, the bullet diving near my feet so
I felt the ground shake under me.

Miss Amelia and I held perfectly still until Miranda
walked over, bent forward, and stood, holding a dead rattler
up by the sides of its mouth.

"Looks like an old guy to me. Been around awhile." She
pointed to its rattles then went back to her whinnying horse
to push the dead snake into the canvas bag.

I pulled in a long breath and gave her a very nervous
smile. "Thanks, Miss Miranda. Glad you got him."

Miranda made a face. "Ain't missed a rattler in seventy-
two years."

"Guess we'll be getting on back to town." Miss Amelia
started toward the car, a little faster now.

"I'll find that letter for you," Melody Chauncey called
out, giving a firm nod along with the promise. "Don't know
where on earth Miranda stuck it, but if it's still in the house,
I'll dig it out all right."

"I'd appreciate—" Miss Amelia began.

"What do you mean 'where I stuck it'?" Miranda interrupted as she flung herself up and over the saddle. "Look to
yerself first."

"I'd say we best begin by going through stuff in that crammed full room of yours . . ."

"I wouldn't go talking about somebody's room being a mess. If Miss Amelia got a look at that pigsty you call a bedroom, why, she'd just think you were a nutcase."

Melody put her foot in the stirrup and swung her skinny body up on her horse, as easily as her sister had mounted hers.

"Nutcase, eh?" Miranda reined her horse around and headed back up the road, the way they'd come. Melody was close behind her. "You talk about 'nutcases,' I'd say start looking at yourself and all those old romance novels you got stuffed everywhere I look."

"Well," Melody Chauncey could be heard objecting as they rode away. "At least I'm into literature. And you, Miranda Chauncey, long as I remember, you ain't read nothing but the side of the soap powder box . . ."

Their voices faded. Miss Amelia and I exchanged an exasperated look and climbed back into the pickup.

Down the track toward the main road, Miss Amelia sighed. "Not much from the girls. I'd hoped . . ."

I looked over at my meemaw, whose face was drawn and tired. "I know," I said. "Me, too. I'd hoped they'd have something for us. Maybe just a city where he was heading. Something."

"There's that letter."

I gave her an exasperated look. "You think the Chaunceys will find it?"

Miss Amelia shrugged and pulled her blouse away from where it hugged the sweat across her shoulders. "The girls can surprise you. Always fighting like that, but ask them to do something together and they're right on it. I still think . . ."

I nodded. "Just gotta give it time . . ."

"Could you put that air-conditioning on, girl? Don't know why you're so stubborn . . ."

I was about to answer back, all the while thinking maybe whatever caused the Chaunceys' constant fighting was catching, when I spotted a tall plume of dust heading up the road toward us. Another car. More company. The Chaunceys wouldn't be happy.

Chapter Eighteen

I watched the cloud of dust move toward us from a half mile away and had a sinking feeling I knew who was coming. Hunter Austen, right on our heels. He would be following everywhere we went, I supposed. Or getting ahead of us—which was what I really feared. Much as I said out loud I trusted him to be on our side, the reality of it was—I didn't. I knew Hunter Austen from as far back as before our class in "sandbox," and even then he was one of those straight-arrow boys who had a hard time with a guilty kid saying, "No, ma'am, wasn't me." Like the time I hid candy in my underpants over at Shipley's 7-Eleven and he turned me in, even though I offered to show him my underpants one more time.

I think I still hold that against him.

So it was no surprise to see his low blue-and-white rolling to a stop next to my pickup. He got out pretty quick and ambled around to my open window, leaned in, pushed up his large sunglasses, and greeted us.

"Lindy," he said, nodding. "Miss Amelia."

He stepped back from the car to check out the terrain in all four directions. The armpits of his otherwise crisp blue shirt were damp. Another line of damp ran down his back when he turned to look behind him. His police shirt sported a Riverville Police patch at each shoulder made in the shape of Texas with a wide spreading pecan tree at the center.

"You two paying a visit to the twins?" he asked when he looked around at me.

"Haven't seen the girls in a long time, Hunter," Miss Amelia leaned across me to answer.

He nodded. "So right now, with Justin in jail and a murder out at your place, you two take the time to come calling. Is that right, Miss Amelia?"

I looked over at Meemaw. I wanted to see how she got around telling a lie on this one.

"We had a few things to ask them, Hunter," she said and looked smug about it. "Asking questions against the law all of a sudden?"

Hunter shook his head. The man knew when he was out of his depth. "I just don't want to be worrying about you two out looking for a killer . . ."

"If we don't go looking, who do you think will do it?" I asked him.

"What do you think I'm out here for?"

I shrugged. "Who knows? You said you weren't going to help us . . ."

"Never said that, Lindy. I said I couldn't share privileged information with you. That's my job. But I'm sure not out to hurt any one of you Blanchards. Least of all you, Miss Amelia."

"Anybody hurting a member of my family hurts me, Hunter. You ought to know," she answered and sat back so she didn't have to look straight at him.

Hunter's face grew earnest. He put both hands on the sill of my open window. "I'm not out to hurt Justin, ma'am. He's been a friend a long time."

Miss Amelia sighed and stayed turned away from him, talking as if to herself. "I know that, Hunter. It's not you. It's this big mess . . . Amos and all. So much trouble. I sure wish you'd see your way to working with us, though. I don't mind passing anything we come up with along to you. The way I see it, that's the only way to go. Hope you're of a mind to help . . ."

"Sheriff's got me in charge on this one. He'd knock my head off, he hears I'm sharing . . . things . . ."

"What about the evidence they say they got connecting Justin to him? You know what that is? Seems like we gotta know or we're out here fighting a ghost. Can't fight what you don't know," I said. If friends were true friends—like they said they were for years and years—well, they didn't try to hurt you behind your back. That's how I had friendship worked out in my head.

Hunter took his time answering. "Won't lie to you, Lindy. I know what it is. State's evidence. I'm just not at liberty—"

"That's what I thought." I gunned the motor. I didn't see any sense in wasting more time with him.

Hunter patted the side of the truck then gave me a long, sad look. I could see how torn he was. Awful to add to it, but Justin's life was at stake here. I put the truck in gear.

"I will tell you one thing, Lindy," he said fast, almost as if he was trying to keep me there. "I know you were over to Amos's room at the Conways'. You see that blue book, the AA book?"

I nodded, admitting both to being there and to seeing the book.

"I think that's significant. If Amos was getting help, what the heck did he come back for? If it was to make amends with all of you, like Alcoholics Anonymous wants members to do, then why didn't he get on with it?"

"Do you know where he went to meetings?" I asked.

He shook his head. "Tried. That one 'A' stands for anonymous and that's what they are. Called their offices in Fort Worth and Houston. No information. No records. Nothing. And no way of knowing where he was living before he came back to Riverville. Even checked our local AA chapter. Got more of nothing."

He cleared his throat, rugged face drawing into a frown. "The Chaunceys able to tell you anything? Something from back before he left?"

I shook my head slowly. "Not a thing."

"Didn't leave anything behind, did he? Didn't say where he was going? How about sending his mail on—they have an address?"

Again I shook my head, well aware of lying but not able to trust my old friend any more than he could trust me.

"By the way, you know anything about Martin Sanchez? I stopped by their house a while ago and his wife says he's not around. Doesn't know where he got to. Juanita's not saying much but the woman looks scared, you ask me. I know the man would do anything for you Blanchards. You know anything about his whereabouts?"

We both said no. We said we hadn't seen Martin, but when we did, we'd have him call.

He smacked the side of my truck again. "Let's keep in touch on this. If you hear anything—anything at all—you let me know. Don't go keeping secrets, Lindy. Won't help Justin or anybody else."

"You do the same, Hunter." I wrinkled my nose at him and rolled up my window. I let off the brake and drove away a little faster than I should have, shooting a cloud of dust behind the pickup, enveloping Hunter and making him invisible.

"Well." Miss Amelia relaxed back beside me on the seat. "Guess we better get used to lying to the police . . ."

"And how about threatening friends like you did to Ethelred, bringing up that antique store thing?"

Miss Amelia reddened. "She deserved it."

"How about stealing things that don't belong to us?"

Miss Amelia's face drew in tight. "If you're talking about that letter from Amos's room, well, I say there are times in life that call for desperate measures, and this is one of those times. I don't consider what we're doing immoral or anything like that. We're saving a life, I'd say. And righting a wrong."

"Yes, ma'am."

"Shame on you, Lindy. I'm not sure I like the tone of your voice. Me—the widow of a good politician, and you, one of those magna cum laudies."

She was into sniffing moral outrage, and I tuned her out until she sat back and, after thinking awhile, said, "Ethelred went to the police anyway, I suppose. Why else would Hunter be out there?"

"Only what he'd have to do."

"Then where's Martin? If he's truly missing, Juanita and Jessie must be in a fine state."

We thought awhile as we turned on to the main highway and headed back toward the ranch. After a while, Miss Amelia turned to me. "You don't think it *was* Martin, do you? That he's the one who killed Amos?"

"And destroyed my trees? I don't think so."

"But if he caught Amos doing that? The way he hated him, because of jilting Jessie, and seeing him hurt you so bad—who knows? Like the sheriff said before. Anybody can kill. If the circumstances are right."

Chapter Nineteen

I liked the Sanchez house better than ours because it was the place where my great-grandparents started. Mama told the story of Daddy's grandmother refusing to leave after her husband built the new house. The one we lived in now. That woman was attached to this tall, square white house with brown shutters. I could see why she loved it. For the solidness of it, how it sat two stories high in a land of hunkered-down houses. How the rooms were divided equally, all of about the same size, same height, like magic boxes stuck together. Nothing showy about the old house. It just was, like the people who came to Texas to create lives from dirt and trees.

I liked to think I had a lot of my great-grandmother in me, someone whose sense of place was a secret we hugged inside us, hung on to as tightly as we could.

When the Sanchez family first came to Rancho en el Colorado, twenty-two years ago, the house was assigned to the man who was foreman then. It took a few years, but Martin worked hard, and when the job was open, he stepped right in—with Daddy's help. Now the family had been in this fine old house a long time, almost as far back as I could remember.

On each of the ten tall steps leading up to the porch, Juanita, Martin's wife, had placed a pot of bright red geraniums. At one end of the porch a yellow rose, climbing up a white trellis, bloomed thicker than I'd ever seen a rose bloom. In the shade of the wide porch roof, the old green swing moved in the arid heat, which felt like pins stinging on my skin.

It all made me feel sad, as if I were looking out from old eyes and mourning what used to be. Not anything I really knew, just a child's view of history.

Juanita Sanchez came to the door. Like Jessie, who'd been my friend for a long time now, Juanita was small-structured, almost tiny, with dark hair that looked today as if it hadn't been combed. Unusual in this neat little woman who created tidy spaces around her.

She asked us in, keeping her head bowed and a fist clenched at her chest as she led us into the living room, where Jessie sat at a large, round, lace-covered mahogany table that took up the entire center of the room.

"We ran into Hunter, out at the twins' ranch," I started to say.

Jessie nodded and got up, hurrying around to hug first Miss Amelia and then me. She motioned for us to sit down at the table always set for guests with a vase of artificial white lilies at the center of the lace cloth, teacups turned over in their saucers, spoons tucked beside them.

Juanita, who hadn't said much, quickly offered iced coffee or sweet tea. When we both shook our heads, she sat and laid her hands out, a workingwoman's hands with short, stubby fingers and wrinkled knuckles.

"Where's Martin?" Miss Amelia came right out and asked.

"He hasn't come home since yesterday morning," Juanita blurted out. "I thought he would call by now."

She took the tissue Jessie handed her. She blew her nose and sniffed. "I didn't want to talk to the police. Martin would get mad at me. But Hunter was here. He knows something . . ."

"Knows what, Juanita?"

She shook her head.

I turned to Jessie.

She was looking even more like her mother today. Younger, finer-featured, but just as worried and pale. "Everybody in town knows what my father thought of Amos, how he threatened to kill him if he ever came near me again. It was an awful time for all of us. I was stupid, thinking I could change Amos. Make him into the man he should have been. But my father never hurt anybody. He didn't kill your uncle, Lindy."

I nodded, agreeing. A loyal man, I could see him wanting to deflect suspicion away from Justin. Martin would think that was what he had to do for Jake.

Juanita shook her head. "He would never have killed Amos. That was in the past. Jessie's fine—"

"No, Mama," Jessie interrupted, then looked away from her mother, to Miss Amelia. "I'm not fine. Amos called me when he came back to town. He wanted to see me. He said he was sorry. I said no, I wouldn't see him, but how his voice made me ache. I knew he was in trouble, not doing well. I tell you honestly, I wanted to turn the clock back and tell him to come over, that I still loved him . . ." She closed her eyes. "But I knew better. I couldn't get that woman out of my mind—the one he took up with. So I told him no, I never could see him again. But then I made the mistake of telling Papa that Amos called me. Papa was livid. I tried to calm him but he went to see Amos at the Conways'. He—"

Juanita drew in a long, startled breath. "He didn't say a word to me."

"I know," Jessie said. "And, Mama, he threatened to kill Amos if he came near me again. I'll never say that to the police, but Miss Amelia and Lindy have to know. It is their grandson and their brother sitting in jail for this crime."

"Did Amos see Finula Prentiss again?" I asked because I had no one else to ask.

"You know her?" she asked.

I nodded.

"Amos told me he knew what she did to me, that she came into the library and told me she was pregnant by him. That she said he was going to marry her and not me. I told him that. He said that was why he left town. It was all a lie he couldn't prove. But how could I believe him?"

"He could've waited. Babies don't take more than nine months."

She shrugged. "He said he was afraid she might trick him with another man's baby."

"Did he say where he went after he left Riverville?" I asked.

She shook her head. "He said only that he was clean. Not drinking. But"—she shrugged—"how could I believe even that? I couldn't trust him. That's what I told my father. I would never marry Amos Blanchard. You don't build a life on lies and cruelty."

"Maybe this Finula would know where he went."

"There was never a baby. I talked to people who knew her." She leaned back in her chair. "Imagine. Never a baby. What kind of woman lies about such a thing?"

"She works at the Barking Coyote, doesn't she?"

Jessie shook her head. "I think she's just a regular there. Black hair as black as a dark alley. Skinny. She drives a blue

Mustang. That's what I saw outside the library. I never talked to her again but people told me things."

Juanita moaned slightly and slumped back in her seat. Jessie was up, her arms around her mother. "This is so hard on Mama. She thinks my father is trying to help Justin. That's when it started. Justin called from jail Saturday afternoon. He asked my father to do something for him. Of course, my father ran right out of the house . . ."

"We haven't seen Martin since then." Juanita hung on to her daughter. "It was something about the barns. But I don't know what. That's all I heard. Martin said the police had been going through them Friday night. He didn't know what they were looking for. When I thought about it, after Martin left the house, I told myself it was only ranch business. You know, like don't forget to get that mower ready, or the sprayers, or order something. That's what I thought. Business. And Justin was afraid he wouldn't get to do something so Martin went right out."

"What time?"

Juanita shrugged. "About three o'clock yesterday afternoon."

I looked over at Miss Amelia. "We'd better get out to the barns. Just in case . . ."

Juanita put a hand, holding a white handkerchief, to her mouth. Her dark eyes were huge. "You don't think somebody . . . not like they did to Amos?"

I shook my head. "He's probably still looking for whatever Justin asked him to search for. Or taking care of what had to be done."

"But it's been so long," Juanita said. I knew she was hoping we'd hand her an answer. Not understanding anything myself, I had nothing to offer.

I looked over to Miss Amelia. "Let's get out there. If you're up to—"

She stopped me with a look.

"I've been out to the barns and didn't see anything. But I ran through. I didn't want to leave the phone," Jessie said. "In the middle of all of this, I was supposed to give a party for Sophie Landsdorf last night. She's leaving the library tomorrow. I bought her a gift at the Nut House, because she's going back to Montana, where she came from. Everything was canceled."

"We'll only be a half hour or so." Miss Amelia stood and stretched, then rearranged her Sunday top over her white slacks, which already didn't look as sparkling white as they had before.

"Stay with your mother," she said to Jessie. "Martin probably isn't anywhere on the ranch by now, but we'll stop back, no matter what we find."

We were up and out to my pickup before Juanita and Jessie could complain about being left behind. And before they could think what I was thinking: It didn't take almost twenty-four hours to go through our barns.

Chapter Twenty

We found no one in any of the large, echoing barns. Miss Amelia led me staunchly around huge mowers and benches laden with spare parts, then out into the washing, separating, and packing barn, then a storage barn—one leading to the other.

"Yoo-hoo!" Miss Amelia would stop, from time to time, to call, a hand cupped to her mouth. "Martin!"

"Where is everybody?" I looked around, perplexed.

"Sunday," Miss Amelia said, shrugging her shoulders.

"Justin always had somebody here. This time of year it's so critical. Spraying especially."

Miss Amelia shook her head. "Why hasn't Emma called the men? With Justin in jail and Martin nowhere around, you'd think—"

"Maybe she doesn't know that Martin's missing." I felt obliged to stand up for my mama. Even to my grandmother.

"She would have called him by now. Just to check."

"Unless Justin told her Martin was doing something for him."

She lifted a full eyebrow at me, her pale eyes narrowing. "The trees can't be abandoned like this. You know that better than anybody. Call Emma. Tell her what's going on and tell her about Martin, if she doesn't already know. Somebody's got to do something."

I agreed something had to be done and went outside to the barn, where I could get a cell signal. I called her.

"Oh, Lindy. I'm so glad to hear from you." Mama's voice was filled with worry. "Mike Longway called again. He's coming over. I told him I can't find the old co-op books. And anyway, why would Jake have them? He says Jake had all of them. That he took them home with him before he was killed. But, Lindy, Earline Simmons was treasurer back then and she says she doesn't remember giving them to Jake. Or maybe Chastity was treasurer by that time. I don't remember myself. Mike says old Sam Hickok is making a fuss about missing money and needs to look at the old books. A lot of money, Mike says. Over fifty thousand dollars Jake had set aside when he ran the co-op. It was for a new advertising campaign he wanted to start. Nationwide, it was supposed to be. A new slogan promoting Texas pecans. Sam's saying the money's just gone. Not even entered in the books they've got now. I don't like the way he's insisting, Lindy. Like maybe Jake had something to do with it."

"Mama. Calm down. You know there's no possibility Daddy did anything like that. He didn't need money . . ."

"Well, we were having a tough time that year . . ."

"Would he steal money from the co-op?"

"Never on your life," she said, sounding more like the woman I knew.

"There. It's been five years since Daddy died. For goodness' sakes, Mama! Where've the books been all this time? And why wasn't anybody looking for the money before now?"

"Who knows? I'm not understanding any of this."

"Then don't worry about it. They'll figure it out. Some-body's bookkeeping error." I hesitated a brief minute. "I called to tell you about Martin Sanchez."

"He back? I gotta talk to him. Justin told me to have him call all the men in. Gotta dig deeper drainage ditches."

"He's not back."

"Where'd the man get to? Justin told me he asked Martin to do something for him. Something important. He wouldn't say what, just said it wouldn't take Martin long and that he'd take over everything as soon as he was finished with this other thing. I took that to mean . . ."

"Oh, Lord . . ." She moaned in my ear. "I've got Bethany here in tears, waiting to hear back from that newscaster. Mike's on his way over. Martin's gone, who knows where? I'll tell you, Lindy. I feel like I'm just holding my breath, waiting for the other shoe to drop. What next?"

"Me and Meemaw are out at the barns now. We'll see if we can find anything that'll tell us where Martin went."

"I'll start calling the men myself. Guess I'm running things for a while. Tell Miss Amelia not to worry, I won't let anything happen to our trees. We're going to have to work out the irrigation. Damned drought. I don't know what's ahead, Lindy. Just don't know."

I promised to call her as soon as we heard from Martin.

Back inside the barn, Miss Amelia stood next to one of the workbenches, fingering the handle of a greasy wrench.

"I was just thinking," she said. "If Martin went to the Conways and threatened Amos, Harry might have heard about it. You know Harry. Always on the side of the angels. Maybe he went to the sheriff, thinking he was helping us. Like Ethelred Tomroy, thinking she was helping. Could be he got the sheriff looking at Martin. Maybe took him in to the station."

She hesitated. "That's good for Justin, but so unfair. I

know Justin wouldn't have a hand in throwing Martin to the wolves."

She thought hard a long while. "All we can hope is that Martin's got better sense than to offer himself up as a sacrifice for Justin. Like take off and hide somewhere, trying to throw the sheriff off. He's got to know no Blanchard would want that."

She lifted the greasy wrench again, her face deep in worry. After a few minutes, she wiped her hand on a rag hanging at the front of the bench then looked up at the wallboard behind the table, where someone had drawn the design of each wrench—for hanging and for knowing if one of them was missing.

"Must be so the men don't lose the tools," she said, pointing to the designs. There were two places empty. She picked up the single wrench left on the table and held it in front of the two empty outlines. "This one goes right here," she said. "Leaves one empty. Whoever didn't bother putting that one back will sure hear about it from Martin. He's as finicky about his tools as I am about my baking pans. Kind of makes me think Martin hasn't been around in a while. I mean, if there were men here yesterday and he saw this . . ."

I smiled halfheartedly, having no stomach for any concern beyond where Justin had sent Martin.

"Well." Miss Amelia wiped her hand again and stepped away from the table, her good shoes sticking slightly to the cement floor. "Nobody out here. I think we should get back into town."

"What about those sheds down by the river?" I asked.

At first she made a dismissive noise, then stopped to think about it. "Think they're mostly empty now. What could Martin be doing down there all this time, I can't imagine, but we might as well take a look while we're here."

The two old sheds I was talking about were set on top of

the embankment, above the Colorado. Back in my grandfather's time, they were far enough above the high water mark to be safe from any flood but close enough to where the first trees were planted. The sheds once held equipment, when the ranch was small, before my grandfather built the big barns we had now.

Meemaw and I walked over to the river. It wasn't far. The late afternoon air was surprisingly cool, washed with the smell of river water and the musty patches of thickets along the banks.

I saw parts of the two roofs, dark and mossy tin, almost lost among an overgrown patch of willow.

I heard the noise first and put out a hand to stop Miss Amelia. "Hogs," I said and ran to a nearby tree, where I pulled off a dead branch, as large as I could carry. I ran straight down toward the river.

"No, Lindy," Miss Amelia yelled after me. "They'll attack you!"

But I was in full trot by then, branch high over my head as I ran. I spotted a single dark hog, long snout rooting around the first of the sheds. I stopped only a minute to look for other hogs. If there was a group of them, and they felt threatened, they'd attack me. I'd heard enough about how people were hurt, even killed, by angry hogs.

I screamed at the dark, pig-eyed face looking up at me, puzzled by what was coming at him down the rise of the bank. He stood right where he was, watching me fly toward him with my wobbly stick overhead.

I stopped just short of the animal. He snorted, as if wondering what the heck I was doing there. We exchanged a look. I knew better than to trust him. The feral hogs were one of the worst problems farmers in south central Texas had to face. From open fields to the piney woods, hogs knew how to live and breed and kill and take care of each other.

At Texas A&M, where one of the pharmaceutical professors had discovered a form of birth control for hogs, the only question was: Who's going to make them take it?

Behind me, Miss Amelia stopped short, searching the ground for any weapon she could get her hands on. When she picked up a little stick, I rolled my eyes at her. Instead of going on the attack, she shouted at the hog: "Go away, ya hear?"

I found small rocks at my feet, picked them up, and pelted the beast. He snuffled and snorted. He shook his head when a stone hit him on the snout. In the waddling way of wild hogs, he finally turned and took off slowly down the embankment, getting lost in the tall weeds at the river's edge.

"Shouldn't take on a hog by yourself, Lindy," Miss Amelia admonished me when she could catch her breath. "Ever."

"All I could think to do."

Miss Amelia wasn't listening. She stared hard at the door to the shed, pointing to long scratches, as if the hog had been butting against it, or scratching at it with his tusks. "Wonder what had him so interested," she said, walking slowly toward the door, then grasping the knob and turning it. The shed was unlocked.

When Miss Amelia pushed the heavy door inward, something stopped it. The interior was dark. Sticking her head inside as far as it would go, she called back to me that all she could see were shadows.

"Door's caught on something right here on the ground," she called over her shoulder.

A deep moan came from inside the building. It wasn't loud, but it was urgent. Definitely the sound of someone in trouble.

"Help me," Miss Amelia ordered as she put her shoulder to the doors. "We've got to get in there."

We pushed hard against the old, surprisingly strong,

wood. When it opened wider, I slid my body through the opening and then into the dark and moldering room beyond.

Someone was laid out on the floor, a body, half rammed against the inside of the door.

He groaned again. It wasn't hard to make out the man I'd known for years. I yelled out, "It's Martin."

"For heaven's sakes! What's wrong with him? He have a heart attack? Pull him out of the way so I can come in. I know CPR, you know."

I reached down and slipped my hands under the man's arms. I pulled, eliciting a small grunt from him. I reached back to open the door wider so I could see what happened in there.

Martin's face was covered with blood. The front of his plaid shirt was wet with it. I had it on my hands. This was no heart attack.

"He's hurt," I called out as I wiped my hands down the sides of my jeans. I looked up for Miss Amelia, her head just coming around the open door. She slid in and knelt beside me, at Martin's side. She took one of his hands in hers and squeezed. He groaned but didn't open his eyes.

"Get on your phone," she looked up at me and ordered. "Call Hunter. Tell him we need an ambulance out here immediately. Martin's been hurt bad. He's alive, but who knows for how long."

Chapter Twenty-one

The ambulance was gone, off to Riverville Medical. The sheriff had ringed the shed with yellow police tape, cordoning off for area for the tech guys, who were inside and outside, hunting for anything that would explain what happened to Martin.

Miss Amelia and I stood behind the tape, going over and over how we found him and why we were down there to begin with.

Mama and Bethany weren't far behind the police cars and the ambulance. After Hunter told them there'd been an accident and he'd be up to the house in a while to talk to them, they left, Mama turning to give me and Miss Amelia a long, pleading look. I gave Mama a smile and a nod, assuring her we'd be all right and that we'd see her in a while. That we'd explain.

As if I could explain anything that was happening.

Juanita and Jessie had gone with the ambulance. They'd come running at the sound of police sirens, too, following the screaming cars down to the place just above the sheds.

Shock. Distress. Every emotion possible was written over the women's faces. And then quiet as they stood beside the stretcher where Martin lay. Juanita clutched his hand. Jessie kept one hand on his legs, under the white sheet, as the EMS rolled him up to the ambulance.

And then they were gone, along with the frantic pace. Men and women moved in to scour the site while Miss Amelia and I stood off to one side, telling our story to Sheriff Higsby and to Hunter again and again . . .

How Martin had been missing since Saturday morning.

"Why didn't his wife call us sooner?"

She thought he was somewhere on ranch business. With Justin in jail and all . . .

Hunter stood back behind the sheriff, making notes.

"Why did you come down here to look for him?"

We were searching the whole ranch. It was the last place we thought to look . . . The hog . . . The scratches on the door. The moans.

"Could've fallen in there." Sheriff Higsby sniffed and motioned toward the shed. "Hit his head."

"A blow that severe?" Miss Amelia said. "You really think so?"

"Seen worse."

"He's unconscious."

The sheriff nodded and walked off as if he'd had enough of an old woman who spoke too much good sense.

Miss Amelia moved in close beside me.

"Poor Juanita. All she asked those EMTs was if Martin was going to live."

"You saw his head, too. So much blood . . ." I shivered. "Too much to look at. Worse than Uncle Amos. What's going on, Meemaw? What's happening to all of us?"

Miss Amelia shook her head.

In a few minutes one of the techs, in full white protective

suit, down to his booties, came out with something held over his head. He called the sheriff over.

Miss Amelia leaned toward me. "A wrench," she said and fell into deep thought. "You notice the shape of it?"

I didn't have a clue.

"Back on the barn wall? One missing from that pegboard. Shaped just like it."

"That means whoever it was saw Martin going toward the sheds."

She nodded. "Attacked and almost killed right there. The thing is . . . why?"

We waited as Hunter and the sheriff conferred with the tech. I could see Miss Amelia was anxious to tell them she recognized where that wrench came from, but when she went "Pssst" toward Sheriff Higsby, he only waved a hand in our direction, signaling for us to hold on.

It was Hunter who came over finally. It was Hunter who brought us other news, after hearing Miss Amelia out, nodding along with what she told him. It was Hunter who said, "Found your missing trees, Lindy. Guess Martin was hiding them right there in that shed."

My trees!

He lowered his voice. "Sorry, but the sheriff thinks you're all in on this, protecting each other." He shook his head then looked me straight in the eye. "Not me, Lindy. I know all of you too well. There's something else going on here. We've got to get together. We've got to talk—the three of us."

He nodded toward Miss Amelia. "We need what your grandmother's got—a deeper way to see what's going on."

I took a quick breath. Everything so terrible around us, but at least we had Hunter back. This single part felt good, and familiar. I nodded fast. We'd meet and talk.

My trees, I thought again and almost felt happy for a minute, until I realized Martin could have died for those trees.

Chapter Twenty-two

It was after midnight when Hunter called and I drove out to meet him where we hoped nobody would see us, out near a bend in the river, where we used to swim as kids, swinging out into the water on a rope, sometimes skinny-dipping because, back then, when our bodies looked almost the same, the one big difference between us was of interest for only a few minutes. Hunter was already there, waiting in his blue Passat. I turned off my lights and sat worrying about how far I could push him, while he got out of his car, opened the door to mine, climbed in, and settled beside me.

"Lindy." He nodded a nod I felt more than saw.

"Hunter." I nodded back, not able to keep myself from mocking his formality, but the mood was light for only a minute. The weight of why we were there settled in on us fast.

"Miss Amelia couldn't come?"

"Sound asleep. I didn't want to wake her up. A lot's happened lately and I figured the two of us could talk first. I'll pass everything on to her."

He seemed to nod again. "Gotta tell you. I wish I had your grandmother on my side in this. The sheriff's on the wrong track. Nothing he's got against your family. It's just . . . well . . . you know, since losing Dora, it's like he's got to hold on tight to everything, walk the straight and narrow, or he'll lose all he's got. I'm just afraid he's in way over his head. You know, Lindy, this business isn't like anything we've ever handled before. He's trying to be fair . . . but . . . in this case, I'm coming to think our regular training's just getting in the way. There's something so much more . . ."

He stopped, unable to put the rest into words.

I agreed though I truly understood nothing. "Why were my trees in that shed? That's one thing. Was that what Martin was looking for? Did he somehow know they were there? Or did he stumble on them and whoever did this to him? And why were the trees spared in the first place, only to be left behind? What's going on, Hunter? If the trees were here all along . . ."

I looked at him but could see only the smallest glint of his eyes, shining in the moonlight reflecting off the river.

"That's the big question, isn't it, Lindy?" he said. "What were they doing in that shed if somebody who's not with your ranch did all that damage, and killed Amos? What I'm saying is it seems to me the only reason for saving those trees was to make sure you still had stock to work with. Or make it look like somebody from the ranch maybe used all that destruction to cover one thing—Amos's murder."

"We know it's not us, Hunter."

"I know that. But stick with me here. Getting these trees returned kind of puts you back in business, your research can go ahead where you left off."

"I'll still be behind but . . . you're right, I guess. At least I've got something to start with. The trees are more advanced than the seedlings. When can I get the trees back? A few more days without care and I'm not sure they'll make it."

"Evidence," he said.

"Of what? Being trees?" I shot back.

"You tell me what to do and I'll see to it they get the care they need. Get them released to you as soon as I can."

We didn't say anything for a while. Then I had to ask. Had to get information from him. It was what Miss Amelia would have done if she'd been there. I'd told myself, before coming to meet Hunter, that I would just think the way my grandmother thought. Get to the heart of things.

"Hunter." I looked directly over at him. "What was on Amos's body that made the sheriff think Justin killed him? My grandmother and I can't fight what's happening without knowing what we're up against."

He didn't say anything for a while. "I don't know," he said then stopped. "I want to help you but . . ."

"What if I offered something we found? Like a trade?"

He was quiet again. "You've got something you didn't tell me about? How's that supposed to help find—"

I cut through his umbrage. "A trade. And after this I'll tell you whenever we find anything you need to know. Is that a deal?"

Finally he simply said, "A deal."

"And you tell us whatever you've got?"

Again he agreed.

I took a deep breath. "We found a letter from a woman named Virginia in Amos's room over at the Conways'."

I quieted his sputter. "It was after you already searched. In a boot, down under the sole."

"I'll need to take it. Could be valuable evidence. So where's it from? What's it about?"

"A letter. No envelope. This Virginia talked about having a package Amos gave her. She talked about him following the 'program.' Miss Amelia and I think that's Alcoholics Anonymous. We've been trying to find out which city he was in at the time. Where he went to meetings. Things like that."

"Chauncey twins told me Amos didn't leave a forwarding address," he said. "Makes it hard to know."

"Talking with the police doesn't sit well with the Chauncey twins. What they told us was they had something that came for him after he left. They claim they've still got it. But you know the girls, arguing back and forth about who had the thing last. I'm just hoping they come up with it."

"I'll need to see that, too," he said. "Whatever it is."

"And the Virginia letter, I'll get it from Miss Amelia or have her drop it off right away. But . . . if we're to go on turning over what we find to you, you have to trust us, too. This isn't San Antonio or Dallas. You don't have the resources of a big city and we don't have the information you've got."

"Geez." He wiped a hand over his bare head. "There's my friend Justin sitting in jail and likely to stay there until Ben Fordyce gets him a bail hearing. Now Martin—a man I've known as long as I can remember."

"If you'll just let us help you," I said, and waited for him to stick to our bargain. "And you help us."

He cleared his throat, looked off, then spoke as if to the air. "Justin sure was proud of that belt buckle of his—with the Blanchard crest . . ."

"Daddy gave it to him when he started work in the groves. But what has—"

Hunter stopped me. "That's it."

"What? That Justin's got a personalized belt buckle? Like two thirds of the men in Riverville?"

"Always wears it."

"Not recently . . ."

"Seen enough to seem like it's every day."

"He's proud of the family, and the ranch."

Hunter nodded. "That's what we found on Amos. Like the buckle was torn from the leather. Amos still had it in his hand."

"What?" I said. "That's it? It was only a few days ago I asked him why he wasn't wearing Daddy's buckle anymore. He said he hadn't been wearing it for weeks, the belt broke out in the groves. He picked up the pieces and stuck them in a drawer in the big barn." I leaned closer to make sure Hunter understood. "He hasn't been wearing that buckle in almost a month, Hunter. Anybody could have taken it from the barn at any time."

"Somebody like Martin?"

"Don't be silly. You know Martin better than that."

"So does everybody in town, Lindy. But the way it's looking . . . Justin. Martin. Could've been either one."

I tamped my anger down. We needed Hunter. And he needed us. There'd be a time, somewhere in the future, when I could tell him how he made me feel.

And time, in that future, for him to air his complaints about Miss Amelia and me keeping evidence from him. Plenty of time. Right now, all we had was one another.

Chapter Twenty-three

I fell dead asleep when I got home and would have slept on into late Monday morning except that somebody shook me gently. I groaned and slapped my pillow over my head. The pillow was peeled away and a careful hand shook me again until I opened my eyes and stared up into Meemaw's concerned face.

"Thought you were going to sleep all day," she said as I checked the clock. Eight. I didn't have to get up at eight. Or nine. Or ever—if I didn't want to.

I kicked off the sheet I'd pulled across me and sat up at the side of the bed, head in my hands. I was feeling beaten down. I was feeling like a traitor to Hunter—lying as much as I could to get the information we needed. There was no way we'd give him anything we learned if it would hurt Justin.

And I felt like a failure that here it was Monday, three days after the murder, and we still didn't know where Amos had been for the last two years.

"Got to get up, Lindy. Miranda just called. The twins found what they were looking for and are gonna meet us at the Nut House in an hour. Where were you last night? Heard you come in pretty late."

I told her about meeting Hunter, and telling him about the Virginia letter. "I said I'd give it to him today."

She frowned hard.

"And he told me what they've got that looks so bad for Justin. His belt buckle. The one Daddy gave him. Found it on Amos. I told him Justin hadn't been wearing it for a month or so. Said the belt broke and he left it in the big barn 'til he could get it fixed."

"How'd it get out of the barn?" she asked. "How'd Amos get it, do you think?"

I wasn't thinking. All I wanted to do right then was forget the whole thing. I think I groaned. Anyway, Miss Amelia went to my bureau and pulled out a clean white blouse from among clothes I'd left behind when I moved out. Not as much room in my apartment.

She chose jeans from a row of them hanging in my closet and was going back for underwear when I told her I'd be ready in fifteen minutes and shooed her out of my room.

I didn't want to take time for breakfast but Miss Amelia insisted. "Could be a tough day ahead of us. First the Chauncey sisters, then I want to get over to the hospital and see Martin and Juanita. Talk to her. She stayed there at the hospital last night, her and Jessie both. They're about to break in pieces, those two. Feel so bad for 'em. Doctor told Jessie they're keeping Martin in a coma until his brain stops swelling. Could be weeks. They need our support, Lindy." She gave me a pointed look, the way she always did when getting a message across.

I grabbed a piece of toast and spread pecan butter over

it then poured a cup of coffee for me and one for Miss Amelia.

There wasn't really time to sit down but Miss Amelia insisted, sliding a look toward where Mama and Bethany sat at the table, Bethany with her head leaning on one fist, pushing an egg around her plate. Mama, glasses down to the edge of her nose, flipping pages in a ledger, going over them again and again.

"How's the wedding coming along?" Miss Amelia asked Bethany as she settled in her chair, toast and marmalade in front of her.

Bethany glanced up. She looked close to tears. I wished Miss Amelia hadn't asked.

"We're having a conference call this afternoon. Me and Chet Easton and his fiancée, Christina. I'm so afraid they want to cancel on me. I've already spent money and promised money to the band—even if I cancel, I'll owe them a cancellation fee. This whole thing's going to cost us and I won't be making anything on it." She stopped to sniff. "Oh, Meemaw, I don't know what to do . . ."

"You're not turning it over to Chastity, are you?" Miss Amelia asked quickly.

"I can't do that," Bethany said and wiped away her tears. "I just can't do that. I know she's a friend and all, but I can't come out and say, 'Oh, that's all right. Just take your wedding next door.' And then I'd have to maybe turn all my people and plans over to her because it's getting late for her to make new arrangements. If word spreads about what a great wedding it was, she'll get the credit. And after all my hard work, I don't want anybody but me taking credit."

She looked hard down at her congealing egg. "Maybe that means I'm not a good person but I've worked so hard . . ."

"I'd wait 'til after the call to begin changing my plans,

Beth," Mama said and reached over to pat her child's hand. "Everything might be fine . . ."

"Well, maybe it would've been until they found Martin like that. You know the newspapers all over Texas ran the story this morning." Bethany sniffed again. "That's why Chet Easton called. Said he wants his fiancée to make the decision."

"You keep yer chin up, young lady. A lost wedding's nothing to having your brother in that jail," Mama chided her. "And think of Lindy here. All that work just gone."

Bethany looked stricken, as if she'd forgotten why Justin wasn't at the breakfast table. Maybe even forgotten I was the one propagating new trees, building hope for a stronger business in the future, and most of my trees were gone.

"Oh, Mama." She clamped her hands hard in her lap and lowered her head. "You're right. Nothing compares to what Justin's going through. And you, Lindy. I'm so sorry. I just wish . . . I don't know. I just wish all these bad things would . . . oh, I don't know . . . go away."

Emma looked up at Miss Amelia and me. She didn't say anything for a while, just sat thinking until Miss Amelia asked, "What's going on, Emma? No more bad news, I hope."

Mama shook her head and pushed her glasses up onto her head.

"Mike Longway came by last night. We talked for more than an hour. He doesn't understand it any better than I do. Where those books got to. Chastity says she never saw them. Just started out with what they gave her after Jake died. All she got were older books, before Jake took over. And a bankbook. Bills. Nobody knows where that fifty thousand dollars got to. Mike was thinking maybe Jake mixed it in with our personal funds, knowing he'd take care of it, maybe use it when the campaign got going." She took a breath. "I told him I don't have an extra fifty thousand laying around. When

Jake died, I had almost more bills than money. Things are better now, but I don't have fifty thousand dollars to hand over to the co-op, like a donation, or something. As if my husband did something wrong." She fought back tears. "Then I was going back through Jake's bills and I found this."

She waved a paper at us. "It's a bill from a private detective in Columbus. Name of Fritch. Donny Fritch. The bill says fifteen hundred dollars. Now what in heaven's name would Jake hire a private detective for? And pay him fifteen hundred dollars? I asked Mike if it could be co-op business and he said he didn't think so, but he'd ask around."

She looked at the paper, reading it again. "I went through the check ledger. I found a payment to Donny Fritch for a thousand dollars. There should have been another check, for the five hundred still owing. Nothing there. No more payments to the man. And no bill either. I took care of everything back after Jake died. I would've remembered paying a private detective five hundred dollars."

"Maybe the man heard about Jake's death and didn't bother with the bill," Miss Amelia said.

"That's not how people run businesses," Mama said.

"Well, me and Lindy have got to get going." Miss Amelia stood, taking her dishes to the sink, where she rinsed and set them in the dish drainer.

"Lindy." She tipped her head toward the door.

And we were out of there, Miss Amelia clutching a pie from our freezer. "For the Chaunceys," she told me. "The girls don't have to go without their weekly pie just because I'm mad at everybody else."

We took separate vehicles into town. We had separate things to do after we saw the girls. Miss Amelia wanted to get over to the hospital. I wanted to go talk to Justin. It was bothering me that Justin had been the one to send Martin

out into the barns. I needed to know why and I was willing
to bet—if he'd heard what happened to Martin—he'd be
worrying his head off about now: over Martin, over the
ranch, over all of us.

Chapter Twenty-four

"Amelia, Lindy, we been waiting for you," Miranda greeted us when we hurried into the Nut House. I knew the twins could be testy when crossed, especially if they were stuck with city folks and longing to get back out to their ranch. "Don't like standin' here tryin' to scratch my ear with my elbow."

"Now, Miranda," Melody said. "These two poor souls are caught between a rock and a hard place. Guess we got all the time it takes for the Blanchards."

Agreement didn't come easily to Miranda Chauncey. "Suppose so."

"How's Mama an' them?" Melody smiled, wrinkling up all of those sun wrinkles.

"Everybody's fine, just fine," I assured her. "Considering the circumstances."

Both woman clucked and shook their head.

"Came to bring you that letter we spoke about. And we came to get us a pie. Maybe one of your gift boxes. Want to send something over there to the hospital for Jessie

Sanchez's pa. She's always helping us out at the library. Taught Miranda here how to use one of those computers so we can look up something we don't agree about." Melody glanced toward Miss Amelia and lifted her voice up a notch. "Just don't seem to be any pies around this morning, Miss Amelia. Guess you didn't have the time. That right? With Amos dying and all. Your grandson in jail. Suppose we can't fault you."

"Humph. Amos dying don't seem like an occasion for Blanchard misery, you ask me," Miranda groused and picked a candy out of a sampler dish. "Never cried over a flat rattler myself."

"Don't go blaspheming the dead, sister."

"Humph," Miranda repeated. "Not like we're talking about some kind of saint here."

"Amos had nothing to do with it, the reason why I can't make pies at the moment," Miss Amelia said.

"Guess, with you and Lindy chasing down the murderer, the way people are saying, don't leave a lotta time."

"Who's saying that?" I demanded, not liking the sound of people talking about what me and Miss Amelia were doing.

Melody and Miranda looked hard at each other, their almost identical faces screwing up like prunes.

"You remember?" Miranda demanded of Melody.

"Think it was Charley, over to the drugstore. Or was it Cecil at the diner this morning?"

"Couldn't say for sure," Miranda said, turning back to Lindy. "All over town. People swearing to help you, Lindy. No worry about that. That's why me and Melody came in. Not going anywhere near Sheriff Higsby. Putting Justin in jail, the way he did. The man knows better than that. Oh, and we thought maybe we'd drop over and see Emma. Get her thoughts on this darned drought. We been thinking about asking Morning Flower, over at the Indian store, to do a rain dance, but Melody here says that's not a polite thing to do. Guess not many of the Indians doing dances like that anymore . . ."

Miss Amelia smiled at the twins. "Bet they do. They're more up on their culture than the rest of us folks. Just don't know how much good it'll do."

"Miss Emma in town?" Melody looked slyly over at Lindy.

Lindy shook her head.

"Thought she'd come in to visit Justin. We're going over to the hospital to see Martin. Want to let Juanita and Jessie know we're behind them. Whatever they need."

Word sure was spreading fast through the countryside. Which was maybe a good thing. The more people talking and questioning things they'd seen or heard, the better.

"So now you sure you ain't got even one pecan pie back in that kitchen, Miss Amelia? Me and Melody was looking forward . . ." Miranda turned to Miss Amelia, who'd been quiet, in deep thought.

Miss Amelia snapped to and smiled. She nodded and reached under the counter to pull out the pie she'd brought in with her. There were cackles of glee all around.

"I hope you came in for a bigger reason than pie," I said after Miranda passed the pie to Melody to check out and Melody passed it back to Miranda and they both smiled ear to ear.

"Well, of course," Melody said. "And here we are rattlin' on about nothing. Give her the letter, Miranda."

Miranda's thick eyebrows gathered over her nose. "You got it. I told you I didn't have a pocket . . ."

Melody shook her head. "Gave it to you. Just as we was walking out the door, remember? I had to go back and check the gas stove 'cause you made coffee this morning . . ."

"Nope, that's not the way it went, Melody. I was out front, chasing the dog away from the chicken coop, and you said you'd bring the letter. I remember clear as day."

"Well, let me see here," Melody checked her pants pockets, one by one, pulling out the linings to show they were empty.

"What about that satchel over your shoulder?" Miss Amelia asked. "Think maybe you stuck it in there?"

Melody's face clouded over. "Now that you mention it . . ."

She pulled the old, well-scarred leather sack from her shoulder and searched around inside, coming up with a folded envelope she waved in the air. "What'd you know? Right here all the time."

"Told you so," Miranda said, but with a smile.

"Here's what we told you about. Not much, I suppose. From some clinic in Houston, is all." Melody handed the letter to me. I took it and glanced down at the return address. Spenser Rehabilitation Clinic, Bonest Street, Houston, Texas. I slit the sealed envelope and pulled out the single sheet inside. I expected the letter to be an advertisement, maybe a form letter—an answer to something Amos had sent for in a weak moment.

It was addressed to Amos Blanchard, and went on to confirm that he had an appointment there. The letter was dated June 12, 2011.

Something, at last.

I passed the letter to Miss Amelia, who looked at the return address, read it, then folded the letter and stuck it down into the pocket of her jeans.

"Sure do appreciate you girls coming all the way to town with this." She seemed to forget the letter immediately as she smiled broadly at the two women, who were mollified now that they had a pie to look forward to.

"Gotta pay you for this." Miranda held up the pie box

and the gift box she said she was taking to Martin. Or to Juanita, whoever could eat it. "We don't take nothing from nobody for free."

"Why, sure thing, Miranda," Miss Amelia agreed and led them back to the cash register, where she took the five dollars Melody handed over, never saying a word about pecan pies going for twelve and big gift boxes for twenty.

Chapter Twenty-five

The twins were barely out of the Nut House when my phone rang. It was Sheriff Higsby.

"Need to see you over here, Lindy," he half growled into the phone on his end.

"You at the police station?" I asked, stalling for time; so many things were boiling through my brain.

"Yup."

"What's it about, Sheriff? Do I need Ben with me? You charging me with murder, too?"

It didn't seem to matter much if I was uncooperative. Being cooperative hadn't gotten us very far.

"Don't need to be hostile, Lindy. It's about Martin. Heard maybe it was Justin called him, sent him out to where somebody tried to kill him. Justin's not saying a word. I think one of you better start saying something. Doesn't make it any better for him, you know."

Chastened, and a little frightened, and wondering if Hunter had betrayed us, I agreed I'd be right over. "I wanted to see Justin this morning anyway. He's got to be all broken up about Martin."

I hung up and turned to Meemaw. "That was Sheriff Higsby. Wants to see me. He heard Justin was the one sent Martin to the barns, looking for something."

"Think Hunter will be there?"

"I hope so."

"Then give him this copy of the letter." She pulled the "Virginia" letter out of her pocket and handed it to me. "And I think you better call that rehab place soon as you can. Could be where Amos went—drying out. And if that Virginia was with him, maybe we can find her, too."

I was on my way out of the store when Miss Amelia stopped me. "You know what, Lindy? I think it's time we got over to that Barking Coyote. We've got to talk to that lady Amos was having the affair with. I been thinking about that jilted boyfriend of hers. That kind of thing can simmer on for years. Seems like the place where Martin and Amos locked horns was over Jessie. If the boyfriend knew about Martin and how he hated Amos, he might've used it, like trying to make Martin look like the killer."

I winced. The Barking Coyote Saloon wasn't the kind of place I was used to going. And worse than me, I just couldn't see Miss Amelia in there with the "good ole boys" and the cheap women, all doin' their line dancing and slugging back Garrison Brothers Bourbon.

"Sure, Meemaw, we'll get over to the Barking Coyote as soon I get back from the jail. Right after I call this rehab place. Right after I get over to see Jessie and tell her how sorry we are about all of this. And right after I help Bethany with those damned doves and Mama with her private detective . . ."

"Don't be a whiner, Lindy Blanchard," she told me, hands

on her hips. "You remember who you are. Suck it up. Now, you get your lazy behind outta here."

Told off and knowing I deserved it, I was out the door, almost swooning in heat that hit me like a feather tick, and not a cloud in the sky.

I walked over to the police station from the Nut House, as much to buy a little more time before facing the sheriff, as to get some needed exercise. At the corner, where Alamo runs into Carya Street, I turned and looked over at the Dairy Burst. It was past noon, school lunch hour, and the kids who hung out there were already slouched along the outdoor benches, licking ice cream cones melting as fast as they could lick. It seemed so ordinary, kids laughing and falling over one another. I felt a sharp pang, as if I were an outsider in my own town, somebody who didn't have the right to a normal life. But Miss Amelia's words—"Suck it up!"—ran through my head, and I got over it fast and ran up the steps to the police station.

Deputy Sam Cranston, new to the force, only twenty-eight and good looking enough to seem to be always posing in his short-sleeved blue shirt, stood behind the front desk.

"Hunter's back out at yer ranch this morning," Sam said. "If that's who you're looking for. More tech guys with 'im."

"They bring my trees in yet?"

"Saw 'em out back. Hunter was watering them, last I seen."

"Good," I said, and meant it. "The sheriff wanted to see me. And I want to see my brother." I gave him my best haughty voice. Sam had been behind me at Riverville High School, maybe three years. I knew he'd had a crush on me from afar—way afar since he never spoke to me, only gave me the mooneye when we passed in the halls.

"Sheriff's in his office. I'll clear seein' Justin with him." He blushed, a spreading red that started somewhere around his Adam's apple and climbed slowly to his hairline. "Tell you up front, Lindy, Ben Fordyce is back with Justin now."

"Good," I said, keeping my peremptory voice. "Hope he gets Justin out of this place today."

He gave me a shy, but skeptical, look as I flounced away from him and toward the hall leading back to Sheriff Higsby.

The sheriff stood when I walked in, and tipped his brown cowboy hat my way. He offered a seat and launched right into hearing that Justin was the one who'd asked Martin to go and search those barns.

"I don't know a thing about it, Sheriff," I answered, dropping my officious voice for a sweeter one—a voice I hoped would melt the tin badge right off the sheriff's chest.

"One of my men heard him on the phone Saturday morning. That's what he did with his one phone call."

I sat back, anger boiling up inside. "That's illegal, isn't it? Listening in on a man's one phone call?"

He shrugged. "Mistake. My deputy just happened to be standing there . . ."

"Think I'm telling Ben, soon as he comes outta seeing Justin. Let him file some charges or something." I was really into high dudgeon now, mad as a wet hen.

"Lindy." He put his hands in the air. "Calm down. Maybe you think I'm not on your side in this, but I am. I want to turn Justin loose as bad as you want him outta here. But I can't. Not yet. And after what happened to Martin yesterday, well, I'm thinking Justin's at the middle of this somehow. Maybe not that he did anything. Maybe he's not the one who killed Amos. And sure not the one who attacked Martin. Still, he's a part of all of this. And to tell you the truth, I'm not sure but what he's the next target."

I took in a breath.

He leaned forward, hands together on the desk. "I put Hunter in charge of the case, Lindy. I got a lot of other things to do. I can't really spare Hunter right now, but I think he's the best man to look at everything that's happened and figure it all out."

I slouched back in my chair and nodded.

"So I told Hunter to work with you and Miss Amelia." He patted the air with both big hands when I leaped forward to deny that we were doing anything. Last thing we needed was to have the sheriff horning in, scaring away people who could help us. "You know Riverville. People notice things and people talk. So what I wanted you to know is that Hunter's there to help. Whatever you two ladies find out, take it to him. You wouldn't want to get in the way of justice, would you?"

The tone was patronizing. The smile a grimace. I wanted to growl back at him, but the man was being up front with me—in his own way. I dug down and pulled out my best good girl smile, maybe even batted my eyelashes a few times, and left the office, stopping only to be reassured I could see Justin.

"Soon as Ben leaves," the sheriff said.

Ben walked out forty minutes later, when I was just about to give up and go out to call that rehab center in Houston.

He was his usual self, bent forward a little, bulging brief-case knocking against his leg. His seersucker jacket hung open over his white shirt, and his graying hair stuck up at the back from taking off his white cowboy hat. He saw me. His face took on a somber look.

"Lindy, I was coming out to see you and your mother. You going home from here?"

I shook my head. "Not until this evening, Ben. So much to do."

He nodded. "I understand. Heard about you and Miss

Amelia looking into things yourself. As your attorney, I've got to warn you—"

I put a hand up, stopping him. "Don't waste your breath, Ben. Nothing's going to stop Miss Amelia on a tear. We'll be fine."

"Just that—well, now with Martin. I'm a little worried. Could be some madman out there."

"I know. If only Martin'd come out of that coma. I'll bet anything he could tell us who attacked him and put an end to this whole mess."

Ben bent forward, lowering his voice. "There's something I need to talk to you and Emma about. And Miss Amelia. Something I should've brought up before . . ."

There were dark circles under his eyes. Whatever Ben had to say, it was going to be serious. "I'll call before I come out. Make sure y'all are home."

We left it at that, his seriousness doing nothing to raise my spirits.

Chapter Twenty-six

"I can't believe it, Lindy." Justin leaped from his cot when he saw me. "I did this to Martin. All because I had a hunch . . ."

There was nothing I could say. I let him talk, pour out his guilt at sending Martin out to the barns because he'd figured whoever did that to Amos was after all of us. What I wanted to do was close my eyes and not see him in his orange jumpsuit with RIVERVILLE CITY JAIL written across his back. I wanted none of what was happening to us to be real.

"If I woulda thought it was dangerous, I'd never have sent Martin out there looking for those trees. I just thought maybe whoever did that to Amos might want to make us look guilty. Make it seem all the Blanchards were in on the killing." He shut his eyes and shook his head. "Sounds dumb but . . . Look, I was right. The trees were there in the shed. Somebody put them there for the sheriff to find. And Martin," he moaned. "Poor Martin . . . I sent him out there."

I put my arm around him, led him back to the cot, then sat down beside him.

"Martin will be fine."

"He outta the coma?" His eyes lit up.

I shook my head. "Medically induced. Until the swelling goes down."

He looked away, staring at the wall.

"Who hates us this bad?" I asked him after a while.

"I would've said Uncle Amos, but he's dead." He took a long deep breath. "I've had nothing to do but think since I got here. At first I was thinking some pecan rancher from Georgia or someplace, mad about what you were doing and wanting to steal your work, make a killing off it. I was thinking maybe shoving that plant stake through Uncle Amos happened because the man got caught. That it wasn't something planned. Then I was thinking hiding the trees on our ranch would make it look like we were behind the whole thing. You know, frame me for Amos. Frame the family."

"Or maybe it wasn't somebody out to destroy my work, after all," I said. "Maybe whoever did it followed Amos out there. He was trying to see Mama earlier in the day. Amos could've noticed my greenhouse; it wasn't finished when he left town. Maybe he wandered over to take a look, thinking Mama's office was in there. If that was the case, whoever killed Uncle Amos was after him all along. Maybe what happened to my trees was just the killer going wild when he realized Uncle Amos was dead. You know, went on a rampage, destroying everything right up to my office, then setting the fire, cutting down the trees. An awful rage."

"Or a cold calculation," Justin said. "Cut down the trees to make it look like Amos did it and was stopped. Took five trees . . ." He shook his head. "Why would he do that? Had to load them into a car. No tire tracks."

"No rain. Ground too hard for prints."

"Why didn't Martin see him? He was out mowing all around that area."

"If he came the back way in, from over on the river road instead of the main entrance, he was parked behind the greenhouse. That way's all brush and scrub. I come that way myself when I'm coming in from La Grange."

Justin worked his two rough hands together. When he turned his head to me, I looked into eyes that didn't belong to my brother. Or not the brother I knew. It was the first time I'd ever seen Justin scared, and all that did was make me madder and more determined to get whoever was doing this to us.

"You know how much I held against Amos," he said. "Never kept it a secret. Didn't step away from saying I thought he had something to do with Daddy's accident. And I'll tell you something else, Lindy. Somebody's going to remember what Amos did to Jessie, jilting her the way he did. When they do, the sheriff's going to think me and Martin were in this together."

"But I saw him mowing near the greenhouse."

"Yeah. Near the greenhouse. Think about it. And on top of that, Martin's my only alibi. Saw me take off to go after those hogs. And Higsby's saying they found something in Amos's hand. Something that proves I did it. I don't know what he's talking—"

"I do. Hunter told me."

"What?"

"Your belt buckle. The one Daddy gave you. I asked you about it last week."

"Yeah, and I told you that belt broke out in the grove. I took the buckle back to the barn and put it in a drawer until I could get a new belt."

"Anybody see you do that?"

He rubbed his forehead. "I'm always in the barns. Who

knows who was there one day or the other? People drop by. Lord, how many people on any given day! The co-op people were out a while ago. Neighbors come by all the time. You know how it is yourself, Lindy. When isn't there a visitor or friend or even, once in a while, tourists Miss Amelia sends out from the store to have a look? Then there's all the men who work for me."

"Anyway, that's what the sheriff found. Your belt buckle."

"How'd it get there if—"

I gave him a look.

"Who'd do that?"

"A killer."

"They had to plan ahead. Steal the buckle. Can't be any of my men. No reason. Most of them didn't even know Amos."

"Only Martin."

He gave me a hard look. "The last thing Martin would do is hurt me. And if he killed Amos, how'd he attack himself down there at the shed?"

"Then we're right back to *who* and *why*."

He thought awhile. "About the belt buckle, Hunter told you?"

I nodded.

"You mean Hunter's helping you? I was afraid he'd turned on me."

"And we're helping him. Me and Meemaw."

Justin turned his first smile on me. "Can't quite see Meemaw as some kind of Miss Marple."

"She's good at it. Smart with people, Justin. Just like we always said—that sixth sense of hers when she knew we were up to no good. Maybe it's a thing with grandmothers. People talk to her. They like her. Some, like the Chauncey girls, who would never come to the police, are chipping right in with anything they know."

"Then I guess I'm in good hands. And you, too, Lindy. I don't think any man could ask for a better sister . . ."

I got up to leave before my big brother had me crying.

"Be careful, Lindy," he said from behind me. "And keep your eye on Meemaw. You know she has a tendency to get hardheaded, especially where her grandchildren are concerned. I wouldn't want to be the man crossing her. There could be trouble."

"There already is." I smiled back at my brother. "Remember what Daddy taught us."

" 'Remember who you are.' " He nodded.

"That's all we need, Justin. Like Granddaddy used to say, 'Jist git 'er done. Jist git 'er done.' "

Sam was back, pushing the cell door button.

At least I left my brother smiling.

I ran down the high concrete steps to my truck. Laughter came from the kids over at the Dairy Burst. I glanced at them, almost jealous, then got pulled back from my deep self-pity by my ringing cell phone.

Hunter Austen.

"Gotta see you, Lindy. We need to talk. Something you should know. You have dinner yet? How about The Squirrel? I'm buying. Say forty minutes?"

I agreed.

Chapter Twenty-seven

Out in my car, with the motor running and the air-conditioning on full in my face, I dug out the rehab letter. It was signed by a Dr. Ted Lambert. I called the number on the letterhead.

A woman answered at the clinic and put me on hold while she located Dr. Lambert. The voice, when Dr. Lambert came on, was higher than I'd expected, young sounding, and distracted, as if he was in too big a hurry to take inquiring phone calls.

"Ted Lambert," he declared. "How can I help you?"

I explained who I was and why I was calling. I told him about my uncle Amos. That he was dead, murdered, and we had traced him to the clinic.

"I've got questions, Doctor. We think somebody from his last two years there in Houston might be involved and—"

"I'll stop you right here, Miss . . . eh . . . Miss Blanchard, did you say?"

"Lindy."

"I am not at liberty to give out information about any of our patients."

"This is a police investigation," I argued.

"Then you have the police call me."

"He's my uncle," I protested.

"Have the police call and I'll cooperate all I can. But I'm warning you, a phone call won't be enough. I'll need the officer or detective—whoever's doing the inquiry—to come here, present me with the right court order, and I'll cooperate. You see, Miss . . . eh . . . Lindy, privacy is our first concern here at Spenser Clinic. If our patients ever thought that was being violated, why, we might as well shut our doors."

He hesitated. "Give me that name again? The dead man."

"Amos Blanchard. Was he there? Did you know him?"

"I can't give out medical information about our patients but what I will say is . . . well, he was here. And I liked Amos, Lindy. He was a good man . . ."

"You're talking about Amos Blanchard from Riverville, right?"

"Yes. I'd have to say he became a . . . well . . . friend to a lot of people here at the clinic."

I set that aside—Amos as a friend to anyone. "So he was there."

"That's the best I can do, Miss Blanchard. Just let me . . . well . . . accept my condolences. I know there will be others who would do the same if they could."

"Please, Dr. Lambert. Tell me who these others are. And tell me anything you know about Uncle Amos's time there in Houston—"

He interrupted. "I've said all I can say. As I told you, get an officer over here . . . but forget the legal papers. I just need to know . . . you'd be surprised what lawyers and family do to undermine a person's sobriety. I can't trust anybody's word. Show me a uniform. A badge. Something. Then we'll talk."

He hung up.

When I walked in The Squirrel, I was greeted by a terse "Cheerio" from Cecil Darling, crisp white apron in place, the few hairs left on his bald head swept over to the left and pasted there. Cecil was a man for the bow tie. The exemplary bow tie Englishman. If he could have worn spats and swung a cane while clearing heaps of dirty dishes from Formica tables, he would have been just that bon vivant.

"'Day, Lindy." Cecil nodded toward a corner booth. "Hunter's over there. Looks like you're five minutes late."

I looked at my watch. "Am not," I disagreed. "He's early."

I think there was a comment about "uppity women," but I ignored it as I always ignored Cecil, even as he called behind me, "Finnan haddie today. Probably too refined for your tastes."

"That's from Scotland, not England." I tossed my head, happy to show him I was no hick.

He only laughed behind me. "A lot you'd know." His voice was full of scorn.

I went to the far corner booth, where Hunter had settled in. He had a tall glass of sweet tea in front of him.

"You order?" I asked as Hunter sat up straighter on his side of the booth.

"Chili and cornbread."

"That must've got you a big sniff out of Cecil."

"Don't let him intimidate you. Order a pile of biscuits and gravy, if you want."

I shook my head. "Makes my behind spread. I'm off that stuff."

I ordered a salad. Dinner, which comes in the middle of the day for us Texans, was supposed to be bountiful but I wasn't feeling like taking on a big plate of barbecue or pulled pork, which would only make me sleepy. I had a lot ahead of me and had to stay sharp.

"So." I settled back and took a deep breath. "Justin's pretty broken up about Martin."

"We all are. Just shouldn't have happened. Justin coulda asked to see me . . ."

"Yeah, the guy who read him his rights." I let the sarcasm drip.

Hunter examined the backs of his hands, laid flat on the tabletop. "I got something we gotta talk about," he said. I detected the gloom in his voice and fought the urge to get up and run.

"What now?"

"Ben Fordyce."

"What about Ben?"

"Been looking into people who had trouble with Amos before he left."

"How's Ben fit in that group?"

"Turns out Amos scammed him out of a big chunk of money. And not just him but friends of Ben's, too. A big lawyer in San Antonio, for one. Another one in Columbus. Ben's been paying back the money they lost, but it looks like he's falling behind, can't pay the way he wanted to. You ask me, Lindy, I'd say we're looking at a very angry man under that all-business outside."

I gave him a disbelieving look.

"Sheriff dug it up by looking into Amos's financial dealings. Got a look at things over to the bank from back when Amos still did business there. Supposed to be a big amusement park coming in toward San Antonio is what Cal, at the bank, said. Amos swore it was a locked-up deal. He talked Ben into buying acreage—lots of land—where the park was supposed to go up. Trouble was some pals of Amos's owned that land. There was no amusement park. And by the time Ben found out, it was too late. Owned a few thousand acres of worthless brush and Amos's friends made a killing."

"Why would Ben trust Uncle Amos? He knew what he did to Daddy. All the harm to our family."

Hunter shook his head. "What I heard was people think he did it to help the Blanchards. If Amos got something of his own going—enough money to maybe buy a ranch for himself. You know Ben cares a lot about your mama. Wanted to help."

I shook my head, unable to believe what I was hearing. Ben had always been good to us—like so many in River-ville, but caring about Mama? And doing something as fool-ish as taking Amos at his word? Hard to believe.

"So? What happened to the money after Amos got it?"

"All gone. Nothing in the bank. We're thinking maybe Amos was suckered, too. But that sure gives Ben a reason to hate the man. Seeing him back in town like that."

"Are you crazy? Ben wouldn't hurt a—"

"Yeah, I know. That's what you've been saying about everybody. The trouble with that, Lindy, is that we still got a dead man on our hands, and sure as anything, somebody did that to him. And now this business with Martin being hurt . . ."

I couldn't argue plain facts. "Ben's coming over to our house later. He said he had something to talk to us about."

"Probably this business with Amos. See if you want a different lawyer."

"Different lawyer? Daddy trusted Ben. Mama trusts him."

"Sheriff's looking hard at Ben now. It's up to you folks. I'd think about it if it was me."

Our food came and Hunter dug in. I pushed the salad away. Despite Cecil's arrogance and pretentious daily specials, he wasn't known for his "healthy" food. Most of his salads looked like what I had on the plate in front of me: a whole chunk of plastic lettuce with a glob of dressing dumped on top.

"Is that what you wanted to talk to me about?" I leaned toward Hunter.

He nodded, a large spoon full of chili going in with half a piece of cornbread not far behind.

"Okay. Then I've got something I want to talk to you about. I need your help."

I told him about the doctor in Houston, and the rehab clinic for alcoholics. I told him the doctor admitted Amos had been there but wouldn't give me any information. He wanted someone in law enforcement asking the questions.

I told him how I got the letter about the clinic. He wasn't surprised that the girls didn't bring it to the sheriff. He knew the Chauncey twins and their antipathy to lawmen.

"So you want me to go to Houston and talk to this doctor?"

I nodded. "I want you to go *with me*. Remember that 'Virginia' letter? Seems like that's where she'd be. And if she knew Amos during those two years, she'd know if anybody had it in for him. And she's got a package, something Amos left with her. I really think we've got to find her. Could be what's behind this whole thing."

"Okay. So give me the letter and I'll call. How about tomorrow?"

"Sooner the better."

He nodded a few times. "What else you and Miss Amelia up to? Mind tellin' me?"

I thought a minute then decided, what the heck. "We're going over to the Barking Coyote tonight."

He gave me a disbelieving look. "You're kidding. You and Miss Amelia?"

He laughed enough to choke on his cornbread, then coughed a couple of times. "I'll save the pair of you the trouble," he finally said, an amused look on his good-looking face. "Already been there. Nobody knows nothing."

"You talk to a Finula? She's the one who broke up Jessie and Amos. From what I heard, she showed up at the library one day and told Jessie she was pregnant by Amos. Doubt it was true. She had another boyfriend at the time—but he wasn't a Blanchard, had no money. Probably the name was what appealed to her. Anyway, I heard the boyfriend was out to get Amos. Maybe that's what he did."

"Couldn't learn a thing. You'd think nobody ever knew your uncle, the way they shook their heads at me. What I understood was he went to the Coyote almost every night. Guess all the people who knew him two years ago must've died."

"Let's see what we can find out."

"I don't like it, Lindy." He looked hard at me. "That's no place for Blanchard women."

"Blanchard women go where they have to go, Hunter. You should know that by now."

"Your grandmother isn't a young woman. What if a fight breaks out?"

I had to laugh. "In case of a bar brawl, that'll be me standing behind her. Meemaw's a whole lot tougher than she looks."

When we finished eating, Hunter paid.

Out at my car he asked me to call him when we got back from the Barking Coyote. "I don't care what time it is. And I'll call this doctor in Houston," he said, shaking the letter at me. "You want to leave here about nine in the morning?"

I thought ten would be better, thinking about a night over at the Barking Coyote and what I might feel like come morning.

Chapter Twenty-eight

Back at the Nut House, I walked into chaos. People were everywhere and most of the shelves had been stripped of merchandise, dumped into boxes, and set along the front windowsills.

"We don't know anything for sure, but don't miss a single thing," Miss Amelia was calling out to Mama and Bethany, to Treenie and Miss Ethelred.

I pulled my meemaw aside. "What's going on here? You decide to clean the place right now?"

She shook her head. "I couldn't get that letter Amos wanted to give Emma out of my head. Since we didn't find it over to his room, and the police never came to talk to Emma, I was thinking about where it might've got to, and all I could do was picture him in here. Remember? Tipping over those gift boxes there at the end of the counter? Seems he took a long time righting them before leaving the store."

I saw what she was getting at.

"So we're looking for it," she said.

"Everybody wanted to help." She pointed around the

store where Bethany was stacking boxes and Mama and Miss Ethelred and Treenie were moving bags and stacks of aprons and pot holders into cardboard boxes or from one counter to another, looking in and under everything.

"Nothing so far," she said. "And I was awfully sure."

"It's been four days. If he put it in one of the boxes, it could've been sold."

"Well, yes. We're looking anyway."

I chipped in without another word. I opened gift boxes carefully, checking under the waxed liner and in among the candy packages. There were the smaller boxes with chocolate turtles and spiced nuts. There were the medium boxes with the turtles, nuts, and sugared pecans. And there were the large boxes with all of that plus a generous-sized bottle of pecan oil. There were two-bottle pecan hot sauce boxes.

After a while I fell into a pattern, searching each box and closing them carefully, wrapping a new bow on each one, and setting it aside so we wouldn't go through it again.

Bethany sat on the floor, shaking out aprons and dishtowels with the family crest on them. "I don't think there's anything here," she said, looking up at me then checking her watch. "And I've got to get back to the ranch. Chet and Christina are deciding for sure . . ."

I smiled at my pretty sister, her face more relaxed than I'd seen it in a week or more. "So the wedding's on?"

She nodded and raised crossed fingers at me. "I'm hoping."

When I got the chance, I cornered Meemaw, feather duster in hand, going through the cookbooks. I could see she was using the search as much to give the place a good dusting as anything else.

"I'm going to Houston in the morning with Hunter," I told her, keeping my voice low.

She nodded, whisking her duster across shelves and over

a stack of *Barbecue the Pecan Way* books. "Glad to hear it. I been thinking about that letter we found over to his room. Seems somebody who knows him has got something we need to see."

"That's what me and Hunter been thinking, too."

She nodded fast. "Glad to hear it. And if the man won't tell you anything, do whatever it takes to get inside. Tell him you want to get anything Amos left there. You know, tell 'im 'sentimental value.' All that stuff. Talk to other patients. Do what you have to do, Lindy."

"Is this the same grandmother who taught me never to tell a lie? Something about the truth being all mankind has against evil? And about how a woman should be known for the truths she tells?"

Her face got dark. The duster halted in midair. "Who's asking you to lie? All I'm saying is you should think things out a bit before you get into Houston. Bet Amos leaving Blanchard papers and things behind in Houston never entered your mind, did it? You know he had legal things. Copies of your grandfather's will. Like he could make it read different than it really was, with your daddy left in charge. So where else is all that stuff, I'd like to know? You got answers?"

I had to admit I didn't.

She held her duster still as she thought of something else to tell me.

"And you watch out for Hunter. I know he's sweet on you . . . but right now we can't depend on anybody. Nobody at all. We've got to be looking out for our own interests. Keep your eyes open, Lindy. And your mouth shut."

"Geez, Meemaw!" I was still incensed at the "sweet on you."

She nodded hard. Her eyes narrowed. I knew the last word was coming.

"I'll give you a 'Geez, Meemaw,' young lady. I've seen you around Hunter. I know what I'm talking about."

She went back to dusting so hard a stack of *Pecan Desserts* books tipped to the floor.

I moved over to work next to my mother, thinking it the only safe place in the store.

Mama at least smiled at me, though it was a weak smile.

"So much going on, Lindy. My head's spinning. And still those co-op books. I wanted to ask you for just a little bit of help with something."

"Sure, Mama. What do you need?"

"It's that private detective thing. You remember, your father paid the man a thousand dollars but still owed him five hundred. I asked the men over to the co-op if Jake hired him for some of their business back when he was president. They had Harry—you know he's on the board now—look into it and they can't find anything." She turned to look squarely at me. "You think you could call the man for me?"

"Why can't you do it, Mama?" My head was going to explode if one more person asked me to do one more thing.

She shrugged. "Guess I'm a little scared, Lindy. Jake didn't say anything to me . . . ever. Who knows what he had on his mind?"

I looked hard at her. "You think Daddy hired somebody to watch you? Is that it? Mama, that's crazy."

"I know." She looked away. "But would you do it for me? Just so I don't have to . . ."

"Of course. Give me the number."

She went to the back of the store for her purse. She handed me a piece of paper. It read "Donny Fritch Investigations," followed by a phone number.

She had something else on her mind and was about to say something more when Ben Fordyce walked in the store and stood just inside the door, looking around. Spotting Mama, he headed over to us.

"Why, Ben, you gave me a start," Mama said when she looked up. I noticed she straightened the collar of her blouse, pushed her glasses up her nose, and brushed back the hair from around her face.

"Sorry," he said. "I was going out to the ranch when I drove by and saw you all in here."

"You need to talk to me about something? Getting Justin out of that place?"

I'd forgotten he was coming over that evening, though I didn't forget what Hunter told me.

"Trying. Think I'm making some headway with Sheriff Higsby. He's beginning to see maybe Justin couldn't have killed Amos. And now this thing with Martin. Well, looks more and more like it's somebody else."

"Good." Mama looked relieved. "Just let me know when to pick him up."

"I'll certainly do that, Emma."

"And was there anything else?" She raised her eyebrows at him.

Ben looked at me and then away, as if reluctant to come out with what he had to say.

"I think I know what it's about, Ben," I hurried to reassure him. "I saw Hunter at dinner a while ago."

He flinched and turned back to Mama. "Emma, maybe you could come outside a minute? It's best we get this out of the way."

I could see she didn't want to go anywhere, with anyone. Seemed to me Mama was at an edge where she just might sit down and refuse to listen to even one more bit of misery brought to her by even one more relative, or friend.

Chapter Twenty-nine

It was quiet in the truck at first, and dark, despite the waxing moon. Miss Amelia and I were on our way to the Barking Coyote, but she was still put out with me. I knew my grandmother, and knew that when she got maddest at me, it was when she was maddest at herself.

Since I had no idea what she was mad at herself about, I just let it go, saying I was hungry again and that I hoped the Coyote had decent food.

"People don't go there for the food, Lindy." Frosty voice.

"What do they go there for?"

She sniffed mightily. "You mean to tell me you've never been?"

"I don't think it's the kind of place Blanchards go."

"Amos went there."

"Guess that was different. Maybe if I drank a quart of whiskey a day . . ."

"I'd watch my mouth, Lindy. I'm beginning to think maybe I was wrong about Amos—what with this place you're going tomorrow. If he removed himself from our lives for two years the way he did, and was getting his head screwed on straight, well, it just makes me sad to think of him coming back and getting killed."

"Anything else bothering you, Meemaw?" I asked, knowing there had to be more.

She was quiet. After a while she said, "Things I'm working on, Lindy. Just some things bothering me and I can't put them together. Maybe folks are right about me. Losing it. Like there're these threads in my head trying to make something—I don't know—maybe put a picture together, and I can't get them to move. They aren't making a picture. I'll tell you . . ." She looked over at me. "It's frustrating."

I understood what she meant. Every time I tried to look at what we knew about all of this, the figures changed. One way, it was Amos who was the target of a killer. The other way, Amos came on somebody destroying my trees. Either way what happened to Martin didn't fit in. And hiding my trees, maybe for the police to find? There was no drawing a noose around any of it.

It was almost ten o'clock. We figured that would be a good time to get there, especially for a Monday night. Nobody but the regulars would be around, and Miss Amelia said that was exactly the people we wanted to see.

The saloon was back off the main highway, down a slope leading into a pinewood.

The Barking Coyote sign, standing high between the road and a low, red wood building, blinked a garish red outline around a coyote howling at the moon. The bare lightbulbs, half burned out, bounced a Morse code that flared and died. Meemaw pointed it out to me. "Bet anything it says, 'Beware the Good Ole Boys.'"

"We'll get in there, speak to this Finula, and get right out," I emphasized one more time. "Hope that's understood."

"You think I was staying the night?" She pulled her

blouse down hard over her jeans. "And you listen to me, young lady, I don't want you dancing or anything. Just as you said, this is not our kind of place. Remember who you are, Lindy. Hope that's understood."

"Understood." I nodded. "Just have to keep my baser instincts under control, Meemaw. Good thing I brought you along."

"Say that again."

I nosed my truck in among the other pickups and old Chevys, parked any which way up on the grass. With a deep breath, I got out, helped Meemaw down, and went on ahead of her, through the door and into the smoky saloon.

The place was about what I'd expected. The music was loud. The voices were loud, one trying to outdo the other. Lots of women, young and old, all poured into short, tight skirts, wearing tight tops, and strutting around in shiny leather boots. Or they wore cowboy skirts and shirts with lots of fringe. Either way, the women had big hair and makeup enough to hide a hundred bad years.

Men leaned, backs hunched, along the bar or slumped forward at tiny tables. They were in every kind of cowboy hat imaginable, old boots or new, designer boots, jeans, and flannel shirts. The place smelled mostly of beer, and something I didn't want to think about but could be taken for mold.

The country music was loud, seeming to come from everywhere along the walls. The place was crammed full, five or more chairs pulled up to each table, where people knocked back beer out of the bottle, or straight shots of what I imagined was Garrison's Bourbon. They were laughing, until they turned to stare at me and Miss Amelia as we stood at one end of the old-fashioned bar, taking a good look around.

I was hoping we weren't giving off helpless vibes, like hens in a fox den.

"Help you?" A man seated backward on a chair near a

front table leaned back, got up, doffed his cowboy hat to us, and came over. "Wha'cha doing here?"

"We're here to see the owner," Miss Amelia said. "That's Morton Shrift we're looking for."

"Right down there." The man bent to point toward the far end of the bar. "Hope you're not looking for a job," he added, bringing a guffaw from the people behind him.

"Watch yer mouth," another man, hands cradling a tall beer, called out. "That's Amelia Hastings there. Better show some respect, Bobby, or you'll never get your sorry self a ragin' pecan pie again in your whole life."

The tall man in front of us colored up—to his credit. He touched the crown of his hat and muttered. "Sorry, ma'am. Didn't recognize you. Meant no harm."

Miss Amelia gave him a regal nod. "None taken. Oh, by the way, say hello from me to your mama."

She walked off, leaving the embarrassed man behind her.

Morton Shrift, a wide man with a blue kerchief tied around his thick neck, poured whiskey down a long line of glasses while people in front of him cheered and clapped.

"Didn't spill a drop," he bragged to his admirers.

"Hello there, Miss Amelia," he called out. "What can I get for you ladies?"

He smiled widely. "Bourbon? How about a double shot to start you off . . ."

Meemaw fixed Morton with one of those steely looks I knew so well. "We're here to see Finula. That's the woman who used to be with Amos. Remember? We need to speak to—"

Morton interrupted by pointing to the dance floor, where couples were slow dancing, heads together, bodies barely moving. "That's her," he said, motioning to a couple leaning on each other, dancing with their eyes closed, moving only enough to keep from falling over.

"We'll wait . . ." I started.

"I wouldn't do that." Morton shook his head. "Finula leaves the dance floor only if she's gotta pee. Drinks while she's dancing. Takes care of business while dancing . . ."

"What business would that be, Morton?"

The man smiled slyly at Meemaw. "I guess you'd call it the entertainment business, Miss Amelia. She kind of makes appointments."

Meemaw looked at the woman, who barely moved her feet as the rousing song, about a guy in a bar with no place to go and crying in his beer over the women he lost, throbbed like a heartbeat from speakers around the room.

I walked ahead of my grandmother, parting the crowd so she could follow me to the dance floor. Up close, Finula didn't look any more appealing than she did from far away. The changing gel lights turning her skin red, then blue, then yellow making her appear more harsh and older than her thin body and seductive clothes advertised. Finula danced with her head laid on the cowboy's shoulder, her thick, long, dyed black hair spilling across his plaid shirt. Her bottom, in a short leather skirt, twitched back and forth to a beat of its own.

"Finula?" Meemaw·tapped the woman on her shoulder.

The response wasn't immediate. It took another tap before she blinked around and up.

"Yeah?" she said, continuing to sway against the cowboy.

"Are you Finula?"

"Yup. You got a reason for asking?"

"I'm Amelia Hastings. This is my granddaughter, Lindy Blanchard. We'd like to talk to you, if you've got a minute."

Finula pulled back from the cowboy, who looked around for another partner. Her body stiffened. "You from Amos's family?"

I nodded.

"Well, what do you know? I heard somebody did Amos

in over at your ranch." She motioned us back through the clustered dancers, to a table in a back corner of the room. She nodded for us to sit though I looked down at the overflowing table, filled with empty bottles and dirty glasses, then up at Miss Amelia, thinking the woman would never join a table like that.

Meemaw didn't flinch. She took a chair, sat, and folded her hands over her purse.

"Sorry for your loss." Finula leaned toward us across the small table. "But you have to admit Amos had a way of making enemies. This about his murder?"

Meemaw nodded. "In a way."

"Do what I can for you." She lifted a beer glass, took a swig, then straightened her shoulders and pushed her heavy hair back from her face.

"We were just wondering about a couple of things."

"Like what?"

"How's the baby doing?" I leaned in with a big smile.

Finula sat far back and studied me. "Who told you I had a baby?"

"Got it from a friend."

"Bet it was that Mexican girl Amos was with before me."

I sat quietly.

"Turned out I never was exactly pregnant."

"How do you go about being not 'exactly pregnant'?" I asked.

Miss Amelia rapped my knee hard with her knuckles.

"What happened to the boyfriend you had when you were with Amos?" she asked, her no-threat smile in place.

Finula's face went dark. "What in hell are you really asking, lady?"

"Just wondering, that's all. Heard he didn't much like Amos."

"You can say that again. Like to kick the piss outta him.

But he found another girl and was gone before you could whistle Dixie."

"He's not in Riverville then?"

She shook her head. "Seen nary a hair nor hide.'" She laughed.

"You hear from him?" I asked.

"Well." She drained one of the murky shot glasses. "We weren't on the best of terms when he left, you know. Didn't get no Christmas card, that's what you mean."

Finula drew back and lifted an eyebrow at Miss Amelia. "Bet you're a lot like me, lady. Seen a few things in your lifetime."

Miss Amelia ignored her.

"Before he left, did Amos tell you he was going to Houston?" I wanted the conversation back on track so we could get out of there. I was well aware of eyes turned our way and people talking.

"Think that's what he said. Seemed like he was going to clean up his life. Said something about how having a baby was really waking him up."

"So when he left, he didn't know the baby didn't exist."

"Yeah. I guess that's the way it was." She shrugged.

"Was he having trouble with anybody while he was still here?'

She nodded. "Plenty. First it was just about all you Blanchards. Then that seemed to go away and he was talking about people I didn't know. He was sayin' how he was on to something. I never quite figured what he was getting at. But he sure was worked up about it. Kept saying it was time he stepped up or something. Like people wouldn't believe him, the way he was. But you know Amos, had a way of rambling around the horn and back to get where he wanted to go."

Morton's voice came over the PA system. There was a

line dance coming up. A short cowboy in high-heeled boots came over to ask Finula to dance. She looked him up and down then smiled blearily, showing teeth too perfect to be real and red gums that could have used a dentist.

"Sorry, ladies. Got to get back to business." She took the cowboy's hand in hers. "Nice to meet y'all. Just think, we coulda been kin."

Another man approached the table where we sat. I was still thinking about what Finula had said and putting it down to another mark in Uncle Amos's favor. The man, older, grizzled, looking a little bit shy, bowed to Miss Amelia.

"Sure'd be honored if you'd give me this dance, Miss Amelia. Been missing your pies and thought maybe I could talk you back into yer kitchen while we showed these younger folks a step or two."

"I haven't danced in a while, Jefferson." She smiled up at a man I didn't recognize.

"Bet you didn't forget how. It's the Dean Brothers. 'Waltz Across Texas.'"

"Oh my." Miss Amelia thought a minute then surprised me by reaching a hand up to the man, and standing. She let him lead her off to the dance floor, where other couples were already lined up, row after row. The music came on and people began stepping to their right, then left, in a waltz as formal as a minuet.

My mouth dropped open in surprise, watching my grandmother move sedately along the dance floor. Her back was straight, head up, chin in the air. She looked good and danced like a pro.

Before long a very good-looking guy I'd known in high school came over and claimed me. Since I'd been feeling like a wallflower, I took Jeremy Burset's hand and cut in line next to Miss Amelia.

The music was good. The floor was sticky. The air was

so thick with smoke the tables around the dance floor disappeared in a blue haze.

I settled down to have a good time, though I wasn't above doing a little teasing on the way home about somebody in our family having a shady past—somebody leading me directly to hell in a hand basket.

Chapter Thirty

When the phone rang the next morning, I fumbled around, then happily ignored it until it stopped ringing. I let myself lie still, hoping today would be different, everything would go our way, and the doctor in Houston would clear up where Uncle Amos had been and what he was doing and why he came back to Riverville. And for good measure, I threw in that he would trot Virginia out for us to meet and ask about the "package" Amos left with her. She would look thoughtful for a minute and—in my daydream—walk back to wherever she'd come from and bring us the package. Me and Hunter would open it together, and there was the answer to everything. It seemed he was murdered because . . .

Mama was yelling up the stairs and everything hit the fan just as I was about to solve the whole mess.

"It's the Nut House. Somebody broke in last night. That was the sheriff. He's over there now. Get up! Bethany! Lindy! Come on. We've got to get there right now."

There was banging and yelling back and forth and I was out of bed, washed, brushed, dressed, and downstairs in about ten minutes. Bethany, looking unbrushed and unwashed and almost undressed, in a T-shirt with no bra and a pair of jeans from some back hanger in her closet, was still there ahead of me. Miss Amelia stood framed in the front doorway, as cool as ever, despite her night of pure debauchery. Mama looked flustered, but somehow all the better for being on the job and in charge again.

"Treenie's there," Mama said. "Sheriff told me to get into town. They're going over things but it's a mess. Come on, Lindy. You ride with us."

"How did they get in?" I asked, pushing my feet into sandals.

Mama made a face at me. "How'd somebody get in your apartment? Everybody knows that key's right up there . . ."

Miss Amelia cleared her throat. "I took it away yesterday, Emma."

Mama looked embarrassed and, on her way out the door, leaned up to her mother and kissed her on the cheek. "Sorry, Mama. I shoulda known. Just so much . . ."

The store looked like a dervish had whirled through, front to back. Bottles of pecan oil were spilled over split cellophane bags of nuts. Tins and gift baskets had been emptied on top of the rest of the mess. Cookbooks lay beside jars of dip, dressings, and roasted pecan syrup. A table of Miss Amelia's special pecan and bourbon grilling glaze was upended near the register. Candies littered the floor.

Miss Amelia, standing in the open doorway, made a startled sound then shook herself.

Treenie, back by the kitchen, tears running down her face, ran to comfort her.

Bethany, Mama, and I stood with our mouths open. There wasn't a single package of nuts or candy or bread or anything left intact. Whoever'd been there tore up things the way my test grove had been torn apart.

"Sheriff says they got in a back window. Out in the kitchen." Hunter hurried in, open notebook in his hand.

"What's it like out there?" Miss Amelia demanded, nodding toward her kitchens.

"Nothing," Treenie put in. "Musta come straight in here."

Miss Amelia looked relieved, then settled herself to deal with the mess. I could almost see her mind swinging from misery to the job ahead of us.

"Could it have been kids?" Mama looked up at Hunter, not so much worried as shocked. "Maybe teenagers. There've been times in the past; I remember when the co-op got torn apart, kids after money."

"No idea yet. Sheriff says it looks like kids, because of the damage. No guy out for money would take the time. But you never know."

"Where *is* the sheriff?" she asked, looking around. "I thought he'd still be here . . ."

"Got a call. A wild hog attacked a dog over to the Dolorous Ranch. Said to tell you he's sorry he's not here but most of what we had to do is finished."

"Can we start cleaning up?" Miss Amelia asked.

"Go ahead. Hope you've got plenty of people."

"I imagine, when they hear, we'll get all kinds of folks turning up to help." Miss Amelia rubbed her hands together. "Nothing we can't put right in a couple of days. Still got pecans in storage. Just got to get baking, and candy making, and filling boxes."

I looked around the store thinking maybe I wasn't seeing the same thing she saw: pecan oil soaking into the floorboards. Syrup trickling over display tables. It looked like pure meanness to me.

Mama came from the kitchen with an armful of garbage

bags. Treenie brought in a bucket of soapy water and a bunch of rags.

As if the cavalry were riding into town, the bell over the door rang and Ethelred Tomroy hurried in, her face outraged when she looked around at the damage.

"My! My!" Miss Ethelred, otherwise struck dumb, said as she grabbed a broom and started sweeping.

Behind Ethelred came Harry and Chastity Conway.

"Heard about it," Harry said, shaking his head. "Figured you'd need help."

Chastity hugged Miss Amelia hard then stepped back to look her over while waving away Mama's offer of a garbage bag. "Me and Harry hurried right into town. Got the men out in our grove, spraying and such, but we can't turn our backs on our best friends in their hour of need. That's what Harry said, soon as we heard."

"Just tell us what you want us to do, Emma." Harry turned to Mama. "We're planning on spending the whole day with you."

He rolled up the sleeves on his new-looking fancy cowboy shirt.

"Well, Harry's staying," Chastity smirked. "I've got my weekly hair appointment. But I'll be happy to do some baking for you. Just need your recipes, is all."

Miss Amelia might have had a short comment on Chastity's request and on her priorities except Jessie and Juanita Sanchez walked in right then. Tears welled in Juanita's eyes. She put her hands to her mouth.

Jessie shook her head, looking around at the disorder. "What's happening? Who would do this to you?" She choked on the words.

Then, Tommy Johns, the kid Miss Amelia gave work to whenever she could, came in and went right to picking things up. Morton Shrift from the Barking Coyote, along with his wife, Susie, brought in big brooms and a bucket on wheels. An industrial-sized mop was stuck under his arm.

Willy Shuck, the town miser, sidled in and went to work picking up boxes. Not a word to anyone.

The place was getting noisy with people talking and sweeping and calling out, "Get that bucket over here." "Need another bag." One by one, people came, until the store was filled with friends and neighbors and even some friendly strangers who'd heard and stopped in to see what they could do.

Last to arrive, probably because it took time for word to spread out as far as they lived, were the Chauncey twins. Melody and Miranda wandered in and looked around at the commotion as if they'd landed in the wrong place.

"Whew, look at this place, will ya? Why, Miss Amelia, I don't blame you for swellin' up like an ole toad. Awful. Jist awful. Me and Melody was on our way into town when we heard."

"Terrible. Just terrible," Melody put in, head shaking hard enough to knock her hat sidewise.

"Don't you worry. We'll get all this mess cleaned up in no time," Amelia said. "Look at all this help we're getting. Now you girls here to help . . ."

Melody shook her head. "We was comin' in anyway. It's about that gift box we bought to take to Martin. Never got there. First we had no time to come back to town to go see 'im. Next thing that greedy one there"—she motioned toward Miranda—"was rooting around in the box, opening the cookies and eatin' 'em . . ."

"One cookie, Melody," Miranda snapped back. "Don't go exaggerating. Maybe you don't see things right. Gettin' so old, half the time you don't know whether to scratch yer watch or wind yer butt."

"No older than you." Melody rolled her eyes. "Nothing sacred with this one, I'll tell you. Like we had money for something else to take to Mr. Sanchez. Greedy, that one." She pointed to Miranda.

"What are you trying to say?" Miss Amelia urged Melody out of her new grievance against Miranda.

"What she's trying to say," Miranda took over as Melody kept working herself into a state where she was almost speechless, "is that we found us something shouldn't have been in there."

Miss Amelia reached out to take Miranda's hand as she turned back to her sister. By the look in her eye, she'd just come up with another pithy saying to fling at Melody.

"What I'm saying is we found something in the box. Didn't belong there," she confided.

Miss Amelia put a hand up, stopping her.

She turned to me. I could almost see thoughts leaping through her head. She raised her voice. "I'm gonna take a rest now. You know us old folks." She looked around to see who was listening. She slid a look toward Hunter, to make sure he was busy. "Why don't you girls come out to the kitchen with me? Something I'd like to show you. Oh, and Lindy, don't you and Hunter have someplace you gotta be?"

"Well . . ." I had my hopes up about what the girls found in that gift box and didn't like being shut out of the kitchen conclave. But Miss Amelia was giving me the head nod to get out of there and I didn't want to make her mad at me again.

"Sure thing," I agreed. But it was a reluctant agreement. "Guess we gotta go."

I looked from Melody and Miranda to Miss Amelia. The twins were giving me identical frowns.

"I'll call you, okay?" I said loud enough for everybody to hear.

She lifted a single eyebrow at me. "I'd say that's a good idea. You call me. Just as quick as you can."

Hunter, who'd been standing behind me, ready to go for some time, took my elbow and steered me back through the working townsfolk.

Only Mama stopped me on the way out. "You call that private detective yet, Lindy? I really got to know . . ."

"I will, Mama."

I got a long-suffering look.

"Soon as I get a minute."

What I didn't add was that I had no idea when I'd have so much as a minute to myself ever again.

"Don't forget your truck's at the ranch," she said, waving me away. "Better stop when you and Hunter get back, if you want to come to town."

She looked hard at Hunter, then at me. She almost smiled. I was grateful she wasn't up to teasing me, or that nothing sprang to her mind. I grabbed Hunter's hand and cleared our path the rest of the way to the door.

Chapter Thirty-one

"We're taking the Katy Freeway." Hunter pointed out the obvious, making uncomfortable small talk.

I nodded. He could get there any way he wanted, as long as we got going.

"You know where we're headed?" I asked.

"Got it on my GPS. Over by Memorial Park."

"You call the doctor? We're going to be late, you know."

He nodded as he settled behind the wheel, snapped on his seat belt, and started the car. "Told him we couldn't get there until after lunch. Fine with him. Said he's got morning appointments anyway."

"I hope this isn't a wild-goose chase," I groused because I felt like grousing.

He shrugged as he turned south at Carya and then east on US 10. "You got a better idea?"

"Not at the moment. Just I wish we didn't have to rush out of there."

"Why not? We're late as it is . . ."

"The Chaunceys found something. Miss Amelia didn't

want to make a big deal out of it in front of everybody, but I know they've got that paper Amos wanted to give Mama. I can just feel that's what they were talking about."

"It'll wait."

"What kind of cop are you, Hunter? It's got to be what everybody was looking for. A letter. A document. Whatever Amos wanted Mama to have."

"You said yourself, Houston's the most important thing we've got to do right now." He turned to smile at me. "Your grandma's just as smart as you think you are, Lindy. She'll take care of it. You think I didn't catch on, what was goin' on?"

"'Course I figured. Miss Amelia must've thought you'd grab the letter or whatever, the way you do. It's just that here we go running off when things are—"

"Can it, Lindy. Let's get this done and see where it takes us. We'll be back to Riverville this afternoon. With what we find in Houston and what your grandma's got there, it might be all over by tonight."

I took in a long breath, wanting to believe him but not having much faith in anything right then. "I wish Martin would get better."

"Know what you mean. Me, too. Poor man."

"He's got to know . . ."

"You learn anything at the Barking Coyote last night? And why didn't you call me? Heard you did some dancing while you were there."

"It was kinda late when we got back. I was tired."

"All that dancing, I'll bet."

I ignored him. "We saw that old girlfriend of Uncle Amos's. That Finula."

"Yeah. Finula Prentiss. I tried to talk to her when I was over there. Wouldn't tell me a thing. It was like she never knew your uncle. What did she have to say?"

"That Amos was leaving town to clean up his life. She

said he was all worked up, talking about people she didn't know. He told her there was something going on in town and that it was time he stepped up. She didn't know 'stepped up' to what. That was about it."

"Heard she was pregnant. That's the real reason he took off the way he did."

"Well, seems that baby didn't even exist. Old trick. Maybe this other thing he told her was just a way to get her off his back."

"But he *was* going to this Spenser Clinic. Looks like he stayed awhile."

"There's that. I'm looking forward to talking to the doctor. Sure hope this woman, this 'Virginia,' was there with him at the time," I said.

"I hope she's still got that package. You think the whole thing's for real? You know how Amos liked to lead women on."

"Why would Amos say she should only give it to a cop or some official in case something happened to him? That doesn't sound like a game to me."

We were quiet. I leaned against the seat and tried to clear my head. It felt good to be with Hunter again, as a friend. I was telling myself how much I could trust him when a smarter part of me woke up and warned me to remember we were still on opposite sides of this thing. Hunter was looking for a killer. He could still believe that killer was my brother. I knew Hunter well enough to know that law and truth were important to him. And I knew me well enough to know I'd do anything to prove that no Blanchard did this.

We were getting close to Houston. Soaring cement ramps of other freeways intersected overhead. The skyline was right in front of us, tall buildings against a big flat sky filled with murky clouds rolling in from the bay. I couldn't help thinking of those clouds as traitors, promising much and delivering nothing. Still no rain.

Hunter drove easily in traffic, pulling off the ramp to Memorial Park and going straight to where we found the rehab clinic, set down in a green park with even a few browning palm trees thrown in among the mix of native plants. Sprinklers shot out water, keeping that grass green. People on benches set in shady places fanned themselves with folded newspapers. Children chased a football half-heartedly. Early afternoon, on a sweltering Texas day, wasn't a time for running and playing hard, unless a person courted heat stroke.

The steps to the wide glass doors of the low, stone building were deep, as if to give patients a time or two to think about the commitment ahead.

The receptionist, a typical Texas girl, pretty, with blond hair and a wide smile, offered us sweet tea while we waited for Dr. Lambert to come out to the lobby. We turned her down. I was thirsty, but more than that, I was nervous. So much counted on what the man would tell us.

The doctor was short and wiry. He wore a blue short-sleeved shirt, open at the neck. Not what I had pictured—expecting tall and thin with dark hair and a white coat. Kind of like most TV doctors.

We introduced ourselves, shaking hands all around, then followed the doctor back to his office, down a beige-carpeted hall. Photographs of historical places in Texas lined the pale green walls. Not exactly calming—battlefields and the Alamo.

At his office, he shut the door and took a chair behind his desk. We took plastic chairs across from him.

"So." He laid thick hands on top of a stack of papers and asked to see Hunter's credentials. Everything to his satisfaction, he relaxed back and took a deep breath. "You want to know if Amos Blanchard of Riverville was here and how that went. That about it?"

Hunter nodded.

"I'll tell you, Officer, he was a patient up to a few months ago. He was in and out at first. Then he settled down and worked hard at his sobriety. When he left us, to go back home, he was in great shape. Had a handle on his drinking. Told me he was a changed man."

"You know he was murdered in Riverville?" I said.

"So you told me on the phone. I looked up the news from last week and found the story online. Terrible thing. You get who did it?"

Hunter shook his head. "That's why we're here, Doctor. Did Amos have any problems with other patients?"

The man shook his head. "Nothing. If anything, he made a lot of friends. Amos was here to heal his life. He didn't get mixed up in little squabbles that sometimes get started among recovering alcoholics. Too much time on their hands and too much truth coming at them all at once. We understand that. Amos stuck to his own business. Helped people. Listened to them if they came to him. But otherwise, he was like a man on a mission. Getting well meant a lot to him."

"Did he talk to a psychiatrist here?" I asked.

The man nodded. "To me. I am a psychiatrist."

"Can you tell me anything about what he planned to do when he left? What he was thinking about?"

The doctor shook his head. "I'm sorry. That's all confidential."

"But the guy's dead." Hunter moved uncomfortably in the chair.

"Nevertheless. He was my patient."

I leaned forward. "Did he meet a woman named Virginia here?"

The doctor sat back and looked hard at me. "Why?"

"I've got this letter . . ." I pulled the copy from my purse and pushed it across the desk toward the doctor.

"Hmm . . ." he said. "Sounds like they had something going on, doesn't it? To tell you the truth, I'm glad to hear it."

"What we're most interested in is this package he left with her. She still here?"

He shook his head. "All I can tell you is that, if possible, I will locate the woman. This Virginia. I can't say if she is a patient or if I even know her."

He stood. "I'll do what I can. No promises. There is a great deal of importance placed on anonymity here at Spenser's."

I took out a ranch business card and handed it to the doctor. Hunter made a move to stop me, then sat back in his chair.

"Have her contact me at either number," I said. "And that's my address." I pointed.

The doctor nodded and we left.

Chapter Thirty-two

I bought Hunter a burger at a truck stop outside Houston.
I figured it was only fair. It was his car and gas, and after
all, he bought the food last time.

I didn't let myself think how natural and easy and normal
our conversation was going. Not a whole lot about murder.
More about the master's degree in law enforcement he was
working toward online.

"Only got a year of classes left," he said while digging
into his burger.

Hunter'd left college when his daddy died, to help his
mother in their feed store. When he got the feed store to the
point where it was making a profit, they sold it. Now his
mother was well and happy and working part-time at a dress
shop in town. Hunter had time to study for further advance-
ment in a job he loved. I was glad things were going so well
for him.

Back in the car, pulling out on to the busy highway, when
I'd almost forgotten we weren't together just because we
were good friends, my cell rang.

It was Mama. She sounded as if she'd been crying.

"I had more to say before you left," she began.

"Sure, Mama. I'm still with Hunter. Just leaving Houston. Saw that doctor who treated Uncle Amos."

"You coming back?"

"Be about an hour and a half. I want to see how my greenhouse is coming. And anyway, I've got to pick up my car at the ranch."

"We've got to talk, Lindy. Whenever you get here. It's about what Ben told me last night. I think the whole family has to decide . . ."

"I know what it's about. That deal he got suckered into with Uncle Amos. Hunter thinks it makes Ben a suspect, about as much as Justin and me. But, Mama, you know Ben didn't kill Uncle Amos." I glanced at Hunter, to make sure he heard me. "Why would he be out in my greenhouse? If it wasn't Amos who cut down my trees, you know, sure as anything, it wasn't Ben."

"Oh, I know all of that. Of course it wasn't Ben. Not you either. But, oh Lord, Lindy. We've got to decide what's best for Justin. Should we get him another attorney? All I can think about right now is my son."

"Mama, Ben was the best for Daddy. I'd say we stick to what we know. Like Daddy always said, find that single path and ride it hard. You talk to Miss Amelia?"

"She said the same thing you're saying. It's just that I'm so scared."

"Don't be scared, Mama," I said, glancing over at Hunter, who had to be listening though his eyes were narrowed, concentrating on the traffic in front of him. "Let's have a little faith in justice and friends, and family, Mama."

"You're right," she said. "Of course you're right. You hear about the letter from Amos the Chaunceys brought in here a while ago?"

"Knew of it. I was supposed to call Miss Amelia about it but I forgot. So much going on."

"You gotta read it, Lindy. All about how sorry he was for the things he did to your daddy and me. It's really sad, Lindy. I don't know why he didn't come right over when he got back here in town. At least I woulda talked to him."

Thinking maybe that wouldn't have been the case—too many things in their past—I slid right on by what she was saying.

"I'll be there soon as I can. We'll talk and—"

"Lindy? Did you find the time to call that private detective yet? Seems like maybe what Jake was after plays into what's happening. Me and Miss Amelia talked a few minutes ago. She kind of thinks the same thing. And there's still five hundred dollars owing, far as I can see. I went through everything. Not another bill. You'd think—"

"I'll call right now."

"If we owe the man money—something Jake was supposed to take care of—well, tell him I'd like to pay."

"Of course, Mama. That's what I'll say."

I hung up.

I decided to call the detective after Hunter dropped me back at the house to get my truck. It wasn't that I didn't want him listening in; more I'd picked up on Mama's unease and didn't want any more dirty linen swinging in the wind.

It wasn't a time to be dependent on anybody. Not even Hunter, whose blue uniform was like a blinking red light that could stop people, besides Finula Prentiss and everybody at the Barking Coyote, from talking to me.

Hunter dropped me off and promised to call in an hour or so.

With Hunter's taillights still in sight, I called Meemaw from the front porch. "Just checking in," I told her. "Wanted

to bring you up to date on what Hunter and I found in
Houston."

"You coming to town?" she asked in a bright tone that
didn't match what was going on. I figured there were people
around her.

"Thought I'd stay here awhile. Still I'd like to see that
letter you got from the Chaunceys."

"Well, don't you worry none. And—since you're askin',
we got the place cleaned up without you. I'm still not going
to be baking my own pies, like everybody's asking here. Not
yet. Seems like a fitting memorial, don't you think, Lindy?"

I heard a woman's high-pitched complaint behind her
and figured Miss Ethelred was standing nearby.

"No, no, Lindy. Now don't push me," Miss Amelia kept
on, pretending I'd said something. "Can't do it. Not yet. Even
though all these folks are just begging—"

"Can it, Grannie," I growled into the phone. "I know
you're playing me. And personally, I don't care if I ever have
one more slice of your rotten—"

"Yes, well, you just take your time coming in, Lindy. You
sweet thing, you."

"Think I'm gonna do that. Take my time. I'd rather be
out in my greenhouse anyway."

"Suit yourself. Bye now, dear. Oh, and don't worry, we'll
just bring that other thing along home with us. So many
kind folks here. Can't think about . . . well, you get yourself
some rest, ya here?"

She hung up, giving me an extra bang in my ear. I was
sure, from what Meemaw had just put me through, that she
was still busy with people at the Nut House. That "other
thing" she was talking about had to be the letter. I'd see it
later. And tell her what we'd learned—or hadn't learned—
from the doctor.

I figured I'd take the time to get out to my greenhouse. It had been a while.

A little time to myself sounded awfully good right then.

The private detective, Donny Fritch, wasn't in his office when I called. I was still standing on the front porch when his answering machine came on, telling me to leave a message, which I couldn't do because I didn't know what to say. I'd call later. Mama would keep after me until I did.

With Miss Amelia among all her friends, with Mama upset about Ben—well, time alone with the seedlings I had left seemed like the place where I was needed most. And while I was thinking about it, on the way around the house to get my truck, maybe I'd call the sheriff and arrange to pick up the five trees he was holding hostage. Poor trees. Roots drying out. Dying even as I thought about them.

If I was ever mad about anything in this whole mess— suddenly it was about my trees. With this new drought raging around us and newspaper headlines tolling out bad hot weather news like a funeral bell, my trees were the future. And if the sheriff wouldn't let me have them—as if they would climb up on a witness stand one day and point a long, leafy branch at the killer and, in a long hissing voice, make an accusation—like some Perry Mason moment—well I was going in there and . . .

When I got to the greenhouse, a small, dark man with a wide chest and back stood there. My sentry—on duty. Mama had called the workmen to see if they would take turns keeping an eye on my empty grove and greenhouse. José had been the first to offer, Mama'd told me.

"Hey, José." I was happy to see his smiling face, those big arms, the butt end of a revolver in the waistband of his pants, and those sharp dark eyes looking back and forth.

"We don't want nobody coming back here, Miss Lindy. Finish what they started. And we want to get whoever hurt Martin like that."

He nodded again and again. I thanked him and hurried away. Being tired and depressed, I knew that the one thing that could break me faster than anything right then would be kindness.

First, into the greenhouse, avoiding the burned circle on my office floor. I checked the temperature, then the sprayers above my yellow seedling pods. I checked the water timers, resetting one. I checked to see how well everything had been cleaned up, avoiding the one row where I'd fallen over Amos.

Back inside my office, I settled down with a new ledger, entering tag numbers I'd jotted down in the greenhouse. Although all my old records were gone, I still had the new genera I'd been working with. I had a good idea of what I'd grafted. What I needed to do was fix the records for seedlings I still had, from memory if I had to. The killer had destroyed the notes with grafting dates, seed germination of a particular type of tree I was interested in—one that stood up well to drought. I had nothing on the other trees I'd been working with, but I had a lot of that in my head. I put all of it into the record book in front of me. If I was lucky, I'd have the cleaned greenhouse back on a schedule of individual feeding and watering in a week.

What I faced, I decided, was a bad bump in the road, but not a complete disaster. I thought about climbing back up the hill I'd already scaled and it seemed daunting, but I wasn't a quitter. My work was too important. The only way to stop me now, I thought, laughing to myself, was to kill me, too.

It was a chilling thought. I brushed it away as fast as it came, but not without looking behind me, toward the closed door, and feeling grateful again for José, standing outside the gate.

When I'd wrung my brain dry of facts and dates, I stopped working to try the detective, Donny Fritch, again. This time a man answered. Not a machine.

"Donny Fritch," the deep male voice said.

"Mr. Fritch, I'm glad I caught you . . ."

"Who's calling?"

"I'm Lindy Blanchard . . ."

"Name's familiar."

"You did work for my father, I think. A few years ago. Jake Blanchard."

"Oh, sure thing. Now I recall. Jake Blanchard, of Riverville. I read in the newspapers that your father died. Accident, wasn't it? Sorry for yer loss."

"My mother's been going through Daddy's records and found a bill from you. She was wondering if there's still money owing. It didn't seem you were paid the full amount. At least, not from what she could find."

"Hmmm." He hesitated. Took a deep breath. "Let me think back now. Had some trouble here in the office. Lotta things got messed up. Seems we would've billed the estate if the work was completed. Maybe your daddy canceled the job. Let me go ask my partner what she remembers. That was a couple years ago, but let me see what I can find."

He was gone. I waited. Not long. I heard the faint sounds of voices at the other end before the phone was picked up again.

"Yes, ma'am. Carrie reminded me. She's the one handles the billing. Seems I finished the job your daddy asked me to do. Had a final report, along with records he wanted. Quite a bit of work. I talked it over with my partners here and we decided to close the file after your father died. We don't like springing things, like an investigation with maybe some embarrassing elements to it, on a family once a client has passed."

"Embarrassing things? Was there any of that in what you did for my father?"

Hesitation. "Sorry. Can't do that. I don't know who you are. You're just a voice on the telephone. And to tell the truth, well, it has been a few years. I remember looking into a couple of people for your dad. But not exactly what came of it."

"But you must still have the report? You're in Columbus. I could come there. I'll pay you what's owing. It's important."

Another long pause. "Well . . . Miss Blanchard . . . you see, there's no way I can turn the file over to you."

"I said I'd pay. You worked for my father. I'll bring ID . . ."

"No, no. You don't get it. That bill was paid. In full. Says so right on the invoice. And I don't have the file anymore."

"We didn't find anything in Daddy's papers. You'd think he'd keep something he paid that much—"

"You wouldn't find it. Someone came in just a few months ago and paid it off. The whole thing. Took the file with him. So, Miss Blanchard, you see, you don't owe me anything."

"Paid you? That was my father's property. He'd already paid a thousand, didn't he? Where's the file now? I'm his daughter. I have a right—"

"Well, yes, I guess you have . . . except . . . well, a guy came in and paid the bill, the way I said. I remember my partners and me talked it over and felt—since your father was dead—file's no good to him. I never took another look at the contents. We took the guy's check. He's got full rights to whatever's in that report he bought. Sorry, Miss . . . er . . . that's business."

"Nobody has a right to work that my daddy ordered, and

paid good money for. If I have to, Mr. Fritch, I'll go to our attorney and see about making you hand over—"

"Nothin' to hand over. All gone, Miss Blanchard."

"I don't believe that. I'll bet anything you keep copies of your work. What kind of company do you run that you don't keep copies in case the original gets lost or stolen? Can you tell me the man's name? This man who took what belonged to my daddy? We've had a murder here. He could be the killer for all we know. Your files might be subpoenaed, Mr. Fritch. If I were you . . ."

"Hmm . . . calm down. Got it right here. Copy of a check attached to the invoice . . . let's see. Says Amos Blanchard. Think that's it. Handwriting's a little crooked. I remember now, he said he was Jake's brother. Makes him yer uncle, I'd say. Guess you'll have to take it up with him."

I held my breath. "And you really didn't keep a copy of your report?"

"Funny thing, Miss Blanchard. We always keep copies— just in case. But we got broken into here only a few days after this Amos Blanchard came in and took your daddy's file away with him. Stuff thrown all over the office. Yup, our records of the Blanchard case were just gone, all of it, and . . . I don't remember if anything else was taken. All I remember was we were glad the damage wasn't any worse. Papers scattered all over the place."

"Mr. Fritch." I stopped him. "Amos Blanchard is the man who was murdered."

I heard him suck in air.

"If there's anything you remember about that investigation. Who you looked into. What my daddy wanted to know. Anything at all . . ."

"I would if I could, Miss Blanchard. I'd like to help but . . . five years. That's a lot of time. Lots of investigations since then. Just somebody I had to take a look at. Something about a person pretending to be somebody they weren't. Like it was . . . an attorney or something. Can't say for sure. It was all in the file I gave your uncle. Take a look at it."

I didn't answer. All I could think about was "an attorney." I hung up and called Hunter.

Chapter Thirty-three

"I was just putting together a batch of piecrust, Lindy," Meemaw said when I called her at the Nut House. "Sorry about talking to you the way I did, but Ethelred Tomroy was standing right next to me. Big ears quivering like a parade elephant. She's been getting a few orders for pecan pies. Can you imagine that? Kept rubbing it in, even saying Willy Shuck said he liked her pie better than mine. That old miser. I'd get after him except for how he came on down here and helped with the cleanup. Just you wait 'til he brings her a half-eaten pie and wants his money back. Just you wait and see how happy she is then. That man likes anything he can get cheap and Ethelred's undercutting me by two dollars. Probably using all lard in the crust, I'll bet you. Anyway, I decided I don't care what people say about me, I know what I can do and what I can't do and—"

"Miss Amelia," I had to cut her off or listen to grievances for the next twenty minutes. "Could Treenie take over?

You've got to get home here. Mama, too. Maybe even Bethany. She come back?"

"Girl's scrubbing the last of the floor. Seems she's mad as a person can get. Somebody called that Chet Easton, her Dallas broadcaster, about his wedding. Offered to do it cheaper and better. He wouldn't say, but Bethany thinks he's trying to hold her up for a reduced rate, just because of the murder at the ranch. And she's sure it was Chastity who called him."

"Well, whatever . . . tell her to come home or let her stay and finish. I need to talk to you and Mama most."

"I'll see, Lindy. Emma went over to talk to Ben . . ."

"Oh no, call her, Meemaw. Get her back here. Just as soon as you can. And bring the letter the girls gave you."

That was how I left it because I didn't know what I was most afraid of or what to start warning people about.

And after all, what did I really know? Only that the detective had been investigating an attorney.

In all of this, I knew one thing for sure. That package "Virginia" wrote about in her letter to Amos, it had to be the file Amos bought from Donny Fritch. I was suspicious of the man and willing to bet it cost Uncle Amos a lot more than the five hundred dollars he was supposed to have paid, but pretty sure Virginia's package couldn't be anything else.

If Uncle Amos brought the file back to town with him, somebody would have found it in his room. Hunter would have told me if he or the sheriff had it. If the killer knew who had it . . .

I got the package and will keep it until you tell me what to do with it. Just the way you said, I won't give it to anybody but you, unless the police or some official comes asking.

I prayed fast that it wasn't already destroyed.

We had to find the woman. I put my hands to my head and held on tight. Where to start? I wasn't good at this. I needed Miss Amelia.

The first thing I did, when Mama and Miss Amelia got home, was read the letter Mama held out to me:

Emma, I'm trying my best to clean up my life. I been in AA here in Houston at a rehab center. I'm back on my feet. Got some good friends but one of the things I have to do before my AA program's really in place is make amends for the things I did wrong and the people I hurt. One of my biggest sorrows is what I done to you my own brother's wife. And one of the worst things was—you maybe won't believe this is one of the worst due to all the things I done to you but what I'm almost sorriest for is not admitting I had my suspicions about Jake's death. I did but I was just so mad at all of you I couldn't admit even to myself what I was thinking. That's what I came back to Riverville for. Not to hurt any of you ever again but just to follow something that's been nagging at me since Jake died. I think I know who killed Jake, Emma. And I mean killed. That mower tipping over on him was no accident. I'm almost ready to go to Sheriff Higsby with what I'm finding out. You'll be surprised to hear it was something Jake did that's gonna put this person in jail for a long, long time. Please don't talk about this with any of the kids or Miss Amelia or I could be the next target of this killer. I know you all hate me but I won't let any of you down again. When the time comes, the best thing about all of this is that Justin will understand I didn't kill Jake. That's what I'm hoping for. The

day all of us can be family. That's the day I get your
trust back and feel like a real Blanchard again. Amos

I had to sit down. I wanted to run or cry or scream or do anything but stay in that house another minute. I wanted out of Riverville. Maybe go somewhere on the Amazon where I could find all kinds of new specimens and come back twenty-five years in the future with exotic new species that would save the world . . .

Not Daddy. Not him, too. And *"something Jake did."*

That meant all of this had started back then, when Daddy became suspicious of somebody . . . *like an attorney . . .*

"He was sorry, Lindy," Mama said. "You see that? Amos was sorry for causing us trouble. Jake would have been so happy. That's what he always wanted, just for Amos to get well again, and be the brother he used to be."

"Yes, Mama. Uncle Amos was sorry. Then he was dead because he found out something. It had to be who killed Daddy. If this is even the truth." I shook the letter at her.

"I believe it, Lindy. With everything that's happening now." Tears ran down Mama's face. "I can't stand to think about . . . in his last minutes, my husband faced a killer. Poor Jake. Then Amos."

Miss Amelia put her arm around Mama's shoulders. I envied the two of them. There was still so much they didn't know.

Miss Amelia looked hard at me. "But what'd you find out in Houston?"

I told them about the rehab clinic and how well liked Amos had been. I told them about Virginia, that the doctor would let her know we're looking for her. I told them about the detective. Mama's face went from one emotion to another. Relief, I'd say, on the one hand, about what the detective said. I don't know what awful thing she expected. Then shock, even horror, on the other, when I told them what the man said about his investigation—something about an attorney.

"No," Mama moaned. "I won't believe this has anything to do with Ben. He came right out and told me about the trouble with Amos. He didn't have anything against Jake."

"Depends what's in that report, Mama. Could be something Ben didn't want anybody to know, and then Uncle Amos found out . . . All that money. Think about it."

"Amos blackmailing Ben?"

I nodded. "No big land deal after all."

"Jake trusted Ben. They were friends. And Amos wouldn't have done that. Not knowing somebody hurt his brother."

Miss Amelia had a few words to add. "Remember, Lindy. There was no money in Amos's bank account."

"All we know about, Meemaw, is the bank here. Lots of other banks in big cities like Houston."

I didn't like pushing Ben's guilt on them and something even more important dawned on me. "I'm thinking . . ."

"Me, too," Miss Amelia said right then. "We need whatever this 'Virginia' person has. That's the only answer."

Miss Amelia led Mama over to sit down on one of the living room sofas. "Hunter's got to get some kind of notice out to other police departments about her."

I shook my head. "We can't do that, Meemaw. She's not a criminal. And think about it, if anybody's in danger now, it's her. She's the only one who's got the information connecting whoever this man is to Daddy and to Amos. The killer will want whatever she's got as bad as we do."

"Well, it's doesn't have anything to do with Ben," Mama said then shook her head. "I don't care what anybody says. I know people. And I trust Ben."

We were in agreement, of a sort. Better to do something than nothing. And better not to go jumping to conclusions, the way the sheriff concluded it was Justin who murdered Amos.

I got on the phone to Hunter, telling him about Amos's letter to Mama and how afraid we were for this Virginia who had that "package" Amos talked about. "Could you call that doctor back? Tell him how Virginia's in deep trouble. Could be a killer after her."

And then I told him we were coming in to town see the sheriff about my daddy's death. Hunter, to his credit, didn't try to stop me or say much of anything. Maybe this new information shocked him as much as it shocked the rest of us.

Mama was up and on her phone with the sheriff right then, her voice stronger than I'd heard in a long time.

"Right now, Sheriff," she was saying. "No sir. You stay where you are. No damned hog attack is more important than what I've got to say to you."

Chapter Thirty-four

"All we've got is Amos's word, Emma." Sheriff Higsby shifted hard in his squeaking chair and frowned at us across his littered desk. Amos's letter to Emma was in his hand. "Nothing against the Blanchards, you know that, but the Amos Blanchard I knew wasn't a man of his word. And not above stirring up trouble. Looks like even in death."

"You've got my son in jail. I take that as something against us, Sheriff." Mama sat with her back like a tree trunk and her hands tight together in her lap. Miss Amelia was beside her. Just as upright and just as focused. I sat between the two of them, ready to jump in if the sheriff gave us trouble for long. I wasn't sure what I was going to jump in with, but I knew we were in the battle of our lives.

"Did you read what Amos said there?" Mama leaned forward and pointed in the general direction of the letter. "That's what he came back here to do. Prove that Jake was murdered. You see that? The man had cleaned up his life."

The sheriff nodded and lowered his eyebrows so his eyes all but disappeared.

"He was going to bring proof to you, Sheriff. What more do you need?" Miss Amelia put in.

"What I need, Miss Amelia, is that proof."

"At least you owe us another look at Jake's death." Mama leaned forward.

Sheriff Higsby looked from one to the other of us. "I got Hunter going full-time on Amos's death now. And looking for who did that to Martin, out at your place," he said. "Tell you the truth, I got nobody to put on a revisit to Jake's death. Not without more proof than this here letter."

The sheriff shook the letter in his broad hand. "County board already coming down on me for overtime pay."

Mama fell back in her chair. "For the good Lord's sakes, Sheriff, I'll pay. Whatever it takes . . ."

"Doesn't work that way, Emma."

Miss Amelia spoke up just as I was going to weigh in. "Doesn't take your officers to look into this. Call the new coroner. Have him take another look at Jake's autopsy report and the x-rays."

Mama shivered. The thought of what we were asking wasn't pleasant to me either. A man should, after all, rest in peace.

"That's all we're asking for," Miss Amelia went on. "If he finds something . . . well, we'll know we're after one man who did all of this: Jake, Amos, Martin. But if he doesn't find anything, then I guess Amos was wrong and we'll never know what proof he had. Or if he was even telling the truth."

"Could I just say one thing here?" The sheriff put up a hand. "The way I see what's happened is like this. Amos caught the guy out at your greenhouse, Miss Lindy. Surprised him and was killed by accident. Whoever did it already had those trees of yours in his car and he took off with them. Panicked. When he tried to get rid of them, bring 'em back to the ranch, he ran into Martin. Didn't kill him. Just panicked again." He stopped, cleared his throat. "I'm thinking it's somebody from out of town. All a stupid accident caused by some greedy . . . eh . . . out-of-town rancher.

"As for Amos's accusations." He tapped the letter. "We all knew Amos well enough. When he was drinking, the man was crazy. Looks like he got it in his head to get back in your good graces, Emma. That's all. Looking for a way to weasel his way back into the family, is all. For what reason, we'll never know for sure."

I jumped in. "My uncle's time away from here was spent at a rehab facility. Did you know that? And in AA. He was clean and sober when he came back here, Sheriff. Even Harry said he made Amos pledge he wasn't drinking anymore before he took him on at Rancho Conway."

"Yeah, well, that and a nickel . . . as they say."

"There's more," I said. "I gave Hunter that letter from a woman named Virginia. She sent it to Amos while he was staying here in town."

He nodded. "Hunter showed me the letter."

"She's got a package he gave her."

He nodded again. "Could be anything from dirty socks to legal documents against you folks."

"He told her only to give it to the police, not to anyone else. You don't give dirty socks to the police in case of your death."

He was thinking. And finally listening.

"We're trying to find this Virginia," I went on. "Hunter and I went to the clinic in Houston where Uncle Amos stayed. The doctor there wouldn't help a whole lot, but he said he'd try to get ahold of Virginia and tell her to contact us."

"Not much to go on, is what I understand. Maybe a package."

Miss Amelia stepped in. "There was a private investigator, Sheriff. Jake hired him. Lindy here talked to the man.

He did the work for Jake and closed it out when Jake died. Amos found out and went there. He paid the man off, what Jake still owed. He took that report with him. That's what he had, Sheriff. We think this Virginia's got it. And we think it's what's behind Jake's death and Amos's, and even the attack on Martin."

"Hunter talk to that doctor? Tell him how important it is we find the woman?"

I nodded. "The man wasn't really cooperative, but then Hunter didn't have any legal standing there in Houston."

Sheriff Higsby nodded. "Hmmm . . . what you're putting together sure sounds like something," he admitted. "I'm calling that doctor myself. You got any idea who it is? The one behind all this?"

Mama turned around and looked at me. Miss Amelia avoided looking at either of us. I sat back, pushing down in my chair.

Nobody mentioned Ben's name.

Sheriff Higsby stood and leaned across his desk. "I'll call the coroner. Get this thing moving. If he finds there's any reason to suspect Jake was murdered and not dead from that mower's blades, we're going full tilt after who did it. You've got my promise on that, ladies."

He stood up and pulled at his belt as he sniffed and thought awhile.

"You know what? I'm letting Justin outta here. Dropping the charges. I've been coming to it anyway. That damned belt buckle's not enough reason to hold him. Got nothing else except he hated Amos. And comes to that, how many others could say the same thing?"

I wasn't the only one swallowing hard and taking deep breaths so I didn't cry all over the sheriff's crummy carpet.

"When?" Mama asked.

"Soon as I can. Let me get the paperwork together. You

want, you come back in 'bout an hour and I think he'll be ready to go home with you."

Miss Amelia stood and pulled Mama to her feet. "That will be fine, Sheriff," she said in her best lady-of-the-manner voice. "And you'll contact the coroner right away?"

He nodded. "Yes, ma'am. Get right on that. See what he comes up with."

We walked out, almost tiptoeing, as if anything we said now could upset some delicate balance and keep Justin in jail.

"Ladies," the sheriff called from behind us. "If you're right, we got us a killer out there. Y'all've got to be careful. Don't want anybody else getting hurt."

"You know, Sheriff." Miss Amelia turned to look full at him. "If the doctors bring Martin out of that coma, that will end it. He's got to know who tried to kill him. You think about that?"

He nodded.

"You got a man over there? Watching him, is what I'm asking."

"Juanita and Jessie with him all the time. Got nobody else. Unless we hear he's waking up . . ."

She nodded. "Just wanted to make sure you were thinking about it."

"Thinking about everything, Miss Amelia. Me and Hunter, we been over it. I'll be watching."

Mama turned in the hall outside his office. "When will we know, Sheriff? About Jake?"

He shrugged. "I'll let the coroner know it's a rush. Shouldn't be long. Not like he's got to do the autopsy, just go over the file. I'd say a few days."

He followed us out of the room. "The only thing I still want to tell you is if you've got any idea who did this and aren't telling me what you know, well . . . and I mean this sincerely . . . that's not a game you want to be playing."

I changed the subject. "About my trees. Could be too late already. But I'd like them back; get them in the ground . . ."

"'Course, Lindy. Out behind the building. Hunter's been watering them. Look pretty good, you ask me. Considering what they been through."

I couldn't help my big grin. "Good for Hunter."

He nodded, looking pleased with himself. "We all chipped in. Everybody knows what you're trying to do for the ranchers, Lindy. I'd have an uprising on my hands, I let anything happen to your trees."

I could've hugged the man except he looked too official and lawman-like for hugging.

"You can take 'em now, you got room in your truck."

I did have room and I did take my trees. Miss Amelia and Mama helped load them, all straight and tall and tied to wooden stakes Hunter had found for them. It was like bringing home family.

Well, almost like that.

Chapter Thirty-five

Mama headed back out to the ranch. Her plate was full, with nobody overseeing the work there, and at such a critical time. I could well understand the big smile she gave us when she got in her car. First about Justin, but then about the ranch being taken care of again when he got home.

"I'm coming back for Justin in an hour," Mama called out her open window. "Big supper tonight, I hope. You cooking, Mama?"

Miss Amelia nodded and waved her off.

I dropped Meemaw at the Nut House but didn't go in. I had a couple of things to do before getting the trees home so I stopped at Pecan Park, in the center of Riverville, where the town's streets of houses and rows of shops converged, where the school buses lined up along one side during the school months, and where the town's elderly ranchers met on benches in the shade of live oaks to talk politics and gossip. I parked near the town fountain and ran over to fill a large Coke bottle the sheriff had given me—again and again. I watered those trees lovingly. Touching their leaves.

Patting their pots. Poor trees. They'd been through a lot. Then I thought of what we humans had been through, too, and felt a little less sorry for my pampered progeny.

With the trees watered, I figured I had time to stop by the library and see Jessie, long as I parked in the shade. For just a minute I worried about leaving my babies in the back of the pickup. Then I thought how Riverville hadn't been a raging den of thieves in the past and probably wasn't now. I'd have to start trusting my neighbors sometime. Now was as good a time as any.

I drove around the park and up the Camino Real to the library, turning into the parking lot and into a shady spot. The heat should have been lessening by this time of afternoon, the sun not so fierce, but these were unusual times. Just walking over to the library caused prickles of sweat to run down my back, under my T-shirt. I felt the beginnings of a heat rash on the insides of my thighs.

The long stone building was cool inside. Felt good. I let myself dream, for just a minute, about what it would be like to sit there and read a book and not have another thing to think about.

Jessie, behind the main desk, had a look on her face somewhere between tears and exasperation when she saw me. There was no pleasure there, not with those dark circles under her eyes and her hair tossed up into some kind of messy knot on top of her head.

"Any change?" I asked right away after taking her hands and squeezing them.

She shrugged. "The doctor says the swelling is starting to go down. Could be soon. I just want to see . . ."

She choked on her words.

"I can only imagine," I said.

She nodded. "Just to see him smile at me. Mama hugs him and talks to him—for hours. She reminds him of his mother and father and his brothers and sisters back in Mexico. She talks about coming to this country for a better life, about the Blanchards and what you've done for us. She just talks. And talks. And every once in a while she puts her head back and stares off at nothing. I have to leave the room at those times. It's breaking my heart."

Pain was like a mask somebody'd slapped on her face.

"Why are you here, working? Can't somebody fill in?"

She shook her head. "Sophia left town." She stopped, even smiled a little. "It's what's keeping me sane right now. I don't have to think so much when I'm talking to people about books."

"Is there anything I can do? Pick up things at the house for you?"

"No, I go get clothes for both of us when I can. Mostly I go right to the hospital."

"Oh, Jessie." I wanted to hug her, but I didn't. There were ladies in line behind me waiting to pick up ordered books. They were already making noises. "If you need me to spell you or your mama, give me a call."

"People showing up every day now. Good people. They've offered help if we need them. Just a few hours here and there. Then I take over later."

"Good to hear. Everybody's concerned. Gotta be somebody with him at all times," I said. "You understand what I'm talking about, don't you?"

She nodded. "Don't you worry, Lindy. Not a minute alone. Sheriff's hoping to call in a deputy from the next county. 'Til then we got Harry and Chastity Conway. They come by every day, just to visit with my mama. They stay when Mama needs to do a little shopping for herself. The Chaunceys came this morning. Ben Fordyce stopped by, offered whatever we needed. Perks Mama up, that people care so much. You don't know what a town thinks of you until something awful like this happens."

For a minute, I wasn't comfortable hearing Ben was there. I told myself that was ridiculous. It couldn't be Ben. He was like a member of our family. He never would have hurt my daddy.

Unless, of course, he was hiding something even worse than that land deal with Amos.

I wished I could have talked to Jessie in private. There was our trip to the Barking Coyote to tell her about. No baby. Never was. And Amos's letter to Mama. I knew Jessie pretty well. Despite what Amos had done to her, I knew she'd be happy to hear he'd cleaned himself up and was trying to help us. If he'd lived, I would have bet anything she'd be the next one getting an apology. But still—there was that "Virginia." That he'd moved on to another woman wasn't exactly the kind of news I wanted to bring her.

At a complaint from an old classmate of mine, standing behind me in line and tapping the face of her watch to show she had someplace she had to get to, I moved away, promising to drop by later if I could. I meant to ask if I could pick up the mail or water their plants when I went by their house, but I didn't. Angry ladies behind me, holding large and heavy books and telling me to move on, weren't a group I wanted to stress any more than I already had.

When Miss Amelia called and said she was tired, that she wanted to go home and make something special for Justin's homecoming, I forgot everything else I wanted to take care of that day and went back to the Nut House to get her.

I should've known not to expect anything about that place to be easy.

Ethelred Tomroy was there again. I could see from the way Ethelred and Miss Amelia stood, like two hens about to peck each other, that trouble was brewing.

"What I understood," Miss Ethelred was saying, "was when I agreed to take over the pie making from you, it was only because you didn't want to be making them anymore."

"Never said a thing like that in my life, Ethelred." Miss Amelia reared back on her heels. Her arms were crossed in front of her, face as blank as she could make it. I knew the signs and wished I could go right back out the door and return a whole lot later.

"Why, you did, too, Amelia Hastings. Put that sign right up on your door for people wanting pies to give me a call."

"That didn't mean I was going out of the pie-making business forever. Just for a decent mourning period, is all. Don't know where you ever got the idea I wouldn't be back in here doing my job."

"Why, everybody's been saying it was because you don't feel so good anymore. Too much work for you."

"Really?" Miss Amelia's eyes were almost black. "And who's saying that, I'd like to know? Might be a case of slander, you ask me."

"Wasn't me." Ethelred shook her hands in the air. "I'd never say a thing like that. Heard it from Freda Cromwell. You know Freda. Picks up every piece of news in town. All she does all day, walk up and down Carya talking to this one and that one."

"So just which one of the 'thises' or 'thats' did she get it from?"

"No idea. Just what I was told. I started taking those orders thinking I was helping you out, and now I'm getting cancellations. Treenie's taking orders here, is what people been telling me."

"True." Miss Amelia nodded. "I've been away from my job long enough. Pie dough's already mixed. It's in the cooler."

"Then where does that leave me, I'd like to know—holding the nuts? I bought a big load of pecans, anticipating I'd need them for my pies."

"Where'd you buy them?"

"Over to the Conways'. Got the best price going. Cheaper than anybody."

"Conways? Well, guess you better go talk to Chastity 'bout buying them back."

"Humph. Doubt she'd take 'em. You know Chastity. Deals a deal. People around town saying she's getting a little full of herself. Talking about a store out there by the road. Got that new pavilion. You better tell Bethany to watch herself. Wouldn't put it past Chastity to try stealing events you got planned."

Miss Amelia shrugged and looked over at me. "What do you say, Lindy? Should I go out of the pie-making business?"

I shook my head hard and stepped up next to Miss Ethelred. "Wouldn't give up making the best pies in Riverville if I was you, Grandma. Why, Riverville's known for your pecan pies. Nobody comes close."

Ethelred reared back and gave me a shocked, wide-eyed stare. "For goodness' sakes, Lindy Blanchard. What a thing to say. You know I make a pie just as—"

I shook my head at her. "Not like Miss Amelia's. It was the people coming in and begging got her back at it."

"Begging? Not people who tasted my pies."

"Somebody came in to say the pie they got—I don't know whose pie they were talking about—just wasn't what they were used to."

"For goodness' sakes! That's a hurtful thing to say." Miss Ethelred looked sad and I was sorry I'd taken it just that one step too far. Ethelred Tomroy wasn't a bad person, just one who needed a lot of teasing along to keep her from going off on one of her rants. I was completely out of friendly teasing. Very little left in me that was even very nice.

"Think we better have a talk with Miss Cromwell, Grandma." I turned to Miss Amelia. "Seems she's the one spreading gossip about you."

"Well, for the Lord's sakes, don't tell her I told you where I heard it," Ethelred sputtered. "Woman's got a tongue sharper than an ax. Next thing she'll be after me. Last year she told the Mission Committee I didn't make that pecan butter for the Christmas sale myself. Bought it, she said. Maybe it was the truth, but she didn't have to go telling on me."

Miss Amelia put her arm around the woman, who was blinking away and looking miserable. "Why, bless yer heart, Ethelred," she said. "You look to me like you better run on home and take a rest. People our age—you know, we gotta watch ourselves."

Ethelred nodded and thanked my grandmother for her concern.

"You sure? No more pie orders?" Ethelred called on her way out the front door.

"Sorry, Ethelred. Pies are something I got to see to myself."

Ethelred was gone. Miss Amelia didn't look a bit chastened.

And not a bit tired.

Chapter Thirty-six

We didn't go looking for Freda Cromwell. She was coming down the walk looking for us, shading her eyes from the afternoon sun with one hand while waving and yoo-hooing from a couple hundred feet away.

Funny how fast a person can turn deaf. It hit me and Miss Amelia at the same moment. I felt her tugging at my arm as we headed over to my truck, but it was too late. The elderly woman came flying down the street at us, one hand to her chest like a heart attack could be imminent if we didn't stop. Miss Amelia muttered under her breath then put on a big smile, turned, and greeted Freda.

"Look at you, Freda Cromwell. Gonna give yourself a stroke, running like that at your age."

Freda grabbed on hard to Miss Amelia's arm as if to hold her right there in place until she had her say.

She pounded at her chest with her other hand. I didn't know if she was getting her heart started or waking up her voice box.

"Calm down," Miss Amelia ordered and gave me a look

that told me I wouldn't want to be Freda Cromwell at that moment.

The woman was dressed in a shapeless outfit that kind of skimmed over her body. There were huge sweat circles under her arms and down her sides. She wasn't a big woman but she gave off that kind of feel; as if she needed more space than other women, more air, more words, more time. Something about Freda Cromwell was needy and overbearing at the same time.

"Heard about Justin gettin' out. Hope he doesn't land back in there. Somebody said they got a lot of proof he did that terrible thing to Amos. Not that anybody's blaming him . . ."

"Why, bless your heart for worrying about my grandson, Freda. Sure do appreciate it." Miss Amelia smiled a lip-widening smile, kind of like an ice-carved smile.

She leaned back, looking away from Freda. I could feel the good stuff coming. "But you tell all those nice people to get something else to worry about, would you? Blanchards are doing just fine, thank you."

She turned away from the startled woman. Then she turned back. "And by the way, Freda, care to tell me why you're spreading stories about me going into Columbus to see a doctor?"

Freda smacked her lips a couple of times as if trying to beat words into shape. Nothing came out.

"Now don't tell me it wasn't you spreading the stories. People who care about me said it was."

Freda glowered and swallowed hard a time or two. "Well, now, Amelia Hastings. You believe what people say?"

"Seems you do, Freda."

She nervously scratched at the back of her head. "Let me just tell you who said those things . . ."

We waited while the woman scrunched her face into what looked like thought.

"Well, now . . . She told me not to go passing it around. Said she wouldn't like it if I told people. Knew I was trustworthy, that's what she said. Awful worried about you, Amelia."

"Who, Freda? Who's this 'she' you're talking about?"

She shook her head. "Nope. I can't say. Just can't say. This isn't somebody you want mad at you. Leastwise not me. All I'll say is she just couldn't see you working the way you do, not with that disease she said you got."

"Was it Ethelred Tomroy?"

"Ethelred? Why would she be worried? Worries her most is never winning that county fair prize for her pecan pies. That's the only thing worries Ethelred."

"Are you going to tell me who said those things about me, Freda?"

She shook her head. "Don't think so. Said maybe I'd have a job in that new—"

She threw a hand over her mouth.

I looked at my grandmother and she looked hard back at me.

"Nope." Freda shook her head. "Can't tell. Need that job."

"Well, well, well . . ." Miss Amelia leaned forward and put her arm around Freda's hunched shoulders. "Bless yer heart, Freda. Of course you need a job. Keep you busy. Off the streets. But maybe you can do me one favor? Think you can do that?"

She narrowed her eyes. Freda Cromwell wasn't used to doing favors for people.

"All I want is . . ." Miss Amelia bent close to Freda's ear. "You tell that person with this new job for you, in her new nut store, well, you just go ahead and tell her I'm fine. Just fine. And you tell her Miss Amelia said I thank her for her concern but there's nothing wrong with me now and never will be, I got anything to say about it."

Freda nodded her head. "I'll do that, Miss Amelia. Can't tell you who it is exactly, but I'll pass on the word that you are doing just fine."

Mama wasn't home with Justin yet when we got back to the ranch. Miss Amelia went to the kitchen to whip up some Texas caviar—black-eyed peas and black beans marinated in that spicy mix of hers. She was planning on barbecue, with her Hotter than Hot Pecan Barbecue Sauce.

I knew when to leave her alone in the kitchen and headed out to the greenhouse. There were my trees to plant, which lifted my mood—just the thought of being alone finally, out in my own hallowed test grove, in my greenhouse with five trees back where they belonged, scrawny branches waving in the hot, late afternoon breeze.

José, still guarding the gate, insisted on helping me dig the holes. I took him up on the offer since I figured he had to be bored, a man used to hard, muscle-stretching work, standing at a gate for hours. Other men had already removed the broken trees, filled in the old holes, then dug over and raked the ground so my rows were straight again, and even.

And empty.

While José dug, I mixed my special compound fertilizer, then poured a measured amount down into each of the holes and worked it in. I watered the soil, letting the hole fill up and empty two times. Jose helped me pull each sapling from the pot, then set up the drip irrigation snaking down the rows while I brought five-gallon plastic pails over from the fence and set one next to each tree, dropping a big rock down inside to hold it in place, then filling it with water. I watched to make sure the small holes in the bottom were clear and draining. We staked them then, tied them, and stood back to enjoy the sight: one thing back to normal. I was in business again.

I thanked José and he went back to stand outside the gate, waiting for his replacement guard to come. It seemed like a lot of locking the barn door after the horses were stolen, but I figured it didn't hurt, someone watching. Anyway, having someone out there made me feel safer. I promised myself I'd come back later, after dinner, to get more files ready. With José, or one of the other men standing guard, darkness wouldn't seem so filled with things I didn't dare think about.

I went back up to the house to welcome my brother home from jail and tell myself, one more time, this nightmare had to be close to ending.

"Missed all you women," Justin said and put up with a lot of hugging and a lot of tears when he walked into the kitchen. He took a whiff of the simmering beans and peas and ran to the stove to kiss Miss Amelia on the cheek. "I don't know who does the cooking at that jail, but I'll tell you, almost makes you want to confess and get hung rather than eat another one of those macaroni and cheese bake things—or whatever it was."

We settled into healing by food, a long tradition in our family. First the Texas caviar on tortilla chips, then barbecue that melted when you ate it, mashed potatoes fixed up with lots of butter and corn and carrots mixed in. Salad. And a pecan pie—a very special pecan pie for dessert.

When he'd finished eating, Justin pushed his chair back from the table and stretched.

"Great pie, Meemaw. Over at the jail, they were saying you stopped making them. All the deputies were complaining to me, like I could do anything about it."

"Only stopped for a decent period. You know, after Amos's death. A family member, after all. I got the dough done today and let myself make just one. 'Specially for you."

Pie out of the way and the dishes cleared, we sat thinking and smiling and resting after dinner.

Stretching her arms over her head, Mama finally said to Justin, "We should bring you up to date on what's been happening these last few days."

"Need that, Mama. We've got to talk about the groves, too. Got the men all coming in tomorrow morning."

"There's that. And we gotta think about a funeral."

"They release Amos's body yet?"

"Not yet." Mama bit at her lip. "Think anybody will come if we throw him a big funeral?"

Miss Amelia snorted. "People'll come to anything, you give 'em enough food and plenty to drink."

"I'd keep it small, Mama," Bethany put in. "This doesn't seem to be the time to go all out."

Mama nodded. "Okay. Soon as we get the word. Think I'll leave it up to you, Bethany."

Bethany made a face. "A funeral? How do I make a funeral special?"

"No doves," Miss Amelia said, hiding a smile. "Though that would be pretty—all those white birds heading toward heaven."

Bethany rolled her eyes. "But not until after my wedding. It's next weekend. Please, please, please don't have a funeral procession going one way and my wedding procession going the other."

Mama leaned over and smiled at her so pretty youngest. "We'll do it right after, Baby. Don't imagine Amos will be complaining."

She turned back to Justin. "Got something else to tell you."

"No more bad news tonight, Mama. I'm just so happy to be—"

"It's about your daddy."

He sat back in his chair.

"You could've been right all along. Amos wrote in a letter that he had proof it wasn't an accident took Jake."

Justin buried his face in his clasped hands, but for only a quick minute. "You mean it wasn't Uncle Amos killed him?" he asked when he looked up again.

She shook her head.

"Then—who?"

Mama looked at me, then Miss Amelia. Very slowly she opened her mouth. "We don't know for sure—yet. Your daddy hired a private detective to investigate. We're not sure what the detective found out but Amos got the report. We hope to find it. Miss Amelia and Lindy have been looking into . . . things."

"So? What's the sheriff doing about Daddy's death? Or is he just going to sweep it under the rug?"

I understood Justin's anger.

"The sheriff called the coroner. He's looking through the autopsy report, going over the x-rays, seeing if that first doctor missed anything."

"When will we know?"

"Sometime tomorrow, I hope."

"That pie of yours is putting me right to sleep, Grandma." He got up slowly and yawned. "I never doubted I was right, you know. Now, what I gotta do is get some *real* sleep and maybe tomorrow we'll start hearing some *real* truth."

Over the next hour, the phone must have rung at least six times. People called to say how happy they were Justin was cleared of this terrible thing. Got one crank call, some nut who raved that God would punish all us sinners. Miss

Amelia got that one and set the man straight in a hurry, telling him God may be watching over fools like him but as for her . . . "This is what I think of people who are not only stupid, but cruel." She slammed the phone down.

One time it was for Mama. Ben Fordyce.

"Knew I had to face it." She got up and went out into the hall. It didn't take long and she was back. "Just said he was happy to hear the sheriff let Justin go. Says he got a writ or something to get him out anyway, but glad it was easy, no snags."

She looked around at all of us. "Don't say a word. Nobody. I'm not believing anything bad . . ."

Miss Amelia walked from the dishwasher she was filling, over to put her arm around Mama. "We don't know a single thing for sure, Emma. Not a single thing."

"Ben said Harry's on his way over. Got something he thinks we should know."

I groaned. "You tell him have Harry come around tomorrow?" I asked, impatient to get out to my greenhouse for a couple of hours, make more notes; do more recalling what I could of my grafts and seedlings.

"Ben said it was important."

"You know." Miss Amelia dumped soap in the dishwasher, locked the door, and pushed the button, starting it. "We had a friend once, me and Darnell. Good friend of your grandfather's. Attorney there in Dallas. Somebody got it into their head he cheated them and stole from their parents' estate. First that man spread stories around. Next he took him to court. I remember Darnell couldn't believe the judge took the case. No evidence against our friend. Nothing. Books all straight. It was like crazy people were taking over the court system. Then it came out that man filed to run for district attorney. Running on how he was the one stopped corruption in the system. Except things about him started coming out. He'd done the same thing—singled out an attorney to ruin back in Louisiana, where he came from. People in Dallas learned from that. Not to be led around by the nose. Well, learned for a little while anyway. Makes me think of Ben now. Nothing against him but somebody else's word. Just that one word, Lindy: 'attorney.' I think we gotta pull back here, the way your granddaddy did back then. He got people looking deeper and our friend was cleared completely. That other man went to jail. Been buying votes and paying big into the mayor's coffers. That's where the corruption was."

She hesitated, looking around at all of us. "Do you get what I'm saying?"

Mama nodded. "Makes me think of Amos. How I misjudged him."

I nodded, too.

Bethany looked up and said nothing.

"What have you got going on in your head, girl?" Miss Amelia frowned hard at her.

She shivered. "Nothing. Just thinking. Wondering, you know, how to make a funeral not so . . . depressing."

Chapter Thirty-seven

"Must be Harry," Mama said over her shoulder when she got up to answer the doorbell. "Hope to heaven he left Chastity at home. There are times when that woman . . ."

Miss Amelia looked at me and sighed. "What was it that famous Northern woman wrote? 'What fresh hell is this?'"

Harry was alone. I figured whatever he had to say must be serious; he had that big, fancy cowboy hat of his in his hands instead of on his head. A wide ring of hat hair circled the washed-out hair he had left.

We got through the pleasantries: "How ya doin'?" "How's Chastity?" "How's Justin doin'?" He sat down at the table with me, Miss Amelia, and Mama. Bethany excused herself, said she had something important to start working on, and was out of there as fast as I've ever seen her move.

Harry sat back, spread his knees, and settled down into himself. That Texas-sized belt buckle of his dug into his stomach, making a painful-looking bulge above and bulge below. First he tried a smile. Then gave us a worried frown.

"Might as well get right to it, Harry," Miss Amelia urged.

He nodded at first her and then at me. "This is a lot about you, Lindy."

My ears perked up.

"I been doing some of the same things you been doing."

"What things?"

"With the trees. Trying my hand at some grafts. They teach you right on the computer how to do it. Got some going over there to my place."

I was afraid to speak. All my years of study, my years of experimentation—and he thought he'd learn what I was doing in one computer lesson on grafting?

"No competition with you, Lindy. Just, well, what you're doin' can be worth a lot of money to some people. Seed companies. Pecan growers. I heard you was going to give it away and I applaud you for that. Yes, sir, that's mighty civic-minded of you."

"Maybe not give it away, Harry. Just make what I know available."

"Well, that's what I came over to talk about. It was Amos. He came into one of the back barns one day and saw what I was doing. Said it looked like I was going into competition with you. I swore it was nothing of that sort. Not at all. Then he said he could make it a lot easier for me. Made me a proposition."

"What kind of proposition?" Miss Amelia asked before I could pry my mouth open.

"Said he could get in over here anytime he wanted. If I was interested, said he could put his hands on your research. Might be able to bring me some of your trees. Anytime I wanted, is what he told me."

I sat back, bowled over. Uncle Amos? Worse than I could ever have imagined—Amos willing to steal my work.

"Said he wanted in. A share in the patents. Amos thought that might put the Rancho en el Colorado out of business, with my trees better than yours. You can see where he was going. He wanted a share of my ranch, too. The man wasn't above asking for the moon."

"What you'd tell him?" I asked when I could get the words out.

"Just what you'd imagine I'd tell him. Told him what you were doing here was for all the ranchers, not for just a few of the greedy ones. Told him it was wrong, what he was thinking. Told him, too, I'd come right to you if anything happened to your trees." He nodded hard. "Yup, that's what I told him. Thought I stopped it right there. Then you found him here like you did, Lindy. Makes you wonder."

"I found him dead, Harry."

"I know. I know. Just that, well, I'm feeling guilty that I didn't go to the sheriff with what I know. Chastity said maybe I should come here first. You know, give you a heads-up. We were talking and we both were thinking, this won't look good for you, Lindy, and we don't want to hurt you. You know, like making the police suspect it was you killed Amos all along."

Miss Amelia cleared her throat. "I think what you're saying, Harry, is you're not going to the sheriff with this bit of news because it might look bad for Lindy, is that it?"

"That's what I was thinkin'. There's some kind of code between all us ranchers, don't you think? I mean, I wouldn't do a thing to hurt one of you Blanchards."

Mama stood, smiling the kind of smile that can freeze a kid's blood at a yard and a half. "Well, we're grateful for it, aren't we?"

Mama looked around at all of us. I recognized the pasted smile. "And aren't we grateful we've got a friend like Harry Conway?"

She turned back to Harry. "You do what you've got to do, Harry. We Blanchards do things by the book. That was Jake's motto: Do the right thing. We stand by that."

She walked toward the door, then turned back to look expectantly at Harry, who finally got the message and rose from his chair, settling his hat back on his head.

"Just wanted you to know . . ." He went on with his pitch for keeping news from the sheriff. Since we weren't having any of it, he gave up and left the living room, making his way to the front door alone.

We heard the door close and turned to each other, openmouthed.

"What was that all about?" Mama asked.

"Currying favor," Miss Amelia said. "I believe they're not doing so well over there. Way Chastity tries to get my pecan pie recipe. Way I hear, they're discounting the nuts they got left from last year. And some other things. Now they got that tent they're putting up. It really is a tent. Some kind of army surplus thing. I can just imagine what that store of theirs will look like."

"Mama," Miss Emma falsely chided. "You're not sounding too sweet about those poor people."

"These aren't 'sweet' times, Emma," Miss Amelia said. "These are war times and you gotta call a spade a spade."

Since I was on Grandma's side in this battle, I stepped right in. "Think that was blackmail? Could be he wants in on my new trees," I said. "I always figured I'd run up against a few like that. Poor Harry. Maybe he is in a bad way. Sorry about that but the last thing I want to do is keep everything to myself. They're either available for everybody, or I swear I'll tear the trees out myself."

"Or . . ." Mama stopped us, her face tired. "Maybe Harry's telling the truth. And that letter to me from Amos—was all just another pack of his lies to throw us off our guard."

Chapter Thirty-eight

I slept in my old room again, upstairs, near the back of the house. If ever there was a time we needed to be together, I figured it had to be now. As if the universe had shifted and life was never going to be the way it was, I didn't trust anything I knew and couldn't even guess at all the things I didn't know.

Harry trying to make a dollar off my work. Or maybe he had stopped Amos. It almost didn't matter.

What mattered was that Daddy was dead. Nothing would change that for any of us. But dead because something went wrong and he sort of fell on his sword—so to speak—was different from learning he was dead because someone decided to take his life.

I dug through the old clothes I had left. All I wanted was something clean to sleep in and something to put on in the morning. There was teenage underwear I'd no doubt be tugging at all day, and jeans with the required tears at the knees and just under the butt.

Good enough for morning.

And a pair of pajama pants I could wear with a faded T-shirt to sleep in.

When I hit the bed, I was sure I'd be awake all night. My mind skipped from one picture to the other: trees and plant stakes and overturned mowers. Then back again. I thought if I stayed awake long enough, I'd figure everything out. But I fell into a sleep that closed around me like dark cotton. I didn't stir until a bell woke me. At first I thought it was the bell over the door at the Nut House, and then I remembered I wasn't there. I was home, lying in my old bed, facing my big Willy Nelson poster on the far wall—the poster that ticked everybody in the house off because of his alleged use of marijuana, which had pleased me back then, when I was a teenager and into full rebellion.

The noisy bell was my cell phone ringing, my ring tone being Big Ben or some other large chiming thing. I rolled over to answer it, checking the bedside clock. Six. And then the number on the phone. Not a familiar number. I pressed the answer button and said a sleepy, "Hello."

"Lindy Blanchard?"

The woman's voice was hesitant.

I said, "Yes," hoping it wasn't some survey that would drive me wild since I was on the cell phone "Do Not Call" list and took every infraction as a personal affront.

"I was told to call you. You're his niece?"

I sat up, kicking my way out of the tangled sheet.

There was only one call I was waiting for.

"Yes. I'm Amos's niece. Is this Virginia?"

"I heard you were looking for me."

"You can say that again. You've got something of my uncle's. A package he asked you to keep for him, in case of his death?"

A long pause.

"So he is dead." A weak and trembling question.

I took a deep breath. "Sorry, Virginia. That was insensi-
tive. Yes. He is dead. Killed right here on our ranch. I was
the one who found him."

Only a moan from the other end.

"Hope they get whoever did that. Amos didn't deserve . . .
You know, the only reason he went back to your town was
to make it up to all of you. All his family. That's part of our
program—make amends for all the terrible things alcohol
led us to do."

I quickly thought how Mama would be relieved to hear
that.

"I can imagine it was hard." I wanted to keep her talking,
persuade her to meet me, hand over the package.

"Amos found out something about somebody trying to
hurt your family. That's what's in the package. There's a
police report. Newspaper stories. Some kind of detective's
report."

"Is there a name? The person he focused on? Any clue
who it's about?"

She was quiet a minute. "Amos said I had to give it to the
police in case he died. I think I better wait . . ."

I took a deep breath. "I can come get it from you. I'll
bring a policeman. But we're losing time. We need to know
what the report says, all of it. We need a direction to go in,
a name, any help you can give us."

It was Virginia's turn to hesitate. "You are family. He
loved his family. I guess it's all right."

"Thank you for trusting me, Virginia. Now, can you tell
me who he was looking for?"

"Yes. . . wait a minute, let me make sure . . ." I heard her
leafing through pages. "Here it is. The man's name is Harold
Tompkins. He lived in Terre Haute, Indiana. Seems the man
disappeared. There is a bunch of newspaper articles here.
They're clipped together. You want me to read 'em to you?"

"Wait . . . wait . . . I never heard of a Harold Tompkins."
I was confused even as I felt the need to hurry her along.
"Disappeared? So why the report? What was going on?" I
couldn't work it out in my head. Daddy paid a thousand
dollars to learn about some stranger?

"This first one says the Terre Haute Police need to talk
to Mr. Tompkins. He's what they call here 'a person of interest' in his wife's death."

"What?"

"Eh . . . Here's another article. It's an earlier one. It says
Sarah Mann Tompkins, wife of Harold Tompkins, was
stabbed to death at the Mann Estate there in Terre Haute.
Says here Mr. Tompkins came home and found her dead.
House all torn up. Claims he was in Bloomington all day on
business. Just goes on to talk about what the police think
happened and things like that.

"Here's another one. Police interviewed neighbors of the
Tompkins. . . um . . . two, who knew him. Seems Harold
Tompkins was really in Terre Haute at the time of the murder, not Bloomington as he said. Both of them saw his car
on their street that morning. It gives names. You want
them?"

"No, not now. What year was this?"

"Wait a minute . . . er . . . January 2001. Here's another
one. It says Tompkins disappeared after being asked to come
into the station for a second interview. They're looking
for him and an unidentified woman last seen with Mr.
Tompkins.

She was quiet awhile. "These last articles just tell about
the same things. They talk about the murder and where the
case stands. Last one was a while ago. Mr. Tompkins was
still missing according to the Terre Haute Police, along
with the woman thought to be somebody named Charlene
Cooksey."

It took me a minute to process what she was telling me. Harold Tompkins? Who was he? And who was Charlene Cooksey? I'd never heard either of those names. This wasn't what I'd expected at all. A part of me was certain the name here would be Ben Fordyce. A part of me hoped I was wrong. But not this wrong.

"You're sure about all of this?"

"I'm looking at the papers now. That's what it says."

"What else is in there?"

"There's a picture of Harold Tompkins. Can't see much. He's with a woman. Looks like somebody took the photo from behind. Mr. Tompkins turned around but he's got a hat on and . . . um . . . a small suitcase in his hand.

"And here's a long report about Mr. Tompkins. It's got a cover letter from a detective. Name of Donny Fritch. You want me to read it?"

It was my turn to be very quiet.

"Lindy?" she finally said.

I shook myself. "Sure. Go ahead."

"Gives the man's name: Harold Tompkins. Where he was born. Stuff like that. Married to Sarah Mann in 1998, in Terre Haute, Indiana, where there's a certificate of marriage on file. Then, it says, he went to Ivy Tech and got himself a degree in . . . looks like . . . something about paralegal.

"After that he worked at a law firm there in Terra Haute.

"No kids." She was quiet. "Not much else except a folded paper. Looks like some kind of lab report."

All I could think was "paralegal," not an attorney after all.

And a dead wife left behind him.

"What did Amos say to you about the package?" I asked. "Did he know this Harold Tompkins?"

"He didn't tell me anything. That's it."

"Are you still in Houston?"

Another long pause. "Yes. But not at the clinic. I slipped back. I've been . . . well . . . drinking. Without Amos, nothing seems important enough to fight that feeling."

"You think that's what Uncle Amos would want for you? Quitting because he's not there? Is that what he wanted for the two of you?"

"The two of us." She echoed my words.

"Could you meet me at the clinic?"

"I don't know if Dr. Lambert wants to see me . . ."

"You're not the first, Virginia." I let her think about it. "We need that package."

"All I've got left of Amos. Isn't that a shame?"

"It wasn't meant for you, you know that. He said to give it to the police in case of his death."

"But you're not the police. I don't mean to be a smart mouth, just that it's the last thing he asked me to do and I want to do it right."

"I'll bring a policeman with me. He's investigating Amos's murder. Let's meet right there in Houston. At the clinic. I'll call Dr. Lambert and tell him. He knows us, me and the policeman, Deputy Hunter Austen. You'll be safe. I promise. Or we could call the Houston Police, explain that you're in danger and you need protection until we get there."

"In danger?" The thought was new to Virginia. "Why?"

"Those reports. They name the man who killed Amos."

"Good Lord!" she exclaimed. "I'm not thinking straight."

"Meet us at the clinic."

She didn't hesitate. "Okay. One o'clock all right? Dr. Lambert's not so busy in the afternoon. I'll call him too. Maybe I'll stay there. I mean really get well this time. If you don't hear back from me, just come on in. One o'clock."

I hung up and took a long breath. This could be it. If

Martin couldn't tell us what happened, Amos's report would have to. Who was Harold Tompkins? Was he the man who came to town to kill Amos? Then what about Daddy?

I called Hunter and told him we had to get back to Houston. He understood and didn't ask a single question except what time to pick me up.

Chapter Thirty-nine

The trip into Houston was a quiet one. We had to get there fast. I could feel the urgency. We didn't have hours or even minutes to spare. I was too used to having someone snatch things away from me, someone very evil who watched what I, and Miss Amelia and Hunter, did and laughed at us. I grew more and more afraid we'd get there and Virginia would be gone. I called Dr. Lambert and explained what was going on. One o'clock was fine with him.

"You heard about Martin?" Hunter asked after a while as we made our way by the Columbus exits. He turned his strong, narrow face to me. More as if he was asking some other question.

"He's going to be all right, isn't he?"

He nodded. "Doctor's bringing him out of the coma. Should be awake by tomorrow."

Too much. This could all be over by tomorrow . . . tomorrow . . . tomorrow. That's all I heard: tomorrow. Maybe Martin didn't see who attacked him. Maybe he was surprised.

Maybe he'd just discovered the trees and was knocked out before he heard the man behind him.

"Or by the time we get back from Houston. If we're lucky," he added as if he actually believed it.

"The sheriff called the hospital," he said. "He wanted to make sure somebody would be with Martin from here on in. We've got the feeling this might be a critical time, one way or the other."

Part of my brain took in what he was saying. Martin was in danger too. Like fighting a hydra—arms and heads all over the place. Virginia. Martin. All of us.

"Juanita said she would be there all today and tonight," Hunter went on. "And Jessie's coming part of the time. Guess there are others willing to stay."

"Ben?" I asked, then wanted to bite my tongue.

He nodded. "Ben and Harry and Chastity and Miss Ethelred. Probably anybody Juanita wants will be glad to chip in. Just need folks around him."

"Meemaw and Mama would but for the news they're waiting for."

"Already got it."

"Got what?"

"News."

"About Daddy? And you didn't tell me! Hunter!"

"I told Miss Amelia I'd tell you on the way to Houston."

"Fine. I should be home with my family." I scowled hard at him. "So?"

"I don't know if this is what you're expecting or not."

"Just tell me. Was my daddy murdered or was it an accident?"

"Amos was right. And Justin—right all along."

It was a stunner. Maybe either way would have been a stunner.

"Stabbed in the back, Lindy. What that old coroner took to be mower blade nicks on his backbone weren't. Too narrow for that, this new man says. And too consistently in one place. A mower would have moved on as it rolled over him. This is a tight series of nicks. Stab wounds on the spine."

How could I be any sadder than I'd already been about Daddy dying? Something moved inside me. Hatred. Rage. But not sadness. More like at last we had something to fight. At last we could put Jake Blanchard to rest and know it was done. And at last, there was a tangible thing to look at: knife marks on my daddy's spine.

"You okay, Lindy?" He looked over at me.

"I will be. Soon as this is over. Let's get to Houston."

This time we ran up the clinic's steps as fast as we could run, then over to the front desk. The woman took us straight back to Dr. Lambert's office. I knocked but didn't wait to be invited in.

A woman sat in a chair across from Dr. Lambert. Maybe she was in her forties, but showing a lot of hard wear. Her head hung down between her thin shoulder blades. She turned around, almost cowering in her seat. Her blond hair was thick and badly cut. The outfit she wore—a summer skirt and lace-trimmed blouse—looked as if it had been washed a hundred times too many. Washed out and sad—all of her.

Her hands, worn and red, clutched a manila envelope in her lap.

She relaxed when Dr. Lambert greeted Hunter and me, then introduced us.

"This is Lindy Blanchard, Virginia." The doctor kept his voice artificially calm, the way people do with frightened children. "And Deputy Austen."

I took the chair next to her. "I'm so happy you agreed to

meet us," I said, wanting to take her hand but afraid to startle her.

She nodded at me, and then at Hunter, eyeing him warily, taking in the uniform, the stiff hat he held under his arm, his "at attention" stance.

"Are those the reports?" I nodded toward the envelope she held, getting right to the reason we were there. Every moment felt urgent to me, as if being away from Riverville signaled a kind of desertion.

She nodded, pulled papers from the envelope and handed them to me. With a sigh, she settled back in the chair, relieved of a burdensome duty.

I took the papers into my lap and scanned them once, and then a second time, looking for Ben Fordyce's name—in case Virginia had missed it.

Hunter read over my shoulder until I handed the papers up to him and put a hand over my eyes. He flipped through paper after paper then began to read aloud.

"This one's Donny Fritch's report. It's all about somebody named Harold Tompkins of . . . let me see here . . . Terre Haute, Indiana. Born in 1959, in Lexington, Kentucky, to a Verna and Ferlynn Tompkins. Married a Joslyn Franklin in 1985 and divorced her in 1989. Joslyn was caught cheating and didn't contest the divorce, Fritch says here. No children.

"High school graduate." He went on reading aloud.

"Hmmm . . . says the guy was a traveling salesman for Pullman's Seeds during his first marriage. After the divorce he was an appliance salesman at Sears. That job lasted . . . let me see . . . six months. Seems he was fired for unstated reasons."

I sat up and took the reports from his hands. None of this was about anyone we knew. Why would Daddy have paid a thousand dollars for it? And why did Amos want it so badly he paid another five hundred? Or maybe even more.

Nothing to do with Ben. Ben would have given Daddy a reason to pay the money for the report—believing in his friend. Maybe it would have given Amos a reason to finish paying for it—getting even with the attorney who helped fight Amos off when he was at his worst.

But that wasn't true of Amos anymore. Virginia wasn't lying about Amos coming back to Riverville to make it up to us; nor about Amos knowing something that could stop whoever wanted to hurt us.

This had to be a path through the maze we'd been drawn into. I sensed that these pages and articles would lead directly to whoever killed my daddy and Amos. It would lead to the person who hurt Martin; took my trees; destroyed my records.

So maybe this had been all about my work after all

Or a ten-year-old death in Indiana.

Or one of Amos's scams.

But then how was Daddy involved and why was he murdered back before any of this began?

My head was spinning.

I read on from where Hunter had stopped: "In 1998 Harold Tompkins was in Terre Haute, Indiana, and married Sarah Mann, a wealthy woman. They moved into her estate on Cressley Road in Terre Haute. He wasn't working but went to Ivy Tech for two years, then got a job at an attorney's office in Terre Haute. In January of 2001 Sarah Mann Tompkins was found murdered. Thought to be a suspect in the murder, Harold left town two weeks later and hasn't been seen since."

I read to myself, skipping repetitions. Donny Fritch traced him to California where he disappeared again. That was about all the report said except it included interviews with neighbors and a police lieutenant and mentioned the woman: Charlene Cooksey. She'd either disappeared too or a woman, by that name, never existed.

"It says: 'See articles attached.' " I picked up the yellowing newspaper stories to read from the first account of the murder to a rehash written in 2009, stating that Mr. Tompkins was still missing and wanted for questioning as a person of interest in his wife's murder.

I read the other articles, stopping at the word "estate." Sounded to me as if this Tompkins man had married way up in the world.

All of the articles detailed what the police discovered at the Cressley Street house on that January evening. Harold Tompkins found his wife's body on returning from a trip to Bloomington. The house was torn apart, many items missing, including his wife's jewelry, insured for one million three hundred thousand dollars.

There was a professional photograph of Sarah Mann attached to the article. Surprisingly she was a much older woman. I looked back at the report. Tompkins was born in 1959. Thirty-nine when he married Sarah.

The setting in the woman's photo was very formal. Her gray-streaked hair was rolled up and back from her face; the corners of her mouth were drawn into a pleasant smile. Her eyes weren't cold so much as wary. She was seated forward on a brocade-covered Queen Anne chair; knees together under her blue lace dress; feet, in sensible low-heeled shoes, planted firmly on the carpet; hands folded decorously in her lap. She looked like every moneyed matron ever photographed for posterity, the only ostentatious thing about her being a necklace with a large stone at its center circled by what looked to be diamonds.

Included beneath her picture was a photo of her home, the Mann estate, where she was murdered. A huge, austere house set back on a long lawn, surrounded by well-trimmed hedges.

I went again to the detective's report while Hunter read

the articles. From the Terre Haute Police Lieutenant Donny
Fritch interviewed, I learned that there was something about
Mr. Tompkins's cell phone records on the day his wife was
murdered that raised suspicion. He'd made repeated calls to
a number in Terre Haute around the time of the murder. The
calls pinged off a tower within the city, very close to the Mann
estate, proving he wasn't in Bloomington as he'd claimed.
The police got a court order for the numbers he called and
found that most went to a local hotel, to a room assigned to
Charlene Cooksey.

So that was where the woman came into the story.

I read on. The woman checked out the morning after the
murder. She'd left an address in Bloomington but when the
address was checked the people living there had never heard
of a Charlene Cooksey. She was untraceable. They got a
description from the hotel clerk. She'd been in her forties,
a lot of brown hair piled up on her head. Wore a big fur coat.
High heels.

Could be anybody.

Fritch, in his summation at the end of the report, added
that the police suspected an affair of long standing but found
nothing more on the pair. It was as if they'd vanished. Spec-
ulation was that they'd left the country. A nationwide alert
was sent out but there'd been nothing new until, in 2005, a
piece of Sarah Mann's stolen jewelry was discovered. Sold
to a dealer in Dallas.

After that the trail went cold.

I read the last paragraph of the report. Donny Fritch offered
to do a more exhaustive search for either Charlene Cooksey
or Harold Tompkins if Mr. Blanchard thought it important.

A blurred photograph was stapled to the back of the last
report page. The Post-it note attached said the man was Harold Tompkins and the woman with him was presumed to be
Charlene Cooksey, taken at the Terre Haute International

Airport. It had been taken by a a neighbor of the Tompkins who'd been seeing his daughter off. The man thought it odd to run into Tompkins there, two weeks after his wife's murder, and with another woman in tow. Though the photo had been enlarged, it still looked like something from an old newspaper.

In the picture Tompkins was of average height. His face was turned to look back over his shoulder at the camera. In this bad picture the round face was nothing more than a flurry of dark dots under a hat

A woman walked beside him. She'd turned to the camera, too. Her face was clearer, but nondescript. A woman you wouldn't look at twice, dressed in a dark pantsuit, high heels, a large bag slung over her left shoulder. Her ample dark hair was pulled back away from her face. She wore large sunglasses.

"Anybody we know?" I held the photo out to Hunter.

Hunter shook his head slowly. "That would've been what? Ten years ago? If I've ever seen them, they've changed from what they looked like than."

Dr. Lambert, who'd been quiet while we sorted through the papers, cleared his throat. "I have appointments. Maybe you could take this out to the lobby?"

"Sure. Sure." Hunter collected everything and stuffed it back into the envelope. "Sorry."

The doctor raised his eyebrows.

"Virginia is staying here with us." He smiled at the woman, who turned a relieved face to him.

"I promise I won't break your trust . . ."

We thanked her for meeting us and headed out to Hunter's car.

On the drive to Riverville, I went over everything in the envelope again and found a folded paper stuck near the bottom of the envelope that we hadn't looked at yet.

"You see this lab thing?" I asked.

Hunter shook his head. "Private lab?"

"Wamsley Lab in Columbus."

"Yeah, private. What's it say?"

"They had a fingerprint. Listen to this." I sat up straight, excited. "It says they processed a cellophane wrapper Jake Blanchard had supplied and found fingerprints on the wrapper matched a print from that Charlene Cooksey taken from her hotel room in Terre Haute."

I leafed through the papers, back to the detective's report, and scanned it for the Cooksey name.

"Your daddy gave the lab the wrapper with her fingerprints. That's where the link between all of this comes in." He thought hard. "So it's somebody your daddy knew or met or suspected or something."

A link. It was a relief to finally have something concrete to hold on to.

Charlene Cooksey. Nobody I'd ever heard of. My stomach dropped for just a minute. I would ask Mama, but I was willing to bet she didn't know the woman either.

"That it?" Hunter asked.

I nodded.

"Amounts to almost nothing," Hunter said. "Why did Amos pay five hundred dollars for it? Or even more important, why did your daddy pay a thousand?"

"Because he suspected this woman of something. The fact of the fingerprints is pretty clear."

"Then why was the detective's office broken into after Amos bought it from the man?"

Daddy was murdered and Amos was on the trail of whoever did it. Somebody needed to know what he bought from the detective but got there too late.

"Where's all this leave us?" I asked, tired, sensing defeat.

"I don't know. Your daddy knew this Charlene Cooksey

and must have suspected her of something. He's the one
supplied the fingerprints." He shook his head as if to
straighten out his thoughts. "We've got Martin there in the
hospital, so let's get back to Riverville. This stuff in the
report goes back ten years. Martin's been with your daddy
for a long time. If anybody knows what's going on here, he'd
be the one. And let me take it to Sheriff Higsby, see if he
can come up with more on this Charlene Cooksey. Maybe
something new on Harold Tompkins."

I thought awhile. "First we're showing all of it to Miss Amelia. If anybody can figure this out, it's my grandmother."

Hunter started to argue then thought better of it.

"Okay," he said. "If you let me call the sheriff and have
him talk to the Terre Haute Police in the meantime."

A deal was struck on both sides. Not that I had much
hope of anything coming of it. I couldn't think of a single
reason my daddy was investigating some Northerner who
probably killed his own wife, or the girlfriend who killed
her for him.

The thought that this report wasn't really the one Daddy
ordered was driving a nail hole into my brain. Some last
trick Uncle Amos played?

I didn't have an answer for any one of my questions.

Chapter Forty

As soon as Hunter finished calling Sheriff Higsby, I called Miss Amelia. She was at The Squirrel, having a late supper with Mama. I told her to stay there, that we had Uncle Amos's package and didn't understand a bit of it.

"Bring it on over," she said. "I'll keep Emma here with me 'til you get here."

When we got to The Squirrel, Meemaw was having Cecil's English trifle and, from the look on her face, not enjoying it. "Tastes like paste." She pushed the dish of mushy cake and runny cream away when I sat down next to her.

"Chauncey twins came in," Mama said and handed me a scrunched-down paper lunch sack as Hunter moved in next to her. "They came all the way into town to bring you the rattles off the snake that was about to bite you out there the other day."

Nobody was laughing, but I knew when I was the butt of a good joke. I didn't open the bag and figured I'd leave it behind as a trophy for Cecil.

"You heard about Jake's death?" Miss Amelia dropped

down into dead seriousness. Mama looked away, tears gathering in her eyes.

"Hunter told me."

"So we gonna get whoever did this?" she asked.

"Of course," I said and meant it.

I set the manila envelope on the table and briefly gave them a run down of what we knew: the man, Harold Tompkins; the woman, Charlene Cooksey; the murder of Tompkins wife; the jewelry they got away with.; the fingerprints my daddy gave the detective.

Miss Amelia pulled the papers out and began to read to herself.

"Well." I looked over at Hunter since a lot of what we'd decided on the way home had been his idea. "Everybody over there at the co-op has been hunting for those missing books Daddy was supposed to have, right?"

Mama nodded.

"What we were thinking was that Daddy came across the problem first and it had something to do with that. Maybe looking over the books and finding things that didn't add up. He'd been president for almost two years by then. All those men on the board were Daddy's friends: Bill Hoagley. Jim Pritchard. Fulton Sampson. Who else?"

"Harry Conway. Daddy got him on the board when he first took over as president. Chastity, too. Did a lot of work for the co-op," Mama said.

"So maybe this Harold Tompkins was a buyer, cheating everybody . . ." I said.

Mama frowned at me. "Never heard of him."

"Well, Mama, maybe he's from before you took over. I mean, from before Daddy died."

She shook her head. "I would've known. I always dealt with buyers."

I was getting exasperated with her. "Let me finish . . ."

"This a photograph of Harold Tompkins?" Miss Amelia held up the picture from the file.

I nodded fast. I wanted to get my point across to Mama and not be interrupted.

"Mama. Just listen a minute. Me and Hunter figured out that if Daddy knew these people and you didn't, it had to be through the co-op. This is a pair of murderers—killed the woman for her jewelry. So the worst kind of thieves. If Daddy knew 'em, he had to have met them at the co-op. Maybe a buyer, like I said. Maybe some kind of insurance salesman and his wife. You know how the co-op's always getting these men coming through with surefire plans for selling more pecans, for worldwide markets, crop insurance. All kinds of things."

"So how'd they get their hands on the missing fifty thousand?" Mama demanded, giving me a skeptical look.

"Can't even tell who the man is," Miss Amelia interrupted. "Not from this picture. Who's the woman?"

"They think she's that Charlene Cooksey. Hunter's got the sheriff asking for better photos, if they've got them, from the Terre Haute . . ."

I turned back to Mama. "If Daddy found out about the missing fifty thousand, he could have gone to the co-op men for an explanation. Maybe checks stolen and cashed—something like that."

"Okay, Lindy. That might be the truth behind the missing money. Even why they killed Jake. But what about Amos . . ."

"Same thing," Hunter put in. "Amos found out, too."

"And my trees?" I asked, seeing where Mama was going. We were chasing our tails back into the same old circle.

Miss Amelia, still staring hard at the photo, made a noise in her throat. "I'd know this woman anywhere," she said, tapping the woman in the picture with one blunt fingernail.

I snapped my mouth shut. Hunter and I looked across the table at each other.

"Who?" Hunter asked.

"Just take a look at her," Miss Amelia said. "Don't tell me you don't recognize that wide be-hind?"

I pulled the photo from her hands. Nothing rang a bell.

"I don't see—"

"Lord! Lord!" Miss Amelia was up and pushing me out into the aisle. Her face was white. She grabbed her purse and was on her way across the restaurant and out the door. We all scrambled after her as Cecil called after the disappearing back, "But, Miss Amelia, you didn't finish your trifle!"

Chapter Forty-one

The four of us crammed into Hunter's police car. Once Miss Amelia was settled in the back, she started berating herself for being "so stupid."

"How'd I miss so much?" she was going on. "Should've seen it from the beginning. I pride myself on knowing people—"

She interrupted herself to poke Hunter in the back. "Get on that radio of yours, Hunter. Call Sheriff Higsby. Tell him to get as many men as he's got over to the hospital right away. Tell him, if I'm right, Martin Sanchez could be in big trouble."

He did as he was told, asking no questions. And kept his siren off because Meemaw asked him to.

"We're closest to the hospital," Hunter said over his shoulder. "We'll be there before the sheriff gets the men together."

"Then it's up to us," Miss Amelia said. "You got a gun, Hunter. I'm thinking we've got surprise on our side."

I turned back to Meemaw. "What's going on? We've got to know what we're getting into. You sure don't think Martin had anything to do with any of this. And sure as heck it's not Jessie or Juanita."

"You take a good look at that picture?" She reached down into the manila envelope, brought out the papers, riffled through them, and pulled out the photo of Tompkins and Cooksey.

"Add a bunch of hair on that woman's head," Miss Amelia challenged me. "Slap a thick layer of makeup on her face."

I looked again. "Finula Prentiss? I kind of figured she was in it somewhere. But Finula's skinny."

I pulled the photo up to the end of my nose. "And Finula's got almost no rear end on her. This one's—"

"Now put her in a cowgirl outfit. Color that hair red as a monkey's butt."

Hunter and I looked at each other. In the backseat, Mama gasped.

"Chastity?" I said.

"You're darned right. Told you I know people. Chastity Conway. No mistaking that behind for any other behind. I'm not an expert but . . . Anyway, take a close look at that blurry face. Plain as all get-out unless you add the hair and makeup."

"Throw in a phony drawl wide enough to dam the Colorado," Mama said, sitting up, excited. "And they're deep into co-op business. That's how the books got lost."

"Came here with that million and more from killing Harry's second wife . . ." Miss Amelia, almost breathless, said, "From the size of their house and those new barns—that money's long gone. Stole the fifty. What better after that than to steal Lindy's trees, patent them, and hold the rest of the ranchers hostage—not able to compete with him and his new trees."

"Or," Hunter threw in as he sped around corners, over to Carya Street, and then toward the hospital. "Or sell the trees. Asking anything he could get for them."

"But they hid those five in our shed," I protested. "I thought it was to make one of us look guilty."

"Don't think so." Miss Amelia was holding on for dear life as Hunter took another corner. "More to it. I think those trees got hid because whichever one of them killed Amos—and I'm betting on Harry—got scared when he heard sirens coming and stuck 'em in the shed.

"When one of them, probably Chastity, came back for the trees Martin was there. She had to do something about him. Killing a man wasn't as easy as killing an older woman. And this time nothing was planned. Chastity didn't come to our place with a weapon on her but when she saw somebody down at the shed she picked up that wrench in the barn, snuck down there, hit him, and ran."

"And all that stuff about him doing the same things I've been working on. Him and those grafts he said he was propagating. Learned from some online video." I was spitting mad. "Uncle Amos never offered to steal my trees and files to hurt my work. All Harry's doing. Going to use the trees to make himself another crooked million."

"So where it started here was with that fifty thousand from the co-op. Jake must've known they took it," Mama said.

"That's why he hired the detective," I put in.

"If he confronted them, he would've mentioned the report he was waiting for," Mama added. She pulled in a long, painful breath. "I'll bet anything—knowing Jake—he made a deal with them to pay the money back and he'd keep it quiet."

"They decided to kill Jake instead. Didn't have the money or weren't about to pay back anything," Hunter put in from the front seat as he swung into the hospital's emergency entrance. "Had to be one of them who broke into that detective's office looking for the report."

"By that time Amos had the report. They found out somehow and went after his copy," I said.

"Chastity, I'll bet," Miss Amelia muttered as she unbuckled her seat belt and threw the car door open. "Snooping," she called back over her shoulder at us. "Thank heavens she didn't find Virginia's letter."

"And who knows Rancho en el Colorado better than your fine neighbors?" Hunter loped along beside me. "Knows the back roads in and out. Had access to your barns . . ."

"Those damned killers!" Mama almost stopped running, realizing what Hunter was saying. "That's how they got Justin's belt buckle. Not enough to murder my husband. They went after my son . . ." She sped up, rage pushing her.

Chapter Forty-two

The room was very still, and very white. Martin's bed was empty, remade with white sheets folded crisply over a white blanket. The white pillow, undented by any head, was propped against the gray metal bars of the headboard.

Meemaw, Hunter, and I stopped dead. I'd expected uproar. People in the corridors. Doors slamming. Sounds of voices. At least a patient, or a visitor, sticking their head out from a room at all the noise down the hall.

Nothing.

We'd known there wouldn't be police cars in the parking lot. But something. A warning to Jessie and Juanita that would have had hospital personnel rushing in to stop the Conways.

Nothing.

It was as if we'd walked into the wrong room.

Miss Amelia came trotting along behind me and Hunter. Mama stopped outside to call Bethany then came in to say she was going to pick her up at the store. I could see Mama didn't want us separated any more. We were all suddenly afraid for everybody we loved. It was real now that we had faces to put on what had happened.

But for being real, we had all the more to fear.

"Where's everyone?" Hunter asked, turning fully in the empty room.

"I'll go call . . ." He looked around again, then went out the door, into the corridor.

"They moved Martin." Miss Amelia summed up what we were looking at. "They were bringing him out of the coma today. They've put him somewhere safer. Jessie and Juanita, too. Someplace Harry and Chastity can't get at any of them."

She nodded hard. I knew she was right. It was just that when word got out Martin might be awake and talking soon, I'd expected the Conways to make a move—some horrendous plan to fix this, too, the way they'd fixed people before.

I didn't get a chance to say anything.

"Miss Amelia! Good to see you." Harry Conway was behind us, framed in the open doorway. "I didn't expect anybody else to be here. Jessie said she needed help 'cause she had to get back to the house. You know, get things ready to bring Martin home. Chastity's on her way . . ."

He walked in then stopped, aware of the empty bed. "Lord's sakes," Harry exclaimed, pulling his big hat from his head and holding it at his chest. "Where'd Martin get to? Hope nothing happened to the poor—"

"I think he's with the sheriff, Harry," Meemaw said, smiling wide. "Seems he woke up sooner than the doctor expected."

Harry made a face. "With the sheriff? I don't get what you're saying, ma'am . . ."

"Think you do, Harry." Hunter stood in the doorway, Sheriff Higsby behind him, pushing his way into the room.

"What's this all about?" Harry demanded, his round, red face a mask of irritation. "Just came to do my neighborly duty. Said they'd be bringing him around this afternoon. If the man's better, why, no use in me stayin' . . ."

Hunter was the first to lay a hand on Harry's arm. None too gently.

"I think you'd better hang around, Harry. They brought Martin out of the coma this morning. Fuzzy, but he had a lot to say about who tried to kill him down there at the shed. Guess that was your wife: Chastity, or whatever her real name is. Said, too, he had his suspicions all along. I'd say we've got a whole lot of questions for the both of you. Oh, and some people in Terre Haute, Indiana, looking for you, too. You hear about that?"

Harry's eyes widened. His mouth dropped open with all the anger of the phony innocent.

"Oh, and guess what they found on that belt buckle you stuck under Amos's body, Harry? Found a perfect fingerprint. Wonder whose it is? Care to venture a guess? Not Justin's, by the way."

"I'm arresting you for the murder of Amos Blanchard." The sheriff spun the confused man around and snapped handcuffs on his wrists. Hunter read him his rights and he was gone, swept down the hall and out of sight.

"We've got one more," Hunter came back to warn us, holding up a single finger.

"I'm not going anywhere." Miss Amelia took a seat at the edge of the empty bed. "How about you, Lindy? Want to wait for Chastity?"

The gleam in her eye was wicked. I gave her the biggest smile I had in me. "Bring 'er on, Meemaw." I reached out and patted my grandmother on her back.

Chastity Conway waltzed into the room not five minutes later, surprised, as Harry had been, to see me and Miss

Amelia there and Martin gone. The room filled with the overpowering scent of her perfume—something like long dead flowers. Just the smell of her stirred a memory: that day I found my grove destroyed. Something nauseatingly sweet in the air back then. I'd thought it was blossoms on the trees and spring in general. Now I knew it wasn't. Maybe Harry'd killed Uncle Amos, but Chastity had been lurking somewhere in the background.

Chastity looked at the empty bed then feigned surprise. "Why? Whatever's going on here? Jessie asked me and Harry to take over while Martin was coming out of his coma." She blinked hard a couple of times, then looked around the empty room. "Harry shoulda been here by now. Where'd that man get to? And where's Martin? Don't tell me something happened to him. Not after everything he's been through." She "tsked-tsked" a few times then shook her head. "Not expired, is he? Hope his poor heart didn't take 'im."

"We don't know anything for certain, Chastity." Miss Amelia smiled from her place in the catbird's seat. "Just got here ourselves. Seems something happened. Can't get anything straight outta anybody. Lindy here says she saw the sheriff taking Harry away. You know what that's all about?"

"What?" Chastity's face turned redder than her hair. "Harry? Why on earth . . ."

I watched. It was almost funny, how she tried out one expression after another until she landed on a way out for her.

"I'd better get over there. See what in heck's goin' on. Think I'll just drive by the ranch first . . ."

"Why, I woulda thought you'd want to be with Harry fast as you can." Miss Amelia clucked at her, moving just a little closer.

Chastity took a step back toward the door.

Miss Amelia turned to me. "Isn't that what you'd imagine, Lindy? That Charlene here would want to be with her lovin' husband soon as she can get over there?"

Chastity drew in a breath that stuck her nostrils together.

"What did you call me?" she asked haughtily, cocking her head to one side. I noticed the Texas drawl was missing.

"Oh, sorry." Miss Amelia threw both hands to her cheeks. "Thought that was your real name. Heard it was something like Charlene Rooksey or Cooksey. Something like that."

"You don't know what you are talking about." Chastity Conway turned fast, heading for the door.

Miss Amelia was there before her, reaching out and grabbing on to Chastity's shoulders.

"Why, bless yer heart, Charlene." Miss Amelia turned her, pushing her toward the hall, where Hunter waited. "Bless yer dear little heart. Just look who's waiting to help you outta here. You see Hunter Austen, do you? A fine policeman, our Hunter. One of the best I'll bet *you* ever met in yer whole life. Now just you go along with our Hunter, you murderin' little . . ."

Chapter Forty-three

The day of Bethany's big wedding, the sky turned bloodred just about seven o'clock in the evening. It was after the beautiful outdoor ceremony and when the rollicking reception was already under way.

The bleeding clouds hung above the pecan trees like licks of fire. None of us could believe in a sky that color, one we'd never seen before, and stood around, outside the rocking tent: me and Hunter, Mama and Ben, and Meemaw, marveling at the sky turning the world red.

And marveling at Bethany's success.

Especially when the doves got loose ahead of time and flew at people and the people laughed and ducked and shooed birds out of their food, and stayed good-humored and swore they never had a better time.

Especially when the antenna on top of the cake shaped like a radio station began to fall like something out of a King Kong movie and the guests hovered around, putting down bets as to when the antenna was going to take out the groom,

Chet Easton's, office and cheering it on as it toppled, fell, and took most of the next layer of icing with it.

We hung around outside the tent, nodding to overdressed couples who came out for a look at the sky. Hunter said he hoped nobody took that bloody sky as an intimation of trouble ahead for the happy couple.

"Sure not the kind of trouble the Conways found here in Riverville," Miss Amelia said, smirking around at our group.

I didn't feel the least bit bad about a little gloating.

There was going to be a trial, right there in Riverville. Another one ahead, Hunter had said. Back in Indiana.

Sheriff Higsby thought the co-op's books had been destroyed a long time ago. Maybe before Jake even got suspicious. Didn't matter, though. Not with the fingerprint on the belt buckle. Not with the fingerprint Jake'd checked with the detective belonging to Charlene Cooksey aka Chastity Conway. Sure not with the Conways' past. And not with a bank deposit of fifty thousand dollars at about the time the money came up missing.

On top of that was Martin's testimony.

They weren't going to be tried for my daddy's murder because there wasn't any physical evidence the Conways did it, though there was proof enough in my heart. One way or the other, I figured. As long as the pair of murderers spent the rest of their lives in prison.

The tent couldn't have been prettier, with swags of white and silver tulle and big bows on the backs of the chair covers. Crystal chandeliers hung from the peak of our tent, which was really a solid building that only looked like a tent.

There were huge bouquets of white roses and silver-dipped roses standing everywhere around the huge room.

Seemed Bethany's career path was set. And Meemaw was set, too. Back making her pecan pies.

Bethany came out of the tent to look around for us. Her face lit up with a smile that ran from ear to ear as she almost. skipped over to where we stood.

"Do you believe this wedding?" she asked. "I've already got one person wanting to book a party. Isn't that something?"

We agreed it was and she hurried back inside the tent.

When the food was all served and what was left of the huge radio station wedding cake was cut, Miss Amelia's "special" pecan pies were brought out to a long drum roll with Miss Amelia watching closely after that to see if people liked her pies the way they should.

Even the standing ovation she got didn't convince her they were up to her usual standards. Not until the guests ate second helpings and got happier and happier.

I leaned toward her when the music was at its loudest and people were shaking every body part they had. "You make 'em with a double shot of Garrison's?" I teased.

I got a "Keep your mouth shut" look, followed by a quick nod and a satisfied smile.

With the wedding winding down, Bethany joined us in lawn chairs set out under the trees, a pad of paper in her hands. She turned a worried glance up at the sky, which wasn't so much red anymore as dark purple.

"Hope it holds off just a little longer," she said.

"Can't rain," I said. "Not supposed to rain, though I've been prayin' hard."

"Anyway . . ." She flounced back in her chair. "I was thinking about Uncle Amos's funeral. Maybe I can get some doves dyed black. And I was thinking pecan branches draped across the casket. You know, like the family crest. And, I was thinking, since Uncle Amos had so many friends over at the Barking Coyote, maybe they wouldn't mind dressing in black and doing a line dance at the dinner after the funeral. You know, a slow line dance . . ."

She yawned as she nodded along with her own ideas.

Mama reached over and put a hand on Bethany's knee, stopping her in full flight.

"It's a funeral, Bethany. No dancing. No black doves. No pecan branches. Small. Private. Amos was family, and don't forget it. A true Blanchard." She nodded to her words. "Blood wins out in the end."

And that's when the sky opened and the rains came, and the wedding guests, realizing the drought was over, ran out of the tent to twirl in the downpour. Good Texans, every one of us, hand in hand out in that storm, moving under swaying pecan trees, doing our own kind of happy, pagan rain dance.

Recipes

Miss Amelia Hastings of the Nut House always puts at least a dash of Garrison Brothers Texas Straight Bourbon Whiskey in her recipes because she thinks Garrison Brothers brings tears to the eyes of a real Texan.

You can use any bourbon that reminds you of home. Or leave out the whiskey entirely.

Or if you're having a bad day, leave out the rest of the ingredients and just drink the bourbon.

MISS AMELIA'S SPECIAL PECAN PIE

½ cup white sugar
½ cup brown sugar
3 tbsp. melted butter
½ cup light Karo syrup
3 eggs, beaten
4 tbsp. bourbon
2 cups pecan halves
1 9-inch unbaked deep-dish piecrust

Preheat the oven to 375 degrees.

Mix the white sugar, brown sugar, and butter together. Stir in the Karo syrup, eggs, and bourbon. Fold in the pecans and pour the mix into a piecrust.

Bake in the preheated oven for 10 minutes; reduce heat to 350 and bake until the pie is set in the middle—about 35 minutes more. Use a knife to test if the center is pretty well set.

Allow to cool on a wire rack.

Serve with a side of pecan ice cream, or a shot of bourbon.

CECIL DARLING'S CANDIED NUTS

1 cup sugar
½ tsp. salt
½ tsp. cinnamon
6 tbsp. milk
2 cups pecan halves
2 tsp. bourbon

Combine the first four ingredients in a saucepan. Cook at medium heat until the mixture reaches the softball stage.

Add the pecan halves and bourbon. Stir to coat the pecans with the mix.

Spread on wax paper to cool then separate the pieces.

Store in a covered container.

ETHELRED'S RUNNER-UP ORANGE PECAN TEA BREAD

2½ cups all-purpose flour
1 cup sugar
3½ tsp. baking powder
1 tsp. salt
3 tbsp. salad oil
½ cup milk
4 tsp. grated orange peel
¾ cup orange juice
4 tbsp. bourbon
1 egg, beaten
1 cup finely chopped pecans

Preheat the oven to 350 degrees.

Grease and flour a 9-by-5-by-3-inch loaf pan or 2 smaller pans.

Measure all the ingredients into a bowl.

Beat all together, scraping constantly.

Pour into the pan or pans. Bake 65 minutes or until a knife in the center comes out clean.

Cool before slicing.

Spread with butter or cream cheese or homemade jams.

Freezes well.

OUTHOUSE MOONS

1 cup soft butter or margarine
1 cup sifted confectioners' sugar
2 cups flour
3 tbsp. bourbon
2 cups finely chopped pecans
Extra confectioners' sugar for rolling cookies

Preheat the oven to 350 degrees.

Cream the butter and confectioners' sugar together until smooth.

Add the flour, bourbon, and pecans.

Mix well.

Shape into 2-inch quarter-moon crescents and place on a cookie sheet.

Bake 10–15 minutes.

Keep a close eye on these. They should be set, but not too brown.

When cool, roll in extra confectioners' sugar.

BLANCHARD'S BOURBON BALLS

1 cup vanilla wafer crumbs
1 cup chopped pecans
1 cup confectioners' sugar
2 tbsp. cocoa
2 shot glasses full of bourbon

1½ tbsp. light Karo syrup
Extra confectioners' sugar
or granulated sugar for rolling cookies

Mix the vanilla wafer crumbs, pecans, confectioners' sugar, and cocoa together.

In a separate bowl, mix the bourbon and Karo syrup. Add to the crumb mix.

Form into small balls and roll in extra confectioners' sugar or granulated sugar.

Store in an airtight container.

FINULA'S FRIED DRIED PIES

Makes 8 large fried dried pies or more smaller ones.

DOUGH

½ cup sugar
1 tbsp. baking powder
3½ cups flour
1 tsp. salt
4 tbsp. shortening
2 eggs, beaten
1 13½-oz. can evaporated milk

THE NIGHT BEFORE:

Combine the sugar, baking powder, flour, and salt in a bowl.

Cut in the shortening.

Work in the beaten eggs.

Add the evaporated milk.

Mix well and allow to sit in the refrigerator overnight.

FILLING

Make the next day so the filling will be warm but not hot.

2 4.5-oz. package dried apples
½ cup bourbon
1 tsp. cinnamon
1 tsp. nutmeg
1 tbsp. brown sugar
½ cup chopped pecans

Stew the dried apples in bourbon, spices, and brown sugar until soft. Add pecans at end of cooking process.

Remove one handful of dough at a time from the refrigerator.

Add flour to make the dough stiff enough to roll out.

Roll out to the size of a saucer.

Spread half of the dough with the cooked apple mix.

Wet the edge of the dough with water.

Fold over to form a half round.

Seal the edges with the tines of a fork.

Heat oil in a skillet or saucepan until a small piece of dough browns quickly. Don't let the oil smoke.

Fry each pie until brown, turning once.

Sprinkle with a mix of confectioners' sugar and cinnamon if desired.

*Someone takes decorating for
Halloween to a deadly level...*

FROM NATIONAL BESTSELLING AUTHOR

B. B. HAYWOOD

TOWN IN A
PUMPKIN BASH

A Candy Holliday Murder Mystery

Halloween is on the way, and Cape Willington is busy
preparing for the annual Pumpkin Bash. Local blueberry
farmer Candy Holliday is running the haunted hayride
this year, hoping to make some extra cash. But her hopes
might be dashed when she discovers a dead body near
some fake tombstones. Now, as Candy uses her keen
eye for detail to unearth secrets, she'll discover that
not all skeletons hidden in this small town's closets are
Halloween decorations . . .

"A savory read, which brings the people
of coastal Maine to life."
—*Bangor (ME) Daily News*

INCLUDES DELICIOUS RECIPES!

hollidaysblueberryacres.com
facebook.com/HollidaysBlueberryAcres
facebook.com/TheCrimeSceneBooks
penguin.com

M1373T0913

FIRST IN THE *NEW YORK TIMES* BESTSELLING SERIES BY
SHEILA CONNOLLY

Buried in a Bog
A County Cork Mystery

Honoring the wish of her late grandmother, Maura Donovan
visits the small Irish village where Gran was born—never
expecting to get bogged down in a murder mystery. When
Maura realizes she may know something about the case, she
fears she's about to become mired in a homicide investigation
and has a sinking feeling she may really be getting in over
her head . . .

Praise for the County Cork Mysteries

"A captivating tale—sweet, nostalgic,
and full of Irish charm."
—*The Maine Suspect*

"The setting and local personalities are cleverly woven into
two mysteries . . . A very promising start to a new series."
—*Booklist*

sheilaconnolly.com
facebook.com/TheCrimeSceneBooks
penguin.com

M1376T0913